WHISPERS OF LOVE

EVE'S STORY

MARY TERESA MADDEN

ACKNOWLEDGEMENTS

A sincere thanks to Susan McKenna, Director at Book Hub Publishing for her patience with me while writing this book; book number three no less with her guidance.

To Niall MacGiolla Bhuí from ShadowScript Ghostwriters for his gorgeous book cover design and second run edits. It took us some negotiation, but we got there!

To Dorothy for her lovely text flourishes.

To the endlessly supportive crew at Book Hub Publishing.

Thanks to all my readers at home and abroad for buying my books. You are the reason I keep writing. I hope you enjoy this one.

Last, but not least, thanks to my family and friends for their interest and support throughout my writing journey. It is priceless.

DEDICATION

To the cherished memories of my uncles, Thomas, Ger, Peter,
Brendan and Jimmy.
They are locked in my heart forever.

It never hurts to see the good in someone,
They often act the better because of it.

—Nelson Mandela

The sea, once it casts its spell,
Holds one in the net of wonder forever.

—Jacques Cousteau

CHAPTER 1

Autumn was well and truly in full swirl. Trees along the avenue had transformed from shades of sage to a symphony of burnt orange, fiery reds and murky browns. The last of the leaves were fluttering to the ground, making rusty piles. The damp chill in the air had encouraged Eve to pull on her fleeced lined jacket before going outdoors. The past few months had been hectic for her. She had travelled to five countries promoting her latest styles in dresses and jackets. Pierre was away at sea for the past six weeks and Eve was missing him greatly. She wanted him by her side; she loved him and longed for her handsome French man to accompany her to fashion shows across the globe. It felt like he was never free for her but could go to France at the drop of a hat to please his parents, which he did each month without fail.

Eve Wallace and Pierre Rolf met at college ten years ago. They lost contact when Pierre gave up his studies and went back to France for three years. He returned to Connemara seven years ago and bought a little cottage out in Rossaveal overlooking the sea where he was close to a fishing environment. Eve thought she had moved on with that chapter of her life, but when Pierre returned and asked her out, she fell in love all over again with him. They started seeing each other regularly. Eve was financially stable, whereas Pierre just got by on his small income. Fishing was a constant job, but the revenue it brought in was small.

Pierre loved the sea and made it his livelihood. Eve's mother Julie and father Eric weren't completely sure about Pierre being the right person for their daughter and advised her to be careful in case he was only in love with her for her bank account. Eve insisted he loved her and they would marry some day in the future. She had worked really hard to grow and develop her designer fashion business; she was excited and confident in her designs, which had brought her to many countries who were eager to showcase her innovated designs. With Pierre by her side, she felt life was complete, no matter what her parents said about him she wasn't prepared to lose him.

She was happy to be home in An Spidéal for a week. She liked nothing better than to be out in the country, to walk down by the seashore and watch the seagulls floating over her head, dipping down the odd time to pick up crumbs from the white sand below. Even though grey clouds hung low and a gentle drizzle misted the air, Eve found peace and serenity in this piece of heaven she called home.

She climbed to the very top of the hill and watched as the waves hissed softly against the shore. Looking out towards the sea she could see the far off crests of the waves, with the faint odours of seaweed and the salt water mingling with the scent of ling...heather on the hill-side. She found the atmosphere electrifying. She looked out towards the Aran Islands and it brought back memories of her childhood when her father brought her brother Conor and herself on day trips to Inishmore and Inishmaan many times. She had never been to Inis Oirr, but Pierre promised to take her there on a fishing trip next summer; she wondered would she have the patience for fishing.

As she stood there breathing in the strong fresh sea breeze, she tried not to let the dark cloud of worry dampen her enjoyment. She wondered about her father, Eric. Was he in some kind of trouble? She had noticed him a little withdrawn while she was home on her last visit. She also spotted a van pull up at the gate. A man jumped out and was shouting something at her father, then he jumped back in and drove off, leaving him standing there, shocked, with his hands on his head. He walked back across the gravel, dragging his feet and when he went inside, he went straight to his office. Julie, Eve's mother, was busy preparing for guests arriving that evening and hadn't seen the interaction at the gate. Eve's parents, the Wallace's owned a Bed and Breakfast and Caravan Park on the sea's edge and with the help of Conor, their son, they had established a profitable business. As her father didn't mention the episode, she decided not to bring it up.

Eve busied herself with getting ready for her night out with Pierre. They were going to Galway that evening for a meal and a few drinks. She looked forward to spending the evening with him and hoped he would mention something about their future. Eve was crazy about Pierre and loved being in his company. She felt it was time that they should move in together. He didn't seem to feel the same way and said he wasn't ready to take that step just yet, saying he wanted to be free to come and go as he pleased to France.

Eve was stopped in her thoughts when her mother shouted up the stairs, "Are you nearly ready? Your father will collect Pierre and drop both of you to town, and you can get a taxi home." The city was alight with activity as Eve and Pierre walked hand in hand along Shop Street. After a fabulous meal in Oscar's Restaurant, they visited different pubs, enjoying the music and energy of the crowds. They had a really fun night out as Eve reflected on how much she missed being out with Pierre, enjoying his company. As the taxi pulled up outside Eve's house in An Spidéal, Pierre kissed her on the cheek. "See you in the morning, darling." She thought he was going to ask her to go back to his place to spend the night and was annoyed when he didn't. She was also upset with what he told her earlier. He was going to France for the second time this month, saying his parents were poorly. She had wanted him to travel to London with her next week, where her business associates would also be there and would be accompanied by their partners. She would be alone and she was annoyed with him. She knew Benjamin would attend and his presence made her feel a little uneasy no matter how she tried to ignore it. She was too tired to argue, so she decided to leave it until tomorrow.

She hopped out of the taxi and walked swiftly inside. The following morning, after a restless night, Eve travelled over to Pierre's cottage. This time next week she would board a flight to London where she was joining an elite group of fashion designers for a weeklong conference. Pierre was already outside preparing for a fishing trip. She walked down to the bank where his boat was tied up. Although it was nearing the end of October, the air was misty and the sun was still warm, which was surprising for this time of year. She could hear in the distance the clap of the blueish black sea.

Pierre swung around. "Didn't expect to see you this hour of the morning. Thought you would be having your beauty sleep." He walked over and gave her a peck on the cheek, then turned around and walked back to the boat where he was loading his equipment for his day's fishing. Eve was ratty and snapped, "Can you leave what you are doing and listen to me for a moment? I was hoping you were going to travel with me to the conference in London. I had mentioned it to you weeks ago. You know how much I really want you to come. Everyone is bringing their partner with them. I will be the odd one out. Surely you can spare just a week to travel with me. I think your parents wouldn't mind if you have to change the days to visit on just this occasion. Please this is the only thing that I have asked you to do. It will be fun, honestly. If you are worried about the money aspect, I'll sort that. There have to be easier ways to make a living. Fishing is so precarious and dangerous. I worry about you when you are out at sea. Travel with me." Pierre was shocked and retorted, "Fishing is my passion like fashion is yours and just because I make little money doesn't make my job any less important. If you are not happy with that, then we won't work as a couple I am sorry Eve." She knew in her heart he was annoyed with her. She loved him dearly and didn't want to lose him but was worried that he wasn't as committed to the relationship as her. Looking at the tall, handsome, muscular man standing in front of her with a broad smile and thick dark hair brushed back off his tanned face and his sexy French accent, she felt so conflicted. She didn't want to let him go but equally she needed their relationship to move to the next stage.

Pierre hoped Eve wouldn't leave him because he loved her but also the security she brought with her. She loaned him money on occasions when travelling to France, which left him financially stable. He walked over to where she was standing and took her in his arms saying, "I promise I will travel with you after Christmas on one of your weeklong trips." She nodded and they walked down towards the pier as she watched him board his boat and slowly take off to sea. As he sailed outwards, she watched him go further into the deep dark and distant crests of the waves. There were several other fishing boats far beyond bobbling up and down. One would imagine they were just white dots on the edge of the horizon. Eve knew well that fishing was a dangerous and chancy way to earn a living and a mistake could prove not merely expensive but indeed fatal. Pierre had admitted she was right to be fearful because years ago he had a near death experience himself out at sea. She stood there for some time and listened to the gasp and slap of the waves.

Pierre watched Eve on the pier until she disappeared out of sight. He knew for certain that deep down he loved this beautiful woman with her golden red hair and porcelain skin. Her eyes were of a deep blue, fringed by their thick lashes, and he noted her soft lips were always curved in a smile that lit her entire face. The following week, Eve travelled to Dublin airport to board her flight to London. As she looked out at the clouds below her, she remembered back to when she left school. She wasn't sure what was on the radar for her future. She had an interest in fashion from a very young age and even though she couldn't afford to buy clothes, she studied them in magazines and imagined herself dressed up, modelling on the catwalk someday. After studying art and design, she continued on in her studies and got a degree in fashion and worked with several designers both at home and abroad. Eve launched her first commercial collection after graduating from college. She was scouted and approached by a top fashion house who saw her potential. She became a household name overnight, going from strength to strength and making her name famous in many countries across the world as a unique designer. She was brought back to reality when she heard, "Fasten your seat belts we are about to land." With a busy week ahead, she transformed her mind-set into business mode.

Eve was well and truly in demand at the London fashion show with her autumn/winter collection. She always found the beginning of a new season exciting and welcomed it with plenty colourful and exotic styles. It gave her the opportunity to exhibit her new collections, which were fresh, unique and pushed the boundaries and could set trends. Eve was adamant to stay ahead of the fashion scene. More recently, her designs were admired worldwide. One top designer described them as "Simple pieces of clothing that shout rather than whisper." When asked to speak that evening, she walked on to the platform with the confidence of a woman in charge of her life. She could feel Benjamin's eyes directly on her, but she tried not to acknowledge him.

Benjamin Thatcher, a middle-aged man and one of the top designers in the business, seemed to turn up continually at the fashion shows and conferences Eve attended. She gave a ten-minute talk and finished by saying "I have been very lucky to have met amazing and wonderfully supportive people along the way. I also stress it is so important to stay true to your own creative vision. After all, it's what sets you apart from the crowd." The day was stressful and tiring, so Eve decided to go to her room early and get a good night's sleep. She planned on getting up early morning and taking a long earned walk in the fresh air. She was rushing for the lift and didn't notice the man until she was almost upon him. It was Benjamin. She almost stumbled as she tried to avoid crashing into him. His arms shot out and he held her in a firm grip. Her heart raced at the unexpected closeness of his body. Eve noted he was barely taller than she, his hair was closely shaven, he had a deeply tanned face and his eyes seemed filled with an amused expression. He had a smile around his lips that made him look attractive. He let her go and nodded at her as he walked off and left her standing in limbo. Red-faced she continued on towards the lift and went to her room for a well-earned rest. She pulled her phone out of her bag and checked for a message from Pierre, but there were no messages. She turned her phone off.

It was coming to the end of the season in the guest house for Eve's parents, the caravan park was still full and Conor had bookings up to Christmas and into January. He was very pleased with himself and felt he was doing a good job in looking after his clients efficiently. If any problems arose, he was there on site promptly to put it right. Julie looked out the bedroom window as she called out to Eric. "There is a man at the front gate." 'I wasn't expecting visitors this evening,' she thought to herself. Eric glanced out the door. He called back to Julie "I'll take care of him he must be here to see Conor about booking into the park." Without another word, Eric went out as fast as his feet would carry him towards the man in the white van. Julie went back to dressing the beds and when Eric came in an hour later, he was red faced and weary. Julie enquired to know what the man in the van wanted. He had to think quickly and replied, "He was asking about second-hand caravans for sale." She looked at Eric "Did you tell him we don't sell them we only rent out spots to holiday makers?" He said, "Of course I did," and he picked up the daily paper and began reading. Only he wasn't reading he was just hiding behind the paper giving himself a chance to think about what had taken place in the van at the front gate. He couldn't think straight. He had to meet his friend Paddy in the morning but what excuse would he give to his wife? Paddy, his drinking friend was calling for him at the crack of dawn and he had to be ready to go with him. Eventually, he plucked up the courage to lie. "Julie, I'm going to Maam Cross early in the morning, myself and Paddy are thinking of buying a pony." Julie stood looking at him with her hands on her hips. "Are you crazy what do you want with an animal like that and most important of all where would you house him for the winter?" Eric tried to think of what excuse he would give for having a pony. "Visitors would enjoy feeding him and children could have rides on him in the summer." Julie was perplexed by his suggestion saying, "Forget about it. It's not happening you are not thinking straight. When did you get that crazy idea?" He replied, "Paddy, text me yesterday I must have forgotten to mention it to you."

The following morning, Eric was up early and gone by seven o'clock. Julie went to the drawer and discovered he didn't bring the cheque book and wondered what he was using for money because she knew he was strapped for cash last week. Eric arrived home mid-day, looking drained. Julie asked. "Well, did you buy the pony?" He shrugged his shoulders "Not today. The prices weren't right." Julie knew by his body language he was fibbing. She said sarcastically, "I wondered what you were using for money as you left the cheque book behind." He couldn't let Julie know where he really was with Paddy, so he remained tight-lipped. He went out the back door and down the lawn to the caravan park where Conor was trimming the hedges. Eric was in dire straits and didn't know where to turn.

Meanwhile, Pierre was back from sea and preparing to go to France. Eve was coming home Monday and he was flying out Tuesday night. He knew he had very little time to catch up with his girlfriend and, of course, she would not be happy. Eve drove straight from the airport to Pierre's cottage. She planned they would go into Galway for a meal and catch up on lost time. She hoped to persuade him to go on the next trip with her to Manchester, it would only be a four-night stay, they would fly over next Friday evening and back again on Tuesday so he wouldn't miss out on his sea fishing for a long period.

Pierre was sitting inside when he heard a car drive up towards the cottage. He jumped up and looked out the window. He was expecting to see Eve today but not this early. He tried to think up an easy way to drop the bombshell that he was going to France tomorrow night. She bounced in the door, not able to contain her happiness at seeing him but then spotted the travel cases in the corner of the kitchen. She knew he was heading away soon again and her heart sank. "This is a lovely surprise. I wasn't expecting you yet, Eve," he said. She was quiet, in fact, Pierre found the silence uncomfortable. He knew he had to try to change her mood, so he walked over to face her and took both her hands in his, looked at her deep in her eyes and told her he loved her with all his heart. Eve responded by asking him was he going to France soon again. "I'm flying out tomorrow night."

She couldn't help feeling a stab of bitter disappointment that he was leaving for France after her arriving home to spend a few days with him. She was raging and pulled her hands from his grip. "It's barely a month since you were over to visit your parents. Surely they can't expect you to go back and forth continually. Do they not understand that we need to spend some quality time together it isn't fair? You'll be gone for a week and I will be gone to Manchester when you come back home. I had intended to ask you to join me on this trip it was only going to be for a few days but that will not happen this time either." Pierre searched in his mind to find the right thing to say to her. He didn't want to upset her further as he was about to ask her for the usual loan when travelling to France and this time he needed a little extra, he was overdrawn in the bank already and was practically penniless. Eve went over and stood in front of the open window desperate for a breath of cool fresh air. Pierre stayed standing exactly where she left him and quietly watched her. She swung around to face him her eyes narrowed. "Why are you looking at me that way? You can't expect me to be all about you when I'm just home and you take off again?" Eve's temper was nothing new to Pierre. He felt the brunt of it several times and especially more recently. He tensed as she walked towards the door. "I'm going home now." He looked at her with an expression she couldn't fathom. But he didn't speak. She continued out to her car and started the engine. There was a crunch of tyres on the gravel in the drive way and she was gone. Pierre stood watching until she was out of sight. The evening was grey and overcast, the air was cold and there was a hardness to the wind as if its edges had been sharpened like knives. He was panic-stricken, his wallet was empty and the prospects of travelling looked daunting. Pierre stayed awake until the early hours. Eventually, falling into a restless sleep, it was with heavy eyes and a heavier heart that he faced the next morning.

Julie noticed her daughter pale and tired after coming downstairs. "Didn't sleep well I take it Eve?" She wished her mother would mind her own business. She lay awake all night watching the shadows on the bedroom wall and as the darkness of the night lifted to reveal a crisp and bright morning, she was upset and found it hard to stay in control. Eve felt there was a wedge slipping in between her and Pierre. She wasn't sure if he really loved her but one thing was for certain: she loved him and wanted to spend the rest of her life with him. After breakfast, which was just a half cup of tea, she decided to go back down to the cottage and have a word with him. As she drove towards the house he was packing the last of his luggage into the car. He decided early morning he would travel anyway, even though he had very little money to get by. He glanced up as she walked towards him, his eyes were warm and he had a smile that was completely bright and welcoming. She stood looking at him, her back straight, her eyes burning with both tiredness and mixed emotion. Part of her wanted to go to him and hold him close. Instead, she walked past him and into the kitchen without a word. He followed close behind and he noted her face was very pale. Whatever emotions she was feeling she restrained herself. She took a steadying breath, then turned and looked at him and he felt the tension between them raise a notch. She shot him a furious look. His mouth opened, but no words came out. She said matter of factually, "I presume you are about to ask me for the usual cash." Eve continued to say, "I understand about having to go to your parents but why so often?" Against her will, she took out an envelope and gave him the usual thousand euros. Pierre took the envelope slowly out of her hand and looked at her without speaking, then he focused his eyes on the ground. "I was hoping to get a little more this time. My parents are really struggling with the cost of living at the moment." Her heart skipped a beat. 'Was he taking advantage of her? Surely his parents weren't that strapped for cash?' She was trying to quell her suspicious mind. He folded his arms around her and hugged her tightly, at that minute she hated him. He continued on to say, "I love you Eve and I promise I will pay back every euro." "I have no more on me I'm sorry" she said. She wasn't happy with him asking for so much money, "I'm going home, contact me when you get back and remember things will have to change we can't go on like this." Impulsively, he bent and kissed her on the cheek, but she didn't respond and just walked away.

The following evening Eve was checking on the caravans when she heard her father's voice. She stood and listened and realised he was at the back gate talking to the same man from the white van again. She pulled back behind the hazelnut tree and listened. She was shocked as the man's voice was becoming more threatening and he sounded as if he was about to attack her father. "I told you last time Mr Wallace, Paddy isn't prepared to wait any longer" she heard. Eric was pleading with him, "Please ask him to give me a little more time." "End of the month," the man shouted aggressively as he swung around and jumped into his van and sped off at high speed. Eve was still hiding behind the tree, wondering what was all that about? In fact, she couldn't help feeling anxious that her father seemed to be in some sort of serious trouble. She stood there and watched him walk back through the caravan park and up the avenue to the house; he had his hands in his pockets and was dragging his feet along the ground. He looked dejected, and the hump he carried on his back showed a secret worry.

CHAPTER 2

E ric tried to act normal around Julie and spent the rest of the evening power-washing the outside walls. He couldn't think straight. The trouble he was in was horrendous. If he could go back five years, he'd have stayed away from buying shares. Eric was full of shame for taking out a substantial loan and using the caravan park for security. He lay awake each night racking his brain, hoping he could come up with a way out. He was adamant Eve his daughter didn't find out. He believed she'd have no pity on him because she warned him before about being careless with his finances when she found out he was gambling substantial amounts on the odd horse. He knew well that only for his wife Julie this business would never have materialised. She worked day and night to make it successful. When Conor came of age, they decided to transfer the park into his name and for tax purposes. Eric's name was added to the final documents. He knew Julie would probably kick him out if she found out the trouble he was in, so he had to work his way out of it quietly.

Just then, Julie came out of the house and distracted him from his thoughts. She called Eric, waving an envelope at him. "This came in the late post. It is addressed to you 'private and confidential' will I slip it open?" Eric leaned over and took it swiftly out of her hand. Julie noted he looked alarmed. He slipped it into his pocket "It's a reminder to update my bank details I'll check it later." Julie insisted they never sent a separate reminder before and explained to him that both names were on the existing account therefore any correspondence would have the two names attached. Eric said rather quickly, "It must be the park account." Julie said, "Only Conor's name should be on that post." Eric had to think quickly he looked up at Julie "I got my name in on that account a few years ago. I sometimes lodge cheques for him and if he needs me to enquire about any part of the account, my name has to be in there to have permission to enter his details." Eric's voice was rising "And I don't want you to mention this to Conor because he asked me to keep it between ourselves." Julie was upset she had been left out of this decision. Eric continued to say, "I do most of the banking for him. It saves him from going to town." Julie responded, "I don't know why he doesn't bank on line anyway, it's the way forward."

Eric's heart almost stopped when Julie mentioned banking on line. Conor hadn't gone to the bank for a long while because Eric made sure he carried out all his business for him. Eric had a direct debit coming out each month to pay off the loan he had taken out in the bank under his own name. If Conor looked into it, he would discover the money being debited each month. He remembered back to the day he asked his son if he could add his name to the account. His son found it difficult to deal with paperwork so Eric took advantage and offered to take care of his finances for him. Conor's account was very healthy and Eric got a loan on the strength of the park and the steady cash flow. They both had to sign off on the loan, but Conor didn't read the material just scribbled down his signature, thinking it was to do with his father's name being added to the account. Eric felt guilty but he didn't want to miss out on a chance of making easy money at least that's what he thought back then when the lads convinced him to invest in the shares. They were all doing it, so why should he be the odd one out? It was like a dream come true for the first year. Eric invested fifty thousand euros. He was on the way to be a rich man then he would let his family know his secret. They would be over the moon with their windfall. He would pay back the loan and all would be wonderful. He knew Julie his wife would scold him at first for tricking his son and getting him to sign papers in order to get the loan. Julie knew her son would have just signed the forms without reading the small print and trusted his father. But Eric's world fell apart six months ago when the shares crashed and he realised he had lost all his money overnight and he would never see it again. Unfortunately, the direct debit continued to go out each month. He also had to find twelve thousand euro to pay back to his drinking friend, Paddy. He put it all on a horse that was forecast to definitely come in first. He had planned on giving his friend back the money he borrowed and would have enough left over to bring the bank's payments up to date and a little change for himself. His dream was shattered yet again when at the last furlong the horse fell. He was devastated.

Paddy was demanding his money be paid back. He had sent one of his work colleagues twice already to the caravan park in one of the company vans which Paddy was involved in the management of, 'Fair Field Sand and Gravel Suppliers.' Eric was stuck in a rut. He couldn't go near the Bed and Breakfast account to withdraw money to cover his tracks because it would leave finances short for the day to day running of that business, anyway his wife would spot it straight away. He knew very well what he had to do but how would he explain to his wife and son? The following week he announced he was going to work, separate to the caravan park. Julie snapped, "For God's sake, you're mad there is more than enough work to be done around this place." Conor laughed "Dad, we're making enough money here. There is no need to go to work. There is a good income coming from the park. I have seen no statements lately, but you must know the account is healthy. You keep that part of the business going for me and that is a job in itself." Conor looked at his mother "In fact, I'm thinking of changing my car next year. I should be able to afford it. I'm being very careful, only spending what is needed." Eric's stomach churned with fear as he wondered what the outcome would be when Conor checked his finances.

His head was in turmoil. He stood up from the table saying, "I will be starting work in the next few days with the sand and gravel company. Paddy put in a good word for me." Of course, Eric knew it was in Paddy's interest to get him working because he was demanding his money be paid back. "Conor, I'll still look after your finances but I feel I need to get out into the work place for a while." Julie responded "We won't stand in your way but it is ludicrous to see you out working when there is a good turn over between the two businesses at home." Eric started driving the gravel lorry the following week. Paddy was in charge. He was there to show Eric the ropes and check his credentials making sure his paper work was in order to drive a lorry.

Eric was pleased that he had kept up with refresher courses for truck driving. He had spent his younger years driving lorries and articulated trucks for different companies. Eve realised she was travelling at least half the year with her business and if she and Pierre are ever going to become a proper couple, they would have to move in together and commit to each other. She got the feeling Pierre was holding back on her, moving in with him. She felt there was something secretive about him but couldn't quite put her finger on it. She wondered if he was taking advantage of her wealth. She had been thinking that she could get him into the modelling business some day when she launched her range of men's clothing. Her thinking was that it would be easier and safer than fishing and they could work together. She didn't mention her intentions to Pierre yet, she would have to wait until the time was right.

Eve was spending the week in Manchester exhibiting her new designs and to her relief Benjamin the top designer didn't turn up at any of the fashion shows. Eve was relieved but wondered why she thought of him at all. It was the last evening of her trip and as she was getting out of the taxi; she spotted him across the road. The night was cool and bright and the streetlights gave a warm glow to the houses all around as she continued to walk towards the hotel. He came behind her, "I had hoped to get in early" he said "And go for a drink to discuss the last few days and how business is progressing. Will you come for one drink with me?" He looked down at her and smiled. The moonlight and the gleam from the streetlights illuminated her face, and he thought she really looked beautiful. A little voice inside her head said 'go with him it's only a drink to catch up on the weeks fashion scene.' "Just one," she said. They made their way to the Sky View Bar and two hours later he accompanied her, back to her hotel. As she walked inside, he stood watching her hypnotised by her slender body and glamorous demeanour. She had a little too much to drink on an empty stomach, she was unsteady on her feet and took a couple of tentative steps backward to where he was standing. She didn't mind if he held her, but as she drew nearer, he was uncertain of what to do or say next. He outstretched his hand and steadied her. All he could think of saying was to wish her good night, thanked for her company and reluctantly he parted ways with her.

Eve back from her trip, was standing out on the pier waiting to see Pierre's fishing boat appear. Black storm clouds start hovering out over the sea and the first salt-water droplets of impending rain stung her cheeks. With the wind whipping round her ears, she could feel a shiver go through her body. Eve had big news for Pierre. She had secured a one year contract in France with a prominent fashion house. She was delighted with the opportunity. Maybe visiting and staying with Pierre's parents would be on the cards, but first things first, she had something much more important on her mind. She hoped that maybe when hearing she was going away for a year he might think of proposing. Eve's face lit up as she caught sight of Pierre's boat nearing the dock. He waved to her, "Didn't expect to see you here." Eve shouted excitedly, "Thought I'd surprise you." As Pierre stepped off the boat cold and wet, Eve launched herself into his arms and hugged him tightly. "It is so good to see you again," as she kissed him on the lips. He held her cheeks with the palms of his cold wet hands. "How about coming over to stay with me tonight?" "Of course I will, I can't wait. Let's get back to the house," she said. They walked back hand in hand, silently. She couldn't wait to tell him her good news. She hoped he would support her and understand because it was only for one year. She waited in anticipation while he showered and changed into dry clothes. When he came back into the kitchen she was putting a pizza into the oven and did her best to compose herself. Her mouth was dry, she swallowed hard before she swung around from the cooker to face him and without delay said "I'm going to France for a year, I'm signing the contracts with a top modelling company." He looked at her stunned, "When?" "I'll be going soon." His eyes travelled towards the window and the magnificent view of the sea. Pierre wished Eve hadn't caught him at such a low moment. The fishing had been crap today, and he had received a phone call that had upset him this morning. He had to dig deep to find the strength to pull himself back together. Eve watched him. He looked pale and tired and his body language betrayed his unhappiness with what she'd just told him. He swung around asking, "What about us?" "Let's get engaged," she said, "I want to know where we stand with this relationship before I go away. Let's plan our future together."

He looked away from her. "I'm not in a position to settle down yet. I will probably have to give up fishing and find a better paid job. The income from fishing is so uncertain. I want to be able to provide for us. It's not right that I have to rely on you." She was disappointed with his reply. "Pierre, we need our relationship to move to the next level. We need to commit to each other. We have been together for a long time. I know I want to be with you, but if you can't commit to me I don't think we are going in the same direction. Perhaps the time in France will give us space to think about us." Pierre turned paler than he already was. "Please don't say that, Eve I love you and want us to be together. Please don't leave me like that, I'm nothing without you, we will make this work." He walked over and threw his arms around her "Please Eve don't go at all." She saw tears streaming down his cheeks. "Please don't cry Pierre, I have to do this for me. I can't miss this opportunity. You know that I have wished for this for such a long time. It's been my dream." He nodded and she knew he wasn't happy with her decision. "Go then I won't stand in your way." She was shocked when he asked, "Would it be possible for you to transfer the usual money to my account when you are overseas? You know I will pay back all of it as soon as I get a better paid job." She hesitated "I'll forward as much as I can but the cost of living in France is high as you well know from your parents. I'll do my best and send what I can afford. I have to save some money for the future. That's the reason I'm signing up to the year's contract in the first place." When he had asked about the money, he cheered up. "I'll go into town and bring back a few bottles of wine. We'll have a cosy night in. What do you think?" Eve just smiled and nodded her approval. When Pierre was gone to town, Eve decided to wash up and tidy away papers thrown on the chairs. She was almost finished when he arrived back. She lifted the last bunch of papers just as a note fell to the floor. She picked it up and glanced at it. She scanned the phone number written on top of the note and underneath there were a few words written in French. Eve stuck it into her bag.

Later, she thought to herself that she would hide it in her old tweed purse her grandmother gave her when she was a child. She held on to the purse all her life and kept many a secret note in it over the years. Pierre walked over and left the wine on the coffee table by the fire. Eve took the pizza out of the oven and brought it over and left it beside the chilled wine. They sat on the couch ready to enjoy the food and drink. Pierre looked at her. "Are you happy?" She smiled and answered, "Yes." They ate in silence for a while. Eventually she spoke, asking Pierre his plans for the next year, "Fishing I suppose until I find a suitable job." Eve said, "I haven't decided what I'm going to do about coming home for visits." He looked at her blankly she noticed his face drop a little. "Surely you'll get home to visit your parents during the year." Eve said rather carelessly, "Hopefully." When they had finished eating, she stood up to have a shower and change into something more comfortable. She went into the bedroom and took the purse out of the bottom of her hand bag where she bundled the note into it with some others already there, some were there for such a long time she had forgotten what was written on them. She closed it and buried again it in the bottom of her bag. She went into the en-suite and showered and day dreamt that Pierre might change his mind about getting engaged and put a diamond ring on her finger before going away for the year. He always made her feel like the most beautiful woman in the world. She walked into the sitting room feeling refreshed after a hot shower. Pierre walked over and cupped his hands around her face and leaned into her and kissed her. Then he caught her by the hand and they walked into the bedroom where Pierre had the lights dimmed and candles lighting. They closed the door and spent a passionate night together.

The following morning, Pierre set off to shore for his fishing trip. Eve drove down with him and stood watching him move away slowly, he was going alone today his crew of three were lending a helping hand to the captain of the new trawler 'Ocean Wave.' Eve wondered where they picked the names for their boats, Pierre's was named after the planet 'Jupiter.' She could see her breath turn to steam in the chilly early morning air. The smell of the sea hit her nose and a fair breeze brushed her cheeks. Even though she was snuggled comfortably in her sheep skin jacket with a scarf wrapped in layers round her neck, she could still feel the icy chill of the crisp air invading her body.

After Pierre's trawler drifted out of sight, Eve drove home and looked forward to tonight and the rest of the week, staying with Pierre until she headed on her travels next week. Pierre checked the weather as usual before he left home that morning, but as it was nearing evening, the weather suddenly changed and the water turned rougher than predicted. He pulled in the nets and turned for home. The boat rocked and was very unsteady. Suddenly, an unexpected gale force wind blew over the ocean, bringing with it a freak wave. The boat rocked viciously from side to side with a thick spray completely covering it all over. Pierre held on to the ropes tightly. He prayed intensely for the wind to calm.

Eve was on a shopping spree with her mother, she knew Julie was going through a difficult time lately as her father was ratty and when he was at home; he spent most of the time outdoors. They went into Galway city to spend a girl's day out together, going for a meal then finishing up in the cinema. Eve bought a present for Pierre and hoped he'd like it. His phone was outdated and when she was away, she wanted to be able to reach him without his phone cutting out, which was happening with his old phone. Eve was totally unaware of the danger Pierre was in out at sea. She thought of him and looked forward to the night ahead, and hoped he was on the way back. She thought back to last night and felt a thrill run through her body, which left her longing to see and touch him again.

As wind tore through the water, the boat somersaulted, catching Pierre completely unaware. He was thrown overboard, going underwater in a stunned state. Luckily, he never lost his orientation even before his downward plunge. He clawed against the sea to propel himself back up. When his head broke the surface, he gasped for air. The waves rose around him, but he fought them, trying to focus his mind on that singular need to breathe. He used his arms and legs to create a rhythm matching that of the sea in an effort to keep afloat. He trembled, as the cold water was almost unbearable. He thought he could hear an engine in the distance. Just as Pierre's hands were losing the strength to hold on any longer, a lobster boat emerged from behind a massive wave. It was smaller than his boat but one of the most welcome sights in his life. In a very short time, the crew of three pulled him over the side into the boat and wrapped him in blankets. They brought him into the small cabin at the back. While lying there, he could feel the wind whipping against the bow of the boat. He shivered with a mixture of cold and shock. His eyes were misty and his mouth was dry. One of the crew brought him a mug of warm water to sip and take the dryness out of his mouth as he remained in shock. Another crew member dialled 999 and an ambulance was dispatched for when the boat reached shore. They drove him quickly to the emergency department where he was examined by the doctor on call. After reviewing his condition, he was admitted overnight for observation due to low blood pressure. He rang Eve from the hospital's land line and explained what happened. That night, while lying awake in the hospital he began to worry about his finances for the coming year. He tried to relax and put all negative thoughts out of his mind and be thankful he was rescued with no life-threatening injuries. The following morning, Pierre was discharged from the hospital. Eve was told that he needed to take it easy for a few days, but that he would be fine.

Back at home she handed him a new phone. He was overjoyed, as his own had been damaged in the water. She knew he needed it for business but also so she could contact him. She noticed he was having trouble trying to get the phone set up. "If you give it to me, I'll put in the SIM card," she said. He looked worried, "I'll have a different number then." "No, you won't. It is the same number." He seemed relieved. As soon as she switched it on, it bleeped a few times. They were sitting in front of the fire she had lit earlier in the day as he was talking about the previous day's event and how scared he had been. More messages came in on his phone, which was charging over on the counter where Eve had plugged it in. She was about to go over and look at the screen but he got there before her and snapped it off the counter, pulling out the lead of charger. "Pierre, what is wrong? You almost pulled the wire out of the plug it should be left charging for a few hours." He seemed agitated and came back and sat down, putting the phone into his pocket. Eve wondered was he still disorientated or was there somebody sending him messages? She wondered why Pierre was so bothered and secretive about contacts on his phone.

Eric regretted getting into a money trap blindfolded and giving his son's business as security as he now knew he would spend the rest of his life paying it back. He had concealed the whole sorry state from his wife and son, but now he was about to be found out. He didn't know where to turn. Julie and Conor were about to find out, and he was devastated. Conor went into the bank earlier than planned to arrange finance for his new car and was weak at the knees when he was informed by the assistant that his account was overdrawn and he would be advised not to write any more cheques. He went straight home to confront his father. As he walked into the kitchen, his mother was sitting at the table she looked up at her son who roared "Somebody robbed my bank account, it's in the red." Eric drove up the avenue. He got out of the car forcing a smile as usual when he walked into the kitchen but was shocked to see his wife Julie and son Conor with bank statements laid out before them. Julie pointed to Eric to come over and sit down "Do you know anything about the state of Conor's bank account?" Eric stared at the paperwork. He felt a rush of blood go to his face he trembled as his voice shook. "Well Eric, there is guilt written all over your face," Julie shouted at him. He bent his head and rested it on his hands and began explaining the predicament he was in. Every last euro was gone from Conor's account. The twenty thousand euro overdraft was also used, and Eric knew it was his fault. Julie was hysterical "No wonder you wanted to go out to work. Look what you have done to your son after the way he looked after the business and saved every euro possible. What did you do with the money" she shouted. He explained about buying shares and hoping to get a back a fortune. "Well, you are no part of our lives anymore. You can go where you like and don't come back until you bring back that hard earned money." She was vicious with him. Conor stayed silent feeling his mother was being too harsh on his father but there was no reasoning with her. Eventually, Conor said to his mother, "Maybe dad did it to make us some more money, give him a chance and let him stay." Julie was adamant, saying that she had no intention of changing her mind. Conor didn't want to see his father out of the house but didn't know what to do so he walked out the door, down to the caravan park and sat behind the sycamore tree and cried for a long while. He saw his father walk out of the house, getting into his car and driving down the avenue. He called out to him. Eric stopped for a second and said, "I'll be back later." He went out the gate and his son watched until he was out of sight, wondering where he was going and was devastated by the mess that they now found themselves in.

Eleanor called out to her brother Paddy in the kitchen, "I think there's a knock on the front door. Can you answer it I am busy here?" Paddy pulled himself from the armchair where he was relaxing watching television. He had been out late last night and was feeling a little tender. He opened the door "Eric come in." Paddy noticed how shook he looked. Eric walked into the living room, Paddy noticed he didn't speak. Paddy tapped Eric on the shoulder "Everything alright?" Eric sat down. "Julie and Conor found out about the money and me being in debt." He proceeded to tell Paddy what happened at home earlier that day. "Julie won't allow me back until I put all the money back into the bank and that will be never." It was a comfort to be able to talk to his friend even though he owed Paddy a small fortune as well. Eleanor came into the living room and after a few hours sitting with them both he was about to go when they asked him where he was spending the night. He shrugged his shoulders saying, "I can't go home I need time to think." Eleanor offered him a bed for the night and he was so thankful. At least Paddy was aware of his predicament and Eric had begun to pay him back the money he owed him since he started work in the sand and gravel company. He knew it wouldn't be as simple at home because of the situation he had landed his family in and he had very little money over after paying Paddy the agreed amount each week.

The following morning, Eve dropped home to collect some clothes, she intended on staying with Pierre for a few more days while he was off work. The last two days she would spend at home before travelling to France and on one of the days she had planned to spend it with just her mother on a trip to the city. Julie was really going to miss her, but she was happy to see her daughter being successful in her career. Eve noticed the house was extremely quiet when she walked in home. She called out to her mother but got no reply. She called again, "In here, in the office Eve." "Why are you crying Mam?" Julie told her the story and Eve sat staring at her mother. Eve thought for a while before saying "I think you were very harsh telling him to leave until he brought back the money, he can't get it back overnight and I am sure he meant well and hoped to make you rich." "It's the way he went about it going behind our backs he wiped out all the money in Conor's account. Your brother trusted him when he left him the management of his finances." Eve was concerned for her father. "I wonder where he spend the night." Julie shrugged her shoulders and said sarcastically, "Maybe he stayed with his friends that got him into the mess." Eve was baffled and taken aback at her mother's attitude. Julie got up and went into the kitchen, saying in a high-pitched voice, "It will teach him a lesson not to go behind my back again." Later that evening, Eve contacted Pierre and let him know about the major situation in the family. He was disappointed not to be able to see her, but Eve explained she felt she couldn't leave her mother when she was so upset.

CHAPTER 3

Pierre was annoyed after Eve cancelled staying with him. He knew she had to stay with her mother, but he selfishly wanted to spend as much time as he could with her. Eve switched on the kettle there was a slow rumble from it, it was the only sound in the kitchen. She looked over to where her mother sat, looking tired and worried. Eve made two mugs of tea and handed one to her mother. They sipped their tea slowly both stuck for words. The stove creaked and crackled and the fire was bright. Julie sighed tearfully. Guilt made her hesitate. Maybe she shouldn't have been so harsh with her husband. Even though the fire was warm, she felt cold and shivery to the core. The back door opened. Julie swung round in expectation, but it was only Conor. He looked withdrawn and pale. He pulled out a chair and sat down across from his mother. Julie looked at him "Did your father stay in the caravan park last night?" "No, he didn't I thought he might have contacted you," he said to his mother. Julie shook her head. Eve remarked to them that if he didn't make contact, they would have to find his whereabouts. Conor admitted he rang his father umpteen times yesterday evening but got no reply. "This will have to be sorted out before I go to France, I am worried about him," Eve looked over at her mother. "I'll stay with you for the next couple of nights but I'll be spending the last day and night with Pierre." Eve was getting annoyed with her mother "You will have to let Dad come home and find a solution." Eve thought for a while before saying hesitantly, "I can lend him some money, not a lot mind, to help him out until he makes arrangements with the bank." Her mother was adamant. "He will go to the bank on his own to sort out this mess."

Later that morning, Paddy called to the park. He avoided going up to the house in case he met Julie. He was relieved when he spotted Conor outside and drove over to where he was clipping the hedges. He rolled down the window of the car and told him his father was staying with himself and Eleanor for a few days until he got straightened out. Paddy drove away quickly he didn't want to get dragged into a family row. Conor went up to the guest house and told his mother and sister. Eve was relieved that her dad was ok and had a place to stay, but Julie was raging. "What will the neighbours say when Paddy tells his friends in the pub? We will be the talk of the parish." Eve thought a lot about the situation through the day and by evening, had decided to go over to Paddy's house to see her father the next day. She drove over slowly to the house early afternoon a left turn, a right turn and straight on down to the end of the road. There, in front of her, was the bungalow with a neat lawn all around. It didn't look modern to the eye. In fact, she noted it looked shabby and was badly in need of painting. Her heart was pounding and she wondered why? Because she was here to help her father not to scold him? She parked near the front door got out of the car and as she walked over the noise of the pebbles under her feet seemed to pierce her ears, she lifted her hand slowly and hit the knocker twice, then once again. The door opened slowly. A tall, good looking woman probably in her late fifties stood inside with a stern look on her face. "Yes, can I help you?" she asked. "I'm Eve Wallace. I came to see my father, please." "I'm Eleanor, Paddy's sister," she stretched out her hand and took Eve's and shook it lightly.

When Eric saw his daughter walk in, he was alarmed. He shuffled and moved and the chair squeaked. She spoke to him but didn't know exactly what else to say as she moved over to the window just to avoid his stunned gaze. She crossed her arms as she looked outside. Looking at Eleanor, all she could think of saying was, "You have a lovely view from the window." Paddy didn't speak, and Eve felt uncomfortable. She was struggling to hold back tears. All she wanted was for her father to come back home and everything to be back to normal. She tried her best to control her emotions and sat quietly, wishing somebody would speak. To her surprise, Paddy started to talk and even though it was only shop talk, it was a relief. Eve knew the bank would be open for another three hours. She got up and excused herself and went out to the car and rang the bank and asked if it would be possible to meet up with an official to sort out an urgent matter? The receptionist asked her for her name and she gave her father's name and address. The lady at the other end of the phone said, "Just a moment, please." She came back within seconds and asked Eve for her name and her relationship with Eric. When she said 'daughter' she got an appointment immediately with the manager. All she had to do now was to get her Dad to agree to keep the appointment. She went back inside. Her stomach was rumbling with nerves. Eleanor handed her a cup of tea, which she drank it down. There was too much milk in it and too little sugar, but it bided her time until she could get her father talking. She ignored the plate of biscuits, they would never go down her throat with the tension in her neck. When dinner was finished, Eric sat over at the fireplace. Eve pulled her chair over near him. There was no time to waste. Paddy went out and Eleanor was busy filling the dishwasher. This was her opportunity to talk to her father and, after some persuasion, he agreed to go with her to the bank.

Eric's heart was racing as he they walked in and over to the customer desk. A lady showed them into a room. There were four chairs in front of a desk with a large swivel chair on the other side. After a brief wait, a man in his late sixties walked into the office. He shook hands with them and introduced himself as Oliver Prendergast. The palms of Eric's hands were sweaty and his legs were shaking as he explained his financial state to the manager. Next, Mr. Prendergast asked Eric for his account number. After the manager viewed it for a few seconds, he looked up at Eric. "There are two names on this account." The blood rushed to Eric's face, "That would be my son." Eric continued on talking and explaining about the account being in joint names for the past few years for convenience's sake. The manager turned away from the computer and looked up at him with an authoritarian look. "First Mr. Wallace, you'll need to clear the overdraft before we plan for you to pay back the remaining loan. You will be required to produce up-to-date accounts and a tax clearance cert within the next few days. They will need to be forwarded to the head office. Your son will have to accompany you on the next visit to sign the necessary documents in order to start repayments on the loan, which is now in serious arrears. Unfortunately, if you continue to be unable to make repayments on that loan the bank will have no option but to take the park as collateral." Mr. Prendergast,

24

stood up and shook hands with both of them. The meeting was over.

Eve stayed silent and let her father talk. She was only there to lend support. Her father walked out of the bank in a state of shock. In his wildest dreams, he didn't realise there was so much involved in catching up with repayments. He was frantic. Where was he going to get money to clear the overdraft he was already paying Paddy a hundred euros a week to clear that loan? He began to lose hope. His overdraft was twenty thousand euros that was only half the money due, and to make it worse that was Conor's account. As they neared Paddy's house, Eric said, "I can't do this anymore I'll never be able to pay back the money." Without putting a lot of thought into the matter, Eve said, "I'll loan you the twenty thousand euros to pay off the overdraft. Hopefully, the bank will set up a direct debit from your wages and you can start to pay back the rest of the loan." He couldn't tell her he already owed Paddy twelve thousand euro and that he was pressing him for it. He knew he would have to work two jobs to keep up with his dept but he was so grateful to Eve for helping him out.

The following morning, Eric contacted his accountant and by closing time the next evening all the criteria were forwarded to the bank. Conor was persuaded by his sister to go to the bank with his father and sign the documents, and with that there was a direct debit set up. Eve had already transferred the money from her savings to clear the overdraft. She doubted she would ever see that part of her savings again because if he didn't have it today, where would he get it tomorrow or in the future? At last, Eric was heading in the right direction and could see a glimmer of light at the end of the dark tunnel. Conor tried to reason with his father and asked him to go back home and talk it through with his mother who had now calmed down slightly.

Eve was on her way over to Pierre's house to spend the night with him before traveling to France. She regretted they didn't have more time together but was delighted to have her father's affairs sorted out and hopefully he would go back home soon. She arrived at Pierre's cottage early evening and was ecstatic when she walked into the living room and saw what he had prepared for her. There were candles lit, the table was set and red roses adorned the room. The smell of cooking was divine. Two bottles of Chardonnay stood chilling in the middle of the table. She noticed a little box parcelled and left beside her wine glass. Eve was surprised to see Pierre had dressed for the occasion, and she was touched he had made such an effort. She was pleased that she had tried for him and had worn her star print dress with a drop shoulder and low cut back. Her hair was a few shades lighter, the hair stylist had suggested that last week when she visited the saloon. Pierre was very attentive to her.

He walked over from the cooker and kissed her on the nape of the neck. "Sit down, dinner is ready and by the way you look fabulous." He walked back to the cooker. She watched him while he served up dinner whilst eyeing the little parcel and wondering what it was? She was blown away by the change in him this evening. Eve always tried to keep their love alive, but Pierre took little notice how she looked or dressed but this evening proved he cared. After dinner, he took up the little box and opened it and lifted out a stunning 14ct gold-plated pendent with three sparkling diamonds hanging from a very light chain. She tried to not to show her disappointment, thinking that the little box might have contained a ring. The pendant was beautiful and was one of the most expensive gifts she had ever received from him. He stood up and tenderly placed it around her neck. He caught her by the hand and led her outside. She wondered excitedly what was next. She walked on with him until he told her to stand over at the rock in the middle of the large garden. He walked near to where she was standing and knelt down. Her heart thumped like a heavy metal band. She was watching him intensely.

He looked up at her "This is especially for you." Suddenly, a loud noise and fireworks exploded above her head. Lights of pink, orange, purple and red created a shape of a heart in the sky while the words 'I love you' lit up brilliantly sparkling like silver before vanishing. He walked towards her but it was an anti-climax moment for Eve as she thought the build-up was going to end in a proposal. Unaware of her disappointment he wrapped his arms around her and whispered in her ear, "I know I've been distracted recently and not given you the attention you deserve, when you come back next year everything will be different and we'll make a life together." They walked back into the house. She was relieved when he didn't mention money and they fell into a relaxed and blissful mood, enjoying each other's company. After a few glasses of wine, they went up to the bedroom as they went in the door he reached out and stroked her hair with his fingers. Next moment he was covering her mouth with passionate kisses and they melted away in each other's arms until late morning.

As soon as the overdraft was paid off in Conor's account Julie contacted Eric. He was cool with her and said he would consider coming home in a few weeks' time. One month had now passed into six and Eric had settled into life in Paddy and Eleanor's house. He was working two jobs, meeting his repayments and was content. Eleanor and Eric had become good friends and he refused to go back home even though his son and wife were adamant he return soon. It was a nice bright summer's evening and Eleanor was just back from town. Eric noted her hair was brighter than usual. Paddy came in for his evening tea as he admired his sister's hair. "I got it highlighted today because I'm going to a concert tomorrow night in the city." She looked over to where Eric was standing, with a spark in her eye "Would you like to come with me I have two tickets and Paddy isn't interested in music?" "I'd love to. No point in wasting the ticket." She went up the hall to her bedroom and left the men to chat, feeling very pleased with herself. She opened her wardrobe door and pulled out a multitude of dresses and began fitting them on.

CHAPTER 4

Eve was attending fashion shows all over France and was elated, knowing she would do this for an entire year. Her mind wandered back to the night she spent with Pierre before she went travelling and how wonderful it was. Towards the end of the first month, she found the perfect apartment in a secluded spot central to her workplace. She could see right across the city and at night the vista sparkled with lights. The balcony of the main living area was impressive, the kitchen was small and compact with a wooden floor and open fireplace and a window to the western side of the building, which allowed the light to cascade in during the evening time, further down the hall there was a fabulous bathroom. She was pleased to see the apartment had a designated parking space, as they were so hard to secure. Eve was so busy, time seemed to pass by quickly. Eve and Pierre were in regular contact, with each other, but she had known that it would be very difficult to visit home given her unpredictable hours and the many fashion shows she had to attend. She needed to be at them so that she could continue to make connections for future work and to ensure the people in the fashion world kept hearing her name.

She missed Pierre and really looked forward to talking to him but she was beginning to get upset with him because every phone call or video chat ended up with him asking her when she could top up his account as he continued to promise to pay it back. For the umpteenth time, her mind contemplated whether he loved her or her money more. If he wasn't serious about their relationship, she would not waste much more time with him. She was well aware she wasn't getting any younger most of her friends were settling down and having children and that was her plan too. She mentioned children a few times, but he always put it on the back burner. She was feeling lonely today and thought about home and how she missed its familiarity. She sat daydreaming of when she was a child and would run to the top of the hill and look down on the village below with its smoking chimneys. She would smell the seaweed and hear the chorus of gulls in the distance fighting over some stray food. Then she would run back towards the trees perched on the crest of the hill and sit down and listen to the sound of her father's chain saw cutting timber for the fire. She missed her parents and brother, but time would fly by and she would be heading home on holiday.

Just as tears gathered and welled up in her eyes the doorbell chimed. She grabbed a tissue and ran it across her eyes and opened the door. It was Benjamin she wasn't expecting him. He stood there wearing a smile that lit up his face; he moved towards her and noticed her eyes were red. It was obvious she had been crying. Inviting him in, she walked on before him into the living room. "Tea coffee, I have both." "Coffee will be fine, no sugar, just milk." He continued talking, "There is a busy week ahead with a lot of travelling." She was certain if Pierre knew she was working with Benjamin he wouldn't be happy. He wouldn't understand that Benjamin was well known in the business. It would open up doors for her and would give her an opportunity to expand her business to other countries and make her name known through his contacts. Benjamin noticed her lack of concentration. He looked at her, and the silence that followed was almost palpable. "Sorry I lost concentration for a moment." He continued to say, "I need to run through a few new fashion websites with you before the next show." They sat and scanned the web for hours and several mugs of coffee later it was time for him to go to his next meeting. He was walking towards the door when he turned and asked her if she was free tomorrow maybe to grab a light lunch around mid-day? She took a long, thoughtful look at him. Common sense told her no, instead she accepted his invitation. His Mercedes pulled up outside her apartment early afternoon the following day and she was brought to an exclusive restaurant in the middle of the city. A waiter greeted them and it was obvious Benjamin was a regular there because the waiter called him by his name and was very attentive towards them. He directed them to a table in the corner next to the big window overlooking the beautiful River Seine that ran next to the city streets. She noted Benjamin looked sleek and elegant in his white shirt and blue suit. The navy blue tie with a multitude of colour complimented the outfit. They talked at length as the scorching afternoon dissolved into evening. Eve reminded him about the meeting he had arranged in another part of the city at five o'clock. He remarked that he would have liked to spend the rest of the evening with her as he found her very easy to talk to and they had so much in common. Eve could feel herself slightly blush when he suggested meeting up again for a proper date. She said "We'll see. Call me."

Eric was well and truly settled into Paddy and Eleanor's house, so much so that he wasn't giving a return home any consideration. Eleanor was very pleased with the extra money she received from Eric for his rent even though it was a small amount it was extra money in her purse each week. She was equally delighted with his company; they went to the cinema on occasions and the odd show or concert. It was a new lease of life to her because she hadn't been out with a man since her boyfriend left her for another woman and that was coming up on ten years next month. It shattered her confidence and she was scared to enter another relationship. Eric was different he boosted her self-esteem and made her feel good about herself. She felt like dressing up and going out again. She was hoping he would decide to stay for the long term. Julie, his wife had practically thrown him out over finances and Eleanor hoped Julie wouldn't want him back home. Eric felt very relaxed in Eleanor's company, they had fun together. He thought he would probably go back home some day and try to patch up his marriage, but that would be down the road. He wasn't prepared to go there, yet life was good in Paddy and Eleanor's place. Conor and Julie contacted him constantly over the last eight months to come home, but he declined each time.

Pierre was out fishing from early morning until late in the evening even though it was tiresome he enjoyed the challenge that each day brought with it. It was difficult on occasions heading off in rough sea conditions. He was an ardent fisherman and was addicted to pier-hunting for whiting, rock-hunting for mackerel, surf-haunting for bass. He so often sailed home in the night-tide beneath the moon and stars. It seemed a lifetime since Eve went away even though it was only eight months. The cash flow from her account dried up considerably since she helped her father out, so Pierre scanned the Connacht Tribune newspaper each week to see if he could find a part-time job to make the extra money that wasn't going to come from fishing. The day arrived, the job that suited him was advertised 'Green Meadow Golf Club invites applications from qualified experienced chefs please apply with CV,' they gave their email address. Pierre applied immediately with an old CV he hoped they would accept. He qualified as a chef back in France and cooked in a four-star hotel for twelve months before returning to Ireland. That was when he gave into the longing in his veins and answered the call of the sea and went fishing. He dreaded next week when he would travel to France yet again with very little money.

The Wallace's business was hectic for the past few months. Eve's mother and brother wished their life was back to normal, and it could be if only Eric came home. Conor was baffled why his father refused to come back especially when his mother was prepared to forgive him, move on with their lives and cope with the money problems together. Julie was finding it almost impossible to sleep as she reminisced back to when she met and fell in love with Eric. She was travelling back from London with her friends on a plane. They were waiting for their bags to come through, when a crowd of lads began chatting to them. Before they went their separate ways, Eric and she exchanged contact numbers. They met the following month for a show in the town hall in Galway. She remembered the expectation on the days leading up to the meeting. When she spotted him walking up towards her she gasped, her eyes glistening with excitement. He looked so handsome in his leather jacket and scarf draped around his neck. After the show, he asked her for another date and that was the beginning of their beautiful love affair. She was saddened by the thoughts "Look at where the two of them were today, split up, with Eric living with Paddy and his sister Eleanor looking after him." She never thought about Paddy's sister falling for her husband, as she believed Eric wouldn't be good enough for Eleanor.

A few days later, Julie drove over to Paddy's house to talk with her husband. Paddy was caught unawares when he swung the door open and saw Julie standing there. "Come in," Paddy offered. She was stern. "I'd rather not, thanks. Could you send Eric out please." "One second and I'll let him know you're here." She remarked a wistful note to Paddy's voice as he walked swiftly

31

into the kitchen. After a prolonged period, Eric came out. Julie smiled warmly at him. Eric cleared his throat. "Hello Julie," he said, feeling rueful. She felt her heart beat a little faster as he leaned forward "Talk quietly, no use in ironing our dirty laundry on Paddy's doorstep." She looked at him scornfully. "It's time you stopped this nonsense and returned home." They held eye contact for a moment, then Eric looked at the ground. "I'm not moving back home." Julie kept a neutral expression on her face. He knew the situation ahead would not be easy, but he wanted to be with Eleanor now. He looked at her with a steeliness she hadn't seen before. His words produced a knot of anxiety when she realised he was serious about not returning home. Her stomach lurched, her knees felt weak and a lump formed in her throat, which left her stuck for words. She wiped away a tear "I'm sorry Eric, I didn't mean what I said. You are part of the family. We'll work through this together," she pleaded with him. "Please come home we miss you." Eric shook his head turned around and walked back into the house and left his wife standing on the door step numbed. Paddy was directly inside the door and saw Julie walk back to her car distressed. He walked out after her and caught her by the arm "I'll talk to him and try make him see sense." She just nodded unable to sound her voice without crying out. She got into her car and drove home heavy hearted.

After a busy day, Conor was looking forward to closing the office, going up home and walking into a hot refreshing shower. A darker shade of blue was creeping across the sky and the first stars were already making an appearance. As he turned the latch on the door, he could hear his mother talking to his sister on Zoom. He had explained to her umpteen times there was no need to talk so loud it was the same as being on the phone. Why she felt the need to shout, he'd never understand. She could practically be heard down in the park. By the tone of voice she was using, it was obvious she was upset this evening. He stood in the hall way and was 'all ears.' As soon as his mother turned off her laptop, he heard her crying uncontrollably. She didn't realise her son was in the house. He walked into her office and left his hand on her shoulder. She began to tell him what happened when she asked Eric to come back home. Conor lifted his hand "I heard you telling Eve, my advice would be to leave him for another while, he will come to his senses soon and he'll get fed up living over there," then he smirked "Or rather they will get fed up with him intruding in their lives."

Benjamin and Eve began meeting for lunch occasionally to discuss business. They both looked forward to the meetings and their friendship deepened. It was one of those evenings after they had finished a business dinner and walked outside into the dark night, he left his arm across her shoulders and went near her cheek with his mouth and whispered "Have you ever seen so many stars together?" She looked up and gasped. "They are beautiful." His handsome brow was furrowed and his dark brown eyes flashing as he gazed at her. She gave him a quick glance and then turned away. She didn't intend to give him any indication that she found him attractive. She felt her breath quicken and her cheeks redden, her emotions were running high. The drive back to her apartment was very different from any of the previous evenings. She slipped out of the car without delay and walked to the front door, she reached into her clutch bag to find her key. Benjamin called her name "By the way, you look fabulous in that dress," and then he drove off. She went into her apartment with a feeling towards Benjamin that had unsettled her but in a good way.

As she stood in the hall, she noticed there was a letter in Pierre's writing sitting on her hall table. It was amongst the other letters she had put there earlier when in a hurry to leave. She read his letter and she told herself he was 'the one,' convincing herself that it was only business with Benjamin. Eve sat down that night and wrote a long, loving letter to Pierre, as she put thoughts of Benjamin out of her mind.

The following month, Eve was feeling like she was partly living out of her suitcase as she was travelling from one venue to another. Today, she was travelling back to her apartment on the train. Before it neared the destination her mind wandered and she thought of the note, she found back in Pierre's house all those months ago. She was still curious and decided that she must ring it one day but today wasn't that day, so she put it to the back of her mind. She checked her watch. Ten past five, Benjamin was always punctual unless caught in heavy traffic. Each time she returned from a business trip he was there to collect her and take her back to her apartment. This evening was no different. When the train pulled in, the station was crowded but that didn't drown out the six o'clock ding of the big station clock. It gave her a sense of belonging because that clock was a familiar face looking at her each time she entered the station and it looked at her as if it was welcoming her back again. Eventually,

Benjamin walked through the revolving doors and over towards her, his eyes were crinkling and he held a broad smile. She looked at his handsome face and smiled with a girlish shyness. "I'm so sorry about being a bit late, traffic was heavy." "Never mind. It is good to see you." As they drove along, she told him about her trip and how she felt it had been successful. "I met loads of clients who placed orders for my latest range." He glanced over at her "I'm happy for you that all went well." She was thinking ahead, she didn't intend to ask him in this evening. "I'm completely drained after the long week and the travelling, can't wait for a hot shower and fall into bed." He asked what about food but she said she was too tired to eat. At last, they reached the apartment, she left her hand on his arm "Thank you so much for collecting me and getting me back safe. You never fail to be there." She was looking at him and he looked at her with a smile that radiated his face. "How about coming to the beach on Sunday with me just chilling out and have lunch, the company would be much appreciated," as he searched her face for confirmation. She didn't have it in her to refuse so she agreed even though she knew quite well she was playing with fire.

Sunday morning was bright and sunny and by mid-day the beach was thronged, unbroken sun beamed down on the white sand all day. After sunbathing and swimming until evening they wandered around the holiday village before eating in a seafood restaurant. As the light faded, Eve gazed out over the water, "I can see why people come here for holidays." She took a sip of wine and continued to enjoy the view. Benjamin was looking at her deep in thought. "When do you plan on going back to Ireland?" he asked but didn't give her the chance to reply, instead he leaned across the table and placed his hand over hers, "You and I have a lot in common." She withdrew her hand hastily "I'm due to go home in eight weeks. I'm looking forward to seeing everyone again. It isn't the same over Zoom or WhatsApp. I think Pierre is counting down the days." He thought for a second, "Is he the French fisherman?" She nodded. He wondered why she only mentioned Pierre the odd time during the past few months. "I thought you and he had parted company. You haven't mentioned him much," he said. "No, we didn't," she said, as she started to feel uncomfortable with his questioning. Shortly after, she thanked him for a lovely day and made an excuse about why she needed to get back. "Of course," he said as he drove her back to her apartment with soft music playing on the radio. Both were silent for much of the two-hour journey.

Later that night, Eve sat back with a glass of wine and reflected on the day she spent with Benjamin. She found it difficult to erase him from her mind. Those brown eyes filled with an amused expression. Any girl could easily fall head over heels for him. She went upstairs and filled a bath of hot water and added some lavender oil. She sank into the aromatic water and closed her eyes, sliding down so that just her nose and mouth rose above the water. She lay there in the quietness for some time, trying to gather her thoughts, which were all of Benjamin. She told herself, 'you're not falling for him,' as she blinked away a tear or two. When she finally got into bed, she tossed and turned in confusion where these thoughts were leading. Eventually, she tried to picture Pierre's face and fell into a turbulent sleep.

Pierre was working around the clock trying to earn enough money to pay his way. He was looking forward to having Eve home; he had missed her and he also hoped she would help him with his financial burdens. His last visit to France was a disaster because of being strapped for cash. Fishing hadn't been easy for the past few weeks as cold damp weather swept in and brought with it an early morning mist that frequently lingered until mid-day. It was one of those days and Pierre was feeling really down within himself. Eve hadn't been in contact with him for over a week now. He got out of bed and fetched his phone off the locker, dialled her number and waited for a reply. Eve was up to her eyes this morning, party season was fast approaching it was just six weeks from Christmas. Her phone rang for the third time she saw Pierre's name by looking at the screen, she snaps it up "Hi Pierre, I'm so busy right now I'm attending a meeting I'll call you tonight." He hung up without replying. He felt something wasn't quite right with the tone of her voice but couldn't work out what. His mind went into overdrive, he panicked, saying to himself 'I can't lose her.' He sat on the side of the bed for a long while, contemplating what to do next. She had hinted at getting engaged many times and he ignored her perhaps now was the time...he knew what he had to do. Tonight was the night, he would propose to her even though it would be via Zoom.

It was late morning before the fog lifted and Pierre was drifting out to sea facing the slight wallowing and rushing of the waves, illuminated by the low sun and framed by long shadows. The day was soft and damp, with a haze still to be seen ahead. The ocean was as calm as it could ever be. Even though he only had four hours of brightness, he hoped to catch enough fish for the market in Galway the next morning. It was late evening and darkness seemed to fall quickly. He was glad to be back at shore with a sufficient catch as he stored them in the cool room down by the pier until morning. He walked up the long path and into his house which felt empty and hollow. The creeper outside touching the window filled the room with dancing shadows. He plugged in his phone to make sure it was in full charge. After a shower and before eating anything even though he was ravenous, he went over to where the phone was charging. His mind was racing and his stomach churned with nerves. He had come to this major decision this morning but was unsure what the outcome would be. Proposing via Zoom would be far from romantic. Without unplugging the phone from the socket, he contacted Eve. They greeted each other happily. Pierre said "I miss you so much Eve." She noted a hint of anxiety in his voice. "What's wrong Pierre you look agitated." "Nothing's wrong I'm just tired after a busy day." "How have you been? I guessed you were very busy when you didn't get to contact me during the week," he said. "It was a crazy week, travelling and meetings. It's such a busy time of year." They exchanged pleasantries for the next few minutes. Pierre went silent and was looking at her seriously. Eve was shocked with his next words. "I don't know how to reach out to you. We are so far apart and have been for the past nine months." Eve reflected "What's wrong with you Pierre? I'll be home in six weeks." "Well I can't wait that length of time to ask if you, Eve Wallace will marry me?" The proposal came like a bolt out of the blue. It wasn't exactly the romantic scenario she was expecting. She looked at him muddled and thought 'why like this, could he not have waited until Christmas and do the romantic proposal, flowers, chocolate, the full works, what was the rush for God's sake over Zoom it seemed odd.' It took her a few minutes to reply to him, in which his heart nearly somersaulted out of his chest. He didn't expect her to hesitate. She accepted, but it was so matter of fact almost like a business venture been agreed upon.

They talked for a long while. She told him how business was progressing and bonuses she had received from companies that hired her during the year. She noticed Pierre's demeanour change. She could count on one hand the amount of surprises he had laid out for her in all the years they were together and now here he was promising her the sun, moon and stars. He was exhilarated. He needed to say the right thing at this moment. He gathered his thoughts "Money isn't everything. Time together is so precious, we should make that our priority from now on. I have a surprise up my sleeve for you when you come home at Christmas," he said excitedly. She wondered what that might be. Eventually, they said good night each promising to stay in contact regularly from now on. She lifted her left hand and thought it would be amazing to be wearing a big diamond on her finger. She had been dreaming of her wedding since she was a little girl. She pictured herself in a long flowing dress of white satin with lace around the edges and a small head piece with flowers. She didn't want a veil. She'd hold a bouquet of purple lavender in her hand. Their honeymoon would be spent in Seattle sightseeing, firstly going to the Seattle art museum, then a tour on the waterfront on the harbour cruise. Points of interest for Pierre would be the Apollo 11 Mission at the Museum of Flight and climbing the fish ladder at the Ballard Locks. They would have to visit the Seattle Sky View Observatory and of course Tiffany shopping and last but not least she would like to go to the Paramount theatre before ending what would have been a dream honeymoon. She stopped dreaming and rang her mother to tell her the news.

Before she mentioned the proposal, Eve enquired about her father hoping he was settled back home but no. Julie told her daughter through sobs that Eric didn't want to return home "Worst of all" she said "He ignores most of my calls, on the odd occasion when he talks to me he never mentions home or the business. I think Eleanor has him brain washed." "Don't worry when I get home, I'll have a heart to heart with him." Eve took a deep breath. The excitement she had a few minutes ago had suddenly changed to butterflies in her stomach. This was not the time to be announcing Pierre had proposed especially when it was over the phone. She knew her mother was old-fashioned and wouldn't understand why he couldn't have waited until she got home. "I've news for you." Her mother fell silent. "Pierre proposed to me and I am so happy."

It was as if her mother's phone was muted. There was no sound from the other end. Eve continued in a high-pitched voice, "He has so many plans for us." She waited for her mother to reply. When she didn't Eve asked, "Are you there, mother?" "Yes, I am. I was just trying to take it all in." Eve was disappointed with what she said "I am a little concerned to be honest Eve, I don't fully trust him, he spends too much time away in France. It doesn't seem right that his parents depend on him and his finances. It's a burden on him and it will fall on you when you marry him." Eve thought silently, 'But it is affecting on me already, but I know he will change when we are a married couple I know he will." They talked for a short while and Eve assured her mother she would stay with her for part of the Christmas holiday. She said good night and rang off feeling deflated. Eve pulled back the curtains and admired the bright moon in the clear sky. She stood there in silent thought. She understood why her mother was worried. She herself didn't really understand why Pierre had proposed tonight. She also couldn't fathom out why he was so attached to his parents. Eve pictured her mother's face on the last evening before she left for France. It looked worn and her bright smile was gone. Was it any wonder she was low-spirited with her husband gone from home and practically living with another family?

A week passed since Pierre had proposed and he rang Eve every night to show he was genuinely trying. They made all kinds of plans, everything from work to the design of the house she would like to live in. Then she was planning the wedding, the honeymoon, and next it was the opening of a boutique in the city, selling her exclusive pieces. Pierre listened attentively, but she noted he was slow to comment on any of her plans as she continued to plan their future together. It was Friday evening. Eve hoped to sit in and catch up on Netflix and unwind after another busy week. Just as she turned the key in her door, she had a call from Benjamin asking her to meet him in the local hotel to discuss business. She tried to speculate. There wasn't any urgent business on the cards this week to worry about but decided to meet him for a short while and clear up any matter he had. She braced herself. It would not be easy to tell him Pierre proposed, but she had to because she didn't want to lead him on and she suspected he was getting to like her and she liked him too.

She showered and dressed in jeans and a warm jumper and pulled on her leather jacket. The hotel was within walking distance of her apartment. The night was cold but dry with a soft cream moon shinning. She walked across briskly. Benjamin was already there when she arrived. She spotted his car parked close to the hotel entrance. When she walked into the foyer of the hotel, he walked over to her and directed her to a corner with a small round table and two Sienna chairs made of leather. He caught her by the hand and lifted it to his lips and dropped a light kiss on her fingers "Thanks for meeting me tonight." They sat and sipped on a glass of wine and talked business for a while. Eventually, Eve noticed the conversation had become personal when they compared notes on problems they were having. It was nearing mid-night when they parted company. As they stood up to leave, Benjamin held her jacket for her and she noted he left his hands on her shoulders longer than she would have wished. After driving her back to her apartment, he jumped out and went the far side of the car and opened the door for her. She stepped out and was in close proximity to him. He tried to steady his racing pulse. Nobody had ever made him feel the way she did. He longed to hold and kiss her. Her stomach flipped as he put his arm around her waist she didn't resist when he leaned to her mouth and kissed her lightly. "Benjamin, there is something you need to know." He pressed his fingers against her lips "Shhh now, let's enjoy this moment." They kissed again, then he walked her to the door and watched while she went inside then he drove off into the night.

She went to bed immediately feeling the air in the apartment was filled with confusion. Finally, with both Pierre and Benjamin echoing through her head she drifted into a restless sleep. The following evening, Benjamin called around and Eve sat him down and told him her news. He looked at her with a sense of shock. He moved over to be near her then he took her hands in his and said in a whisper "Eve, I have fallen in love you. The more time I spend with you the more I want to be with you. I know I want to marry you." She blinked and looked at him in disbelief. They sat facing each other in silence.

It was only when the kettle which she had switched on just as Benjamin walked in let out a whistle that they seemed to breathe again. She got up and walked to the press and without a word, took out two mugs and made coffee. Benjamin walked after her and stood close to her. "Eve, I know you feel it too. You can't deny the chemistry between us. We would be so good together." Eve reached out her hand to his cheek. "I'm very fond of you but I'm not in love with you." He looked at her, struggling to take in what she was saying to him. "I'm in love with Pierre and we are going to be married next year." Benjamin was close to tears as he stepped back from her. "No Eve, I know there is something between us and so do you, I can see it in your eyes, the chemistry between us." A thrill ran through her body and an enormous wave of longing swept through her. At that moment she felt a longing to hold him in her arms. She was so confused by her feelings. There was something about the way Benjamin treated her. He was kind, thoughtful and loving and let nothing impede their time together. In comparison, Pierre seemed to have more interest in her money than spending quality time with her. Then she remembered Pierre's promise to her a few nights ago, that time together was more important than money so maybe he had changed. She had decided. Pierre was the one she would devote her life to. She looked at Benjamin "I'm flattered that you feel that way about me but I have made my commitment to Pierre. I am so sorry, Benjamin. I think that the timing of us meeting just isn't meant to be." Benjamin moved back "I have no more to say. I wish you and Pierre a very happy life together." Then he walked out and, like a soft mist, faded away. She stood motionless for a long while and felt the strong bond between them was now broken. Eve hoped she wouldn't live to regret it. Obviously, they would meet due to work commitments but it would be business only. The following few weeks were torture going to work. Benjamin avoided Eve except for the odd business meeting. She found the atmosphere in the office was stressful and wished the holidays would come quickly so she could go home for Christmas.

Finally, the day of the holidays came and she was relieved to be facing a well-earned break from work and Benjamin. She arrived back in Galway 19th December and decided to go and visit her mother before going to Pierre's cottage where she was staying for a few nights. Eve intended to enjoy her engagement, chill-out and recharge her batteries before the build-up to Christmas day. She was looking forward to Pierre spending Christmas day with her family. When she returned home, it was a different mother that greeted her; she looked tired and withdrawn and she noted the house was cold. Julie was delighted to see her daughter. She had missed her. Julie didn't give Eve a chance to enquire about her father, as she started the conversation about him " I don't know what to do about your father, "I'm at my wit's end what to do or think." Eve didn't have time to reply as Conor walked in laden down with bags. "Hello Sis," he threw the bags down and wrapped his arms around her "Great to have you home." Laughing, he said "I could do with some help decorating." Julie remarked rather sombrely, "I don't see the point of celebrating Christmas at all, this year. It was my favourite time of year, but this year I want to blank it all out, now that Eric is living down the road with another woman." "He's not living with another woman he's staying with Paddy," Conor retorted. Then she looked at Eve "He refuses to reply to my texts or calls. I went as far as emailing him last week, but he ignored that as well." Eve was ratty and snapped at her mother, "Why do you think that is? He's waiting for you to go over and reassure him that everything will be alright and that ye will work things out if he returns home soon." "I have already done that twice." "Well go over again now that it is Christmas. He will surely want to be at home with his family."

While Eve and Conor were outside lifting the tree out of the car Conor told his sister that living at home was impossible at the moment "Mum is contrary, it is like walking on eggshells around her most of the time and everything I do is wrong. I'm thinking of moving to Galway and commuting to work every day, obviously I'll give Mum a helping hand with the guests staying over the holidays but it is a quite time in the park and a lot of my work this time of year is maintenance." Conor and Eve began decorating the house. "When will we have these lights untangled?" Eve said impatiently. Her brother laughed, "First, let's plug them in and see if they are still working. Last year I wound the lights around the tree only to find when I plugged them in most of the bulbs had blown." Eventually, with the tree sparkling, they went outside and hung coloured lights all along the front of the house. When they were finished, they noticed to their surprise Julie had decorated each window with lights. Julie praised them for decorating and attempting to capture the magic of Christmas. They knew very well that the celebrations would be tinged with the awkwardness of their father's absence.

Pierre didn't frequent the Wallace household very often. In fact, Conor and Julie treated him like a visitor rather than Eve's boyfriend much to Eve's displeasure, but she got on with it anyway even though she found it exhausting at times. Julie emailed Eric after her son and daughter had left the house. 'As

Christmas is approaching' she began thinking about Eric over in Paddy's house and Eleanor looking after him. In fact, something sour twisted in her stomach and with a sense of mild shock she realised she was envious of Paddy's sister. She knew her daughter was gone to stay with Pierre but had no clue where Conor was. He had got into the habit of walking out, and not saying where he was going and could be away for hours. She'd written in the email to Eric, 'I had really hoped you'd have changed your mind about coming home for Christmas. I was eager to talk with you before Christmas to try to sorts things out but you haven't replied to any of my calls or texts. Can we please meet to discuss things? Eve and Conor are wondering what is going on and I have no answers for them. She looked at the send button for a second, pressed it, and the message was gone. Night time was when she felt most alone and could hear the sound of silence. Julie wished she had siblings, but unfortunately she was an only child and her parents had passed many years ago. Julie closed her eyes and pictured her father sitting on the wooden bench at the back of the garden talking to his sheep dog. He was a tall heavy man with thick white hair combed to the side. He was gentle and kind and always searched for the best in people. Julie wished she could run to him now and fold herself into his arms. Tears fill her eyes and real life intruded on her peace. She went into the kitchen and poured a glass of white wine, her hand shaking a little as she lifted it to her mouth and drank a gulp. She went into the living room area, sank onto the thick, cushiony sofa and switched on the television, flicking through the channels sipping her wine willing the distraction of the screen to chase away her troubles. Before going to bed, she glanced out the window and watched as the fluttering snow became more dense.

Eve went into town after leaving her mother's house and it was evening before she arrived at Pierre's cottage. A dense layer of snow covered the paths and the road, with small hillocks of slush piling against the kerbs as Eve drove up the winding road to his house. The front door was unlocked and she walked in but Pierre wasn't there. There was an appetising aroma drifting around the house. Eve peeped into the top oven and discovered a chicken casserole simmering slowly. Pierre also had a bottle of Prosecco lined up on the counter alongside two glasses. She went outside to see if he was close by. The evening folded into night, snow was still falling beautifully and gracefully.

Eve loved the privacy of the cottage and its surroundings and looking at the big patch of land attached, she decided that was where she would build the house of her dreams. As she walked back into the kitchen, she heard a message coming in on his phone, which was left charging on the coffee table. She pressed the button to read it just as he walked in and swept her off her feet. "I missed you so much Eve, I can't believe I have you in my arms again." He slipped his fingers around her neck beneath her hair and gazed into her eyes. "I will always love you, Eve, no matter what happens." Eve thought it was a strange thing to say. She kissed him "I will always love you too," she said. He stepped back and asked if she was hungry? "Starving," she said to his delight. As they sat at the table Pierre so carefully prepared, Eve thought of the message on his phone. "I forgot to tell you, but you have a message on your phone. I heard it earlier, but when I saw you, it went out of my mind." Pierre walked over immediately to check. She noticed a concerned look on his face. "I hope it is not bad news, Pierre." "No, it's not important, just my boss asking me to work on New Year's Day, he has a party of forty people coming for dinner and the other chef is gone away for a week, it's good to have a part-time job so I said I would." She noted before he served the casserole he powered off his phone and left it away behind the toaster. After dinner, they went up to bed and finished the bottle of Prosecco. Suddenly exhausted by the excitement of the day Eve was sound asleep in the arms of the man she vowed to love.

The following morning, after breakfast, Pierre went down to check the boats. Eve decided to go on a walkabout down to the shore. She had missed it whilst away. She felt the sound of the sea birds, the grandeur of the countryside, the arresting pattern of the stone walls and most of all the clean and invigorating air cleansing her soul. Pierre caught up with her on the way back and they walked hand in hand back to the cottage. Eve knew he had something on his mind because he was flying around the house. Then he announced, "I have a surprise planned. I am taking you on a short romantic trip in the boat." Eve was anxious "Pierre, do you realise it is December and the water looks choppy today?" Pierre was confident "You have nothing to worry about. You are in safe hands I can manage a boat in any weather. It will be an experience cruising with snow-covered hills and fields all around us, honestly it will look magical." She gained confidence, telling herself, 'Pierre is on the sea, every day he knows what he is doing, so why worry, just enjoy the trip.'

Even though there was a strong breeze blowing, Pierre chanced going out to sea as he thought it wasn't going to get rougher. The sun was low and a golden beam shone through the gathering clouds. Eve packed a flask and some sandwiches and they were on the water within the hour. After the first hour, Pierre didn't want to admit to Eve that the sea was much rougher than he had expected and for the first time in years he was slightly nervous. It was late winter and with the turbulence he was witnessing today it was definitely not suitable for going to sea in a cabin cruiser. He planned this trip months ago and wanted it to be romantic. He had a diamond ring hidden underneath the control box and when they reached the shore in the evening, he hoped she would be wearing it. He watched her face for a reaction to the rough sea around her. She seemed to be calm and enjoying herself. The sea grew steadily rougher as they advanced towards the open ocean.

Pierre was determined to go further. Eve still was very calm and said, "The wild sea air is hitting my lungs I love it. I never before had time to relish the excitement of voyaging." After a few hours, Pierre decided to turn back. Eve was hungry, she filled two mugs of tea and while the boat rocked they managed to get a drink intermittently. Eve ate the sandwiches, but Pierre had lost his appetite. The day had not gone as he had planned. He was hoping for a romantic one but it was turning into a nightmare. The weather and the water had become more turbulent. Eve suddenly became frightened. Without warning, storm force winds roared and rushed and swept the wave crests towards the skies. The snow turned to sleet, the boat rocked and the windscreen swept by a long and lazy wiper that juddered ineffectually as it went, left visibility challenging.

Eve shivered with fear as the storm sent a spume of spray into the air covering the boat. The sleet became heavy and the wind went howling through the canopy, ripping it on either sides. Eve became violently sick and while hanging her head over the edge of the boat she looked towards the long seemingly endless ocean and over the massive waves and was very frightened. If this was Pierre's notion of romance, it didn't look very promising for the future. Pierre was staring at the disturbed ocean, scared of the situation he was facing.

He was unsure if he would be able to control the boat. Panic was setting in, the sky was darkening, the short December evening was turning to dusk as the sun set beneath the western horizon. He had to ask Eve to assist him, as she was the only crew on board. As she tried to hold herself steady with one hand, she took the controls with the other unsure of what to do. Pierre kept shouting instructions at her. He had to keep the boat afloat at all costs two lives were at risk. Eve's hands were beginning to go numb and there were times when she had to check and make sure she was still holding the steering wheel. She felt hot tears stinging her eyes and her stomach churned. She swallowed hard feeling a crack in her voice but before she could speak Pierre shouted at her "You have to be strong, I need your help to get this boat back to shore before all light is gone from the sky and visibility gets worse."

Eve did her best to follow Pierre's instructions until eventually he caught, with exhilaration, a glimpse of the shore at Rossaveal. He took over the steering wheel from Eve and held it steadily and as the boat went from side to side he tried to break the waves and get to shore safely. His phone was ringing for the fourth time. Eve took it out of the box which was under the steering wheel and looked at the number she didn't recognise it. As soon as he had the boat tied up safely, she handed it to him saying, "You have a missed call, in fact, the same number came in four times. He took it from her and without checking it he powered it off immediately. As they disembarked the boat, the icy wind cut into Eve's face. It was zero degrees outside with a full moon and even though the air was freezing, it was sweet and fresh. As they drove back to the cottage Eve was in a real mood and refused to talk to Pierre. He caught her hand and entwined his fingers in hers she quickly wriggled her hand away and stared straight in front of her.

When they reached the cottage, Eve was so cold it took her some time to motivate her body to get out of the car and as she did the icy cold took her breath away. The thick snowflakes that had fallen again came whirling down from a smudged grey sky and they stung her face and ears. Pierre was distraught he had put the diamond ring into his wet pocket after tying up the boat, he was certain by Eve's body language this would not be the night to introduce it. He would hide it away until he could come up with another romantic setting. There were only two days left before Eve went home to her mother for

Christmas and he'd have to plan quickly if he was to propose properly to her. Pierre hoped she would forgive him for the traumatic trip on the boat in treacherous weather. He had apologised to her since getting off the boat. "I'm going for a hot bath," she said. The heating had been pre-programmed to come on earlier and the house was warm.

After going to the bedroom and getting clean clothes, she went to the bathroom and filled the bath three quarters way up. She emptied the last of her lavender oil into the bath and got in and sank into the aromatic water. She closed her eyes, sliding down to immerse her body, that was still in shock from the traumatic ordeal. She was willing to put today behind her and not let it spoil the Christmas holidays. Her mood changed and after the relaxing bath she went into the kitchen and suggested making a curry to warm them up after their difficult day. Pierre was relieved and wondered how her mood had changed from sombre to light-hearted, but it didn't matter at least she was talking to him. He was elated, saying to himself 'maybe all is not lost for today' and he thought about the diamond ring on top of the press. Before going up for a shower, he snatched the ring down and decided he would hide it in the oven gloves because Eve never lifted out a dish of curry without using them. She prepared the curry and put it into the hot oven and when he came down, it was almost cooked. He looked around for the gloves and spotted them on the sink. Eve went outside briefly that was his chance to slip the little heart-shaped box into one glove. He walked back to the table swiftly and pulled out his chair and, taking the remote control off the shelf he turned on the television.

He sat nervously watching her every move she had already said yes to his proposal but he wanted it to be more intimate and couldn't think of anything else he could do at that moment. Eve was getting tired again and she didn't notice the jar of curry sauce left so near the oven gloves as she was about to pick them up she turned the jar over and covered the gloves in sauce. Before Pierre spotted what she was doing, she threw the gloves in the washer with a few towels and turned it on to a quick wash. She rushed over to the table, holding the dish with a hand towel. His eyes widened and his heart missed a beat. He jumped up. "Eve, where are the oven gloves?" She said with not a care in the world, "In the washer, I spilt sauce on them don't worry they will come out like new, sit down and enjoy the curry."

He ran to the washer and put it to drain and stood there for what seem an eternity. He was speechless. Eve couldn't fathom what the fuss was about especially when he kept telling her she wouldn't understand. His face was scarlet red, he knelt down on the cold tiles, "I have to wait until the washer stops, it's not the gloves it is what I had hidden in them and he eventually told her. Eve was mortified and she knelt down with him until the washer stopped and the door clicked. He pulled it open and shook the wet box out of the glove. He pulled it open and took Eve's hand and slipped the ring on her finger they were both laughing as they kissed. "That was the most unromantic proposal ever," Pierre said. "Let's put it this way. It was different and one that I will never forget," Eve said, smiling. She stretched her arm out and admired the beautiful solitaire ring on an embellished band of white gold on her finger. She threw her arms around him "I can't wait to let the world know we are getting married." "Let's go over and eat," he said relieved that she loved the ring. She noticed during the course of the evening that when she brought up marriage and dates, which she had umpteen times he ignored her. Something was holding him back, but she wasn't sure what. They planned to spend the next day Christmas shopping and getting presents for her family. She intended to go home on Christmas Eve and help her mother prepare for the big day, she was over the moon when her mother invited Pierre to stay until New Year's day with them.

Eric's family had no idea of the excitement that had taken place in Paddy's house lately. It was exhilarating. Likewise, neither of the three of them could quite believe what was after happening. It still felt surreal because these things always happen to someone else, but Eleanor won the Lotto. They travelled to Dublin to the Lotto headquarters last week Eleanor had gone shopping into Galway and bought an expensive outfit. She had to look her best for the photographs! Paddy and Eric went along. She gave Paddy her credit card to get suits for both of them after all she had just won five hundred thousand euro even if it wasn't in her account just yet. Eric was dumbfounded. He didn't know whether or not to be excited and wondered if Eleanor would help him out and ease his financial problems. He felt they were getting on so well together, enjoying each other's company, going sightseeing, shopping and being together. Eleanor had started to tell people, and arranged for a bus to collect herself, Paddy and Eric plus a small group of close neighbours to bring them to the

Lotto headquarters to collect her fortune. When they arrived, there was a reception of champagne and finger food. Eleanor was then brought into a room where the procedure was explained to her and if she needed advice, they could recommend professionals.

Eleanor spoke to them for some time then they asked Paddy to come into the room. He was surprised when they informed him that his sister wished to make out a cheque from her winnings for a substantial amount to him, he was elated and hugged her repeatedly. Eric was outside in the waiting area and was oblivious what was happening. When they presented the cheque to Eleanor all the occupants of the bus were present and they excitedly clicked glasses of champagne together and after some photographs they were on the bus and starting on their journey home. The fun on the bus was sensational with the crowd signing all the way home. Eleanor never felt as happy in her whole life and Paddy was feeling very pleased with his newfound fortune. The following day she went to the bank and lodged her big cheque. She couldn't wait for it to hit her account and realise this fortune was hers. She intended on giving Eric a gift of five thousand euros, that would get him over Christmas and it would leave him in a position to pay an instalment to the bank. Eleanor had no intention paying back bank loans with it, she had never gone into arrears herself even though there were many times she was short of money. Her motto was 'don't spend what you don't have.'

When she got back home Paddy and Eric were in the kitchen and they had dinner ready for her. She enjoyed the shepherd's pie and Eric took the credit for it. Eleanor sat back while the men filled the dishwasher, topped up the stove and Eric started cleaning the oven. She couldn't believe her eyes. The men listened to Eleanor planning out loud what she was going to do to celebrate. She said, "I rang the girls at the book club last night we are planning a holiday after Christmas, Portugal I think then in the spring we will head for the Canaries." Eric wondered would he be brought for a break to an exotic island later in the summer but didn't want to ask. He was hoping she would help him financially perhaps she would realise he was struggling to meet repayments each month and had very little money for spending. After the excitement Paddy went about his usual business at the sand and gravel company until they closed for the Christmas holidays and would reopen on the 3th of January. Eric was finishing work two days earlier but the excitement he had when travelling to Dublin seemed to fade quickly. One evening, Eleanor called out from the kitchen to Eric who was watching racing on television. "How about going to town tonight and having a few drinks I want you to meet the girls?" "Great," he said rather confused.

Eleanor was on cloud nine and talking in a high-pitched voice. He hoped the lotto win wasn't gone to her head and he worried in case she'd lost interest in him. He didn't want to go back to his old life. Up till now, he was having an excellent time. He felt like a teenager again in Eleanor's company. They went out almost twice a week and they brought the youthful spark back into each other's eyes. He had grown to like her a lot and he was almost certain she felt the same. He didn't want to ask her for financial help as he didn't want that to change their relationship, but he hoped she would offer. Having his debts paid off would be a huge relief for him and allow him not to have to worry about money all the time. Eleanor introduced Eric to the girls from the book club. "This is Eric, my brother's friend. He is lodging with us for a while." The girls looked from one to another. They greeted him almost in tandem. After a few drinks, Eleanor began telling the girls about her plans for spending some of her winnings. She talked about the car she was intending on buying next year and the places she intended going to visit and building on an extension to the house. The girls were excited for her and were looking forward to the planned holiday after Christmas. Eric felt left out as she didn't mention him at all in her plans. The taxi collected them after midnight; Eric was worn out listening to Eleanor ranting on about her fortune. He went straight to his bedroom after going home. He felt Eleanor had changed overnight. The money had definitely gone to her head. But he knew he had to bide his time and let her enjoy her new found fortune. He would still be there to catch her when she fell back down to earth and hopefully she would send some of her fortune his way. The following morning, just as Eric sat down to breakfast Eleanor patted him on the shoulder "Don't worry I'm not forgetting you. There is a little gift in this envelope," and she handed it to him. Eric stared at her and his smile broadened. He felt a surge of excitement at the idea of a lump sum of money in his hand.

Eric went outside and pulled the envelope open with great expectations, but to his astonishment the amount was much smaller than he initially thought.

Eleanor walked over to where he was standing her voice cut into his thoughts. "Did you hear what I said? I'm hosting a party after mass tomorrow night for our friends and neighbours. It is a tradition we carry on every year on Christmas Eve Paddy looks forward to meeting up and wishing them a happy Christmas?" He lifted the envelope and half heartily said thanks for the money. "It's a little gift to help you out over the festive season," Eleanor said rather gleefully. She noted Eric's expression was anything but festive.

He was nauseated at the amount of money she gave him. It was of no use to him. He owed so much and thought she would clear his debts. He went to meet his daughter in town a short while after. Eve was waiting for him in the bar. She was uneasy but she greeted him with a smile when he came in. "Hello dad, how have you been?" He shrugged his shoulders "I'm ok." "Dad, when are you coming home?" "Not until I have every euro reimbursed to the banks and, of course you have to be paid back your money at some stage." Eve looked at him pitifully "It will take small steps to get back to where you were before all this happened but you must decide to come home." He was silent for a long time. With excitement she exclaimed, "Look Pierre and I got engaged." "Congratulations love, I am so happy for you" he said as he embraced her. "I wish you the best of luck" but there was no excitement in his voice at all he sounded like a man with low spirits. Eve noticed her father's face looked thinner and there were lines on his skin that made him look twice his age. She realised he was getting older every day and losing precious time with her mother.

He spoke sharply, "I won't go back to your mother ever again I have grown apart from her now." Eve was speechless and hurt she jumped down off the high stool "Don't say that Dad, you only say that because you don't want to face what has happened, it's easier to stay away and ignore it. You owe it to Mum to at least discuss this with her. You can't keep hiding from the issues. You are being selfish now." Eve was raging with him. She handed him his Christmas gift even though she didn't want to and said "It's time for me to go home." Before she walked out, she said, "You had better think long and hard about your decision." He watched her until she got into her car and he whispered "Happy Christmas Eve," he wished he wasn't upsetting her.

It was Christmas day and Eve had returned home the morning before. She was up bright and early preparing the dinner and looking forward to Pierre staying over for the holiday period. She was happy that her mother invited him over; he had only visited her parent's house a few times in the year because Conor and her mother didn't understand him or why he had to spend so much time in France.

Julie decided she would be cheerful today for the sake of her children and told Conor under no circumstances would she answer her phone if Eric called anytime during the holiday period. That evening Pierre said to Julie without thinking, "I love Christmas and always have done, it's not the presents or even the food it's about family and friends getting together and having fun." Julie tried to be cheerful but disappeared into the bathroom and let the flood of tears flow down her face. Over the next few days they sat around, relaxed and enjoyed each other's company Eve was thrilled to have Pierre with her family and looked forward to the celebrations on New Year's Eve night, she told Pierre they usually ended up in the corner pub in town singing in the new year. So that is what they did. As midnight approached, the crowd poured out on to the street and joined hands to form a big circle in readiness for "Auld Lang Syne." The following morning Pierre went back to work and Eve stayed with her mother and began taking down the decorations. Conor announced during the holidays that he was taking a few days off and going on a city break with some friends that he had gone to college with. Eric was back to work and feeling low. Eleanor had changed. She went out socialising and partying all over Christmas, leaving himself and Paddy at home. Eric had fallen for her and enjoyed the good time they were having until she won the lotto. Then he felt as if he didn't seem to matter to her anymore.

When the holidays were over, Paddy felt it was time to have a serious talk with Eric, as he didn't seem to address the problems in this marriage or home life. "I think it is about time you went home to your wife and try to sort out your lives. You are a married man. You can't be considering a relationship with my sister, it won't work, you have a wife." Eric was determined to stay put. "Paddy, I really have fallen for Eleanor and want to be with her." "It won't work Eric, you can't commit to her, you are married, move home and sort out your life. You are not being fair to Julie or Eleanor, you can't continue like this." After that discussion, living in Paddy's house was very uncomfortable. He watched their every move and Eleanor started going out without inviting Eric.

She came home late most nights. Eric peeped out the window one of those nights and watched as an older, distinguished man walked Eleanor to the door and kissed her before she came in. He knew at that stage it was time to move out but where would he go as he was adamant he was not moving home?

CHAPTER 5

Benjamin was back at work after a delightful Christmas break staying with his parents. After Eve turned him down he was heartbroken. She had been clear with him she was committed to Pierre, he knew he would have to move on. Over the Christmas period, he met someone completely unexpectedly. He had no interest in going to the party that he and his parents were invited to, but they wanted to go and were insisting he join them rather than stay at home so he relented and went.

Immediately after going into the party, Benjamin noticed a beautiful woman standing on her own looking a little lost. He chatted to the people on either side of him; he was a complete stranger so tried his best to mingle, making small talk about Christmas and holidays and so on. The woman he had noticed when he arrived made her way towards him and stood right by his side. "Enjoying the party?" she asked. Her face was slightly flushed she wasn't sure what to say to him. She had dark hair, deep brown eyes and an infectious smile that gave off an aura of warmth and friendliness that was contagious. "Hi, I'm Rachael," he stretched out his hand "I'm Benjamin, pleased to meet you." Rachael explained it was her aunt and uncle who were hosting the party and she was just helping them out. Benjamin tried to find out more about her without sounding pushy or too nosey and could establish that she had come alone as most of her friends were with family for the holidays and she was divorced. "Lovely room," Benjamin remarked. "My aunt had it restored a few years ago" she replied. She watched his eyes rove around, taking in the cornice ceiling with the chandelier, the elegantly carved fireplace, classical and strictly in proportion, until his gaze returned to her. "Beautiful," he said. "Thank you," Rachael was pleased. She introduced him to her aunt and uncle and to different people and he found to his surprise that he really enjoyed the night. After midnight, his parents were exhausted and it was time to go home. He felt an instant attraction to Rachael and didn't intend on leaving without getting her phone number. As he said goodbye to her he asked maybe if they could exchange numbers. He looked at her with a hopeful expression on his face. She was hesitant, then she said, "Why not? I'm back to London next week for work." Benjamin couldn't believe his ears. "I moved to London myself before Christmas. I am based there now my office is in central London." Rachael seemed pleased. "That is a coincidence as my studio is right in central London and within walking distance from my apartment." "What do you do?" he asked. "I'm a designer with an emphasis on sustainability in my clothes. I am lucky as there is a real demand to alternatively eco-friendly made clothes." Benjamin was impressed. She looked at him enquiringly. He guessed she was waiting to hear what he worked at. "I'm in the fashion business," but didn't reveal he was a multi-millionaire. His parents walked over beside him and reminded him it was time to go. He looked at her with assurance. "I'll contact you after the holidays." She smiled at him sweetly and they parted company.

Julie felt lonely this morning, it was the first week of January and severe weather had brought snow and ice blanketing down across the country side. The sky resembled a dense murky cloak pressing down on the front lawn. Underneath, a cloud of hailstones bumped against each other before falling to the ground. She was sitting in the lounge gazing out at her garden, wishing for spring to come. She remembered back to happier times when Eric would mow the lawn and they would both weed the flower beds. She missed those days and yet they did not have to be over if he would only come home. She decided she would go over to Paddy's once more and ask Eric to come home and try to get their life back on track.

Eric had moved out of Paddy's even though Eleanor said he should stay until he arranged a proper place to live. Eric felt he was left with little choice given Paddy's discussion and reaction when he told him about his feelings towards his sister. "Don't look so worried I'll be out of the house as soon as I make a reservation in a hotel," he informed Eleanor. She didn't like the unfriendly look flickering in his eyes. Eric swallowed a spark of vexation, he had believed that Eleanor was falling for him but now realised he was only fooling himself. His eyes were opened wide since she won the money. Eleanor had no problem going out alone and having a good time meeting single men and going on dates. He couldn't stay under her roof for another day given his feelings for her, even though he had no place to go. He had the money she gave him and that would pay his hotel accommodation for a short while. He intended to find some place for himself in Galway eventually and pay his way. He didn't need any woman in his life, he would go it alone from now on. The loans would have to be paid so every euro he put aside would be eaten up by the banks.

It was early evening when Eric went up to the bedroom and packed his belongings into the large travel bag he bought yesterday. He walked down and out the door into the cold snowy evening, there was an inrush of freezing air, and he could have cried. The snow was thick hard and icy, and he was careful not to slip. The windscreen of his car was frozen, but he refrained from going back into the house for warm water. The can of de-icer he had in the glove department was empty, he turned on the ignition and waited for the car to heat enough to get the fan hot and get the window cleared. He looked towards Eleanor's bedroom window and there she was looking out at him when she caught him looking she shrank back.

As he drove towards Galway, his eyes watered from the cold, at least that's what he told himself. It was just the cold and not the disappointment of the dreadful turn his life had taken. He arrived at the hotel he had booked online, there were only a few cars in the underground park and he was glad it would be quiet so nobody would notice him because he certainly didn't have the look of a tourist about him and he certainly didn't feel like one. He went over to reception and the girl behind the desk began taking his details. She looked at him questionably "Will you be staying long with us sir?" He paused unsure what to say as he hadn't thought about this himself. He just knew he had to get out of Paddy's house. "A few weeks maybe." She handed him the paper work and key card, he in return paid the deposit. "Your room 120 is on the second floor, the lift is right behind the double doors, enjoy your stay with us and of course you will have the use of all facilities while you're a resident."

He walked into the room where there were two single beds, he threw his bag on to one and sat on the other. He felt like a lost soul. He lay back on the bed and looked at the thick snow falling and flying against the window until he fell into a deep, disturbed sleep without undressing.

Julie had decided she was ready to go over to Paddy's and talk to Eric. Conor offered to go with her, but Julie shook her head "I need to talk to your father alone." She ran the back of her hand across her eyes, wiping away her tears. Julie experienced a sliver of remorse when she thought back to the day that she argued with him. Conor wished he could have accompanied her and be of some support. She drove towards Paddy's house and forced herself to focus her mind. 'Almost there' she felt her heart hammer. They hadn't seen each other for a while and the last time they'd argued. Of course, Eleanor no doubt would be full of herself after her big win, but Julie decided not to mention it at all. It was none of her business. She pulled up outside the house and felt her shoulders droop as she saw the front door opening. Giving herself a shake, she stepped from the car. Taking a deep breath and straightening her shoulders, she headed for the open door. Paddy was standing inside in the hallway. "Hello Julie, come in." She glanced around the living room. "Is Eric here?" she asked. Paddy hesitated. "No, he left Julie. He said he was moving into a place of his own but didn't say to where." Paddy didn't elaborate. He noted Julie's expression was flustered, upset even. She looked motionless at Paddy. "He's gone." "Yes, he has. I've no idea he just up and left without telling us where he was going." Paddy didn't mention that he had a few words with Eric prior to him leaving. He felt sorry for her "Will you sit and have a cup of tea?" "No thanks," she looked distraught as she pulled her jacket around her with an irritable shrug and began walking towards her car saying to herself that she couldn't believe this was happening. Paddy watched until she drove out the front entrance briskly. Eleanor came down from her room just as Paddy closed the door. "Do you have any idea where he is?" she asked her brother. "No idea what so ever as far as I'm concerned I am his foreman at work and his private life is his own business. I hope Julie and Eric manage to work things out. They have been together for such a long time it would be a shame if they didn't try." Eleanor stayed silent, she sat down, took up her book and started to read.

Conor was waiting for his mother when she arrived home, he had news for her and was eager to share it with her. He didn't like the expression she had on her face as she walked into the living room. She sat at the counter and spilt out the story about his father. Conor was raging. "I'm stuck in the middle of this rift between you two, and I have had enough of it. I'm moving to Galway after the weekend. I found myself an apartment so I'll be commuting each day to run the park. Both you and Dad have acted so juvenile and stubborn in this and allowed it to spiral out of control when it could have been resolved much sooner." Julie looked at him blankly and said, "If that's what you want to do, go ahead I won't stop you." Conor couldn't believe his ears she wasn't shouting or protesting, did she really mean it or would the protest come later?

Before Conor went out for the night, he handed the reservation book to his mother "I wrote a booking down for you, a man has booked into the bed-and-breakfast for at least six months, he's an architect and his name is Sam Weston." She barely looked at it and put the book back in the drawer then, as an afterthought as her son was walking out the door she asked 'Did you ask him for a deposit?" "No," he said he would call round next week when visiting for a look around and would drop the deposit off then."

The following week, Conor moved to Galway. He felt the time had come to move out and live independently. His mother and father had issues. He had tried to help them but realised he couldn't solve them. This was down to themselves. Since his father left home, living with his mother had become impossible. Conor's girlfriend of two years lived outside the city with her sister and mother, she hoped to move to Galway soon, as she and Conor were making plans together.

Julie didn't recognise the number when her phone rang for the third time. "Hello, am I through to the Sea View Bed and Breakfast?" "Yes," Julie said efficiently. "My name is Sam Weston and I was talking with your son a week ago about staying for a few months. I am in the area today and would like to call and pay a deposit if you are at home?" "Yes, I'm here. You are welcome to call anytime" she replied. Julie noted he was very polite on the phone. She was delighted to get the business and could definitely use the extra cash this time of year, as guests were scarce.

He arrived in the afternoon. She welcomed him in as she treated all her guests with a cup of coffee. He gave her a warm handshake as he came in through the front door. She directed him into the guest sitting room. They talked for a long while and before going he paid his deposit and agreed to sign the contract for the room. He would live in for at least six months. He was planning to move in earlier than expected because of his work schedule. When he was gone, she sat and thought about how well he looked. He had a sturdy build with broad shoulders and his dark hair was newly groomed. Julie couldn't help but notice his eyes were an unusual hazel-brown colour. He was a good-looking man with a quiet, reserved manner that made him easy to talk to. Julie sat inside the big window looking across the bay in a pensive mood, while time passed she watched the sun balance on the horizon, casting a glittering path across the water, it hovered for a while, lighting up the waves before it slipped beneath the sea. Sam had momentarily lit a spark within her, one which she didn't know was there. After going to bed that night, she fell into a deep, unguarded sleep. It brought her to a place where dreams soften with memories and left her feeling completely relaxed.

CHAPTER 6

Eve and Pierre arranged to meet in the evening for dinner to discuss their wedding plans as Eve was due to go to London the following week for the start of the spring fashion shows. She browsed around Shop Street in Galway waiting for Pierre to finish work as he was on a long shift. Jokingly, she warned him the night before not to taste the food when preparing the meals today, otherwise he would be too full for dinner with her. She was pleased he was working in the hotel and within a short period he had become very popular with his French cuisine. He was receiving a good pay packet which would make all the difference when they got married. She was adamant she wanted to discuss the wedding with him this evening, so they could start thinking about what they might want to do for it. Even though it was early February, the streets were busy and on the pavement city shoppers were rushing back and forth. She walked into a flower shop to admire the array of bouquets on display; she loved flowers but Pierre never seemed to bring her any. Her mind wandered back to the last bouquet she received. They were from Benjamin. She could almost smell the fragrance of them now. They were a bunch of roses with pink, yellow and white petals set against glossy green leaves. She wondered where he was and who he was with.

As she exited the flower shop, she spotted Pierre rushing down the street. "Sorry 'I'm late." He gave her a peck on the cheek and they walked up towards the restaurant. "Nice place here," Eve declared. "They revamped it last year and made it very cosy," Pierre replied. Eve straightened herself in her chair and cleared her throat. "I was hoping to discuss our wedding plans this evening." He looked at her with an uninterested gaze. She continued talking, "We need to book the church, hotel, music, flowers and a photographer. First, we should go and see the priest." Pierre was as about as communicative as a brick. "You're not listening to what I'm saying." He did one of his long sighs, which he was prone to each time she mentioned the wedding. It was disheartening when he refused to discuss their future with her. She bit back tears "You seem to be totally disinterested in discussing the wedding with me." He had noticed her face drop and held her hands across the table. "Love, when the time is right and we can afford a lavish wedding, then I'll talk it over with you. You know I want the best for you." "But you are working more regular hours now and I have savings set aside, so where is the problem? We have been together for a long time. Why wait?" She waited for him to reply to what she just said. "Let's enjoy our meal and I promise it will all work out for us and you will have a magical day to remember." "I really want to meet your parents soon," she said. His jaw tightened when she mentioned going to France to his home place. He turned a whiter shade of pale. 'I can't tell them I'm planning to get married just yet, because I think they always held out hope that I would return to France to live and I guess to care for them, eventually." "Are you ashamed of me or what is the matter?" "Of course not, nothing's the matter. I will prepare them for your visit when I go over next week." Red flags began to fly for Eve. She was disillusioned with how the evening had gone.

She had made no progress with her plans. Mid-week Pierre flew to France and Eve was now on a flight to London. As the plane took off from Shannon, she sat back and closed her eyes intending to sleep until the plane landed in Heathrow. She was absolutely shattered after spending all of yesterday cooped up in a stuffy office preparing for the next seven days. She took a deep breath and tried to get her brain to switch off. The note she found amongst the papers in Pierre's house while tidying came to the forefront of her mind again. The number on the note kept whirling around in her head. At last, the plane landed and instead of being rested, she was in a tizzy.

The next week would be spent launching her latest fashion collections, which comprised of bold and bright shades designed to flatter all age groups. The fashion shows would take place all over the city. After a very successful week, the last night was upon her. All the top names in fashion attended. As the models walked the catwalk and wore her designs, the interest throughout the venue was overwhelming. Designers surrounded her. Compliments were flying. Suddenly, she was the centre of attention.

At that moment, she had no clue why, but somewhere deep in the recess of her mind a vague memory of Benjamin appeared and she wished he could have witnessed how successful she was this evening. Eve was home two days now and went to visit her mother and brother who were delighted to hear of her success. Pierre was due home the next day from France. "Have you many guests staying?" Eve enquired. "I have three rooms booked and then a guest named Sam Weston staying for six months. The caravan park is booked up to the end of July," Conor added. She plucked up the courage to ask about her father, neither of them had mentioned him and it felt like he never existed. Her brother and mother looked at each other, before Julie walked hurriedly across the floor and began emptying the dishwasher. "We haven't been in contact lately I don't know where we stand at this present time," Julie said. The front door opened while they were talking Julie swung around from the dishwasher. Both Conor and Eve noticed their mother beamed as Sam the lodger walked into the kitchen. He walked towards Julie, smiling broadly and Eve noted his dark-lashed eyes were twinkling and she could almost swear her mother had a dreamy look in her eyes when she saw him walking into the house. Eve barely spoke, instead she rushed out almost knocking him over as she walked past him. Julie looked forward to Sam coming in from work each evening. He was company and interested in listening to her talk.

They began to share stories of their past lives, and what they hoped for the future. They laughed and joked and on occasions listened to music with a late night cup of tea. Julie felt a connection growing with him, she liked the way he looked at her with that soft glint in his eyes. There was something hypnotic about them. They stood for a brief moment, looking at each other. Suddenly she froze, what on earth was she doing surely she wasn't falling for the lodger, her thoughts were scattered in all directions. She turned and moved over to the cooker and informed him that dinner was ready. Julie cooked dinner for guests on occasions when requested and this was one of those evenings.

Eve was anxious about collecting Pierre from the airport the following day. She loaned him her travel bag when he was going to France and forgot to take out the old tweed purse which she had hidden under the lining. The flight was forty minutes late and she was already waiting for him. When she spotted him coming towards her, she ran and threw her arms around him. "Good to have you back." He responded, "It's great to be back." "Here, let me help you with your bags" she said. She took the travel bag out of his hand and wondered was the purse intact. She hoped so. After they got back to the cottage and Pierre had showered, they went to dinner, as Eve had planned. Later that night, after they got back and were relaxing with a glass of wine she asked, "How are your parents?" The purse was the main thought, but she had no opportunity to open the bag yet. He seemed hesitant in divulging information about his home visit. He looked pale and tired. She scrutinised his face. He had a frown on his forehead, his cheeks were high coloured and he had a faraway look in his eyes. "Pierre, I think you could do with an early night you certainly look worn out, finish up your drink and go up to bed." He took her advice, went up to bed and slept immediately.

Eve stayed up and poured another glass of wine and sat back on the couch she needed to marshal her thoughts, her head was buzzing. After an hour, she crept up to the room where she heard him snoring then went back down into the hallway where his bags sat. She opened the travel bag and searched the lining, but the purse was gone. She stood up straight and stared in front of her, looking at the wall that needed painting badly. Her heart started to miss a beat 'where did it disappear to?' she thought and was more curious about it now and wondered if it had been lost on the journey.

The following evening out of the blue Pierre said "By the way, I found a purse inside the lining, did you put it in there?" She tried to keep calm and said flippantly, "Oh that old purse I got it from my grandmother, it has a load of rubbish inside it but it's of semimetal value that's all. Where is it?" "I shoved it in with my passport and bank card. It is up in the press with the books." She gestured with her hand, saying "I'll get it later" and she breathed a sigh of relief.

Later that day, she got the purse and shoved it down to the bottom of her handbag again for safekeeping. It was Eve's last afternoon before going back to work and she suggested going to Salthill for a stroll, along the 'Prom.' When they arrived at the seafront, the sun was bouncing on the surface of the rippling water. As the sun glared, he noticed her hair gleamed in the light of the sparkling sun and she could see him study her face and she smiled warmly at him. They sat for a long while overlooking Galway Bay. Eve turned to Pierre "What about getting something to eat? I think I fancy some fish and chips. The fresh air must have made me hungry," she laughed. He jumped up "I'll go across the road and get some." He took up his coat which he had left on the seat beside him and pulled out his wallet and threw the coat back down again, he didn't seem to feel the cold like she did, years of being on the sea she thought and he set off.

She sat there inhaling the fresh air into her lungs. His phone rang she let it ring for the second and third time and pulled it out of his coat pocket. "Hello" it was a woman's voice and she had a French accent. "Is Pierre there?" she said, sounding a little subdued. "May I ask who's calling?" "I'm his parent's carer." "Ok, he's not here at the moment can I get him to call you back." The phone went dead momentarily. She looked back to see if Pierre was on his way back. He wasn't, so she searched for the tweed purse and pulled it out to see if the note with the number on it corresponded with the number on his phone, it didn't.

Pierre came behind her unexpectedly she had the phone in one hand and the note in the other. "Oh, I forgot my phone, had I a call?" "Your parent's carer called it seemed urgent." She handed him the phone, "Call her maybe one of them is sick." He looked down at the note in her hand "Did she leave a number for me?" "No, that's just a note to remind me of a message I have to get for my mother" as she bundled it back into the bottom of the tweed purse and shoved it into the bottom of her hand bag. He looked at his phone "I'll call her later the signal is poor." "I don't think that's a good idea, I could hear her clearly," Eve said. "No, I'll leave it until later." Eve wondered why he wasn't eager to know what the carer had to tell him. They tucked into the fish and chips viewing the wavy blue sea. She noted Pierre was extremely quiet after the call. Suddenly, the atmosphere between them was so tense that she could feel it cold through her veins. It was clear to her that Pierre was upset and the evening was spoiled. "Are you worried about your parents?" he nodded in response. As the evening drew to a close, they went back to the car arm in arm, but Eve was in a confused state she couldn't make sense of the phone episode.

'This is the life,' Rachael thought as she stretched her long legs out on the sun lounger and raised her extravagant cocktail in a toast, "Just you and me, here's to us." "To us," Benjamin grinned, clicking his half-empty glass against hers. Benjamin and Rachael had been seeing each other regularly since meeting at her aunt's party at Christmas when he drove his parents there. It was early evening and the sun was losing its intensity but sitting on the beachside sun loungers they were still benefiting from the warmth of its rays without feeling the need to put a top on. Benjamin was pleasantly relaxed, the disappointment of the past few months seemed to fade. He had fallen in love with Eve over the period of them working together, but she had made it clear she was going to marry Pierre, so he had to try to forget about her and move on. He liked Rachael she was good company and easy to be with, she was thoughtful and kind and was helping him to move on with his life.

Julie's mobile rang she barely heard it over the hum of the vacuum cleaner. She had already worked her way through the house and was doing the living room for the second time, adding the nozzle attachment to make sure she hovered up every speck of dust between the cushions. She stopped and listened then switched off the vacuum and pulled her phone out of the pocket of her fleece jacket. "Hello, Julie Wallace speaking." There was a pause. "Hello Julie," the voice at the other end of the phone was Eric. When she heard him speak her pulse began thumping in her throat, she wasn't quite sure what he was going to say. "I have been thinking of home a lot these past few months. I miss everything about the place and that includes you Julie," in the next breath he asked if he could come back. She sounded harsh, he guessed he had expected that given how things had been between them and he wasn't even sure she would want him back in the house. Julie surprised herself with her response to him "If you return there will have to be changes, you can move into the bedroom at the back of the house, the lodger has the master bedroom and the rest are for the guests, I moved into the single room after you went away. So, I won't stop you from coming home, but things definitely have changed between us. He noticed her voice was icy cold and a shiver crept down his spine. He knew things had changed for them as she continued, "You will have to go to work and continue to earn enough to meet your repayments. Also, I know you were dating Paddy's sister. It will take me a long while if ever, to forgive you. I suppose when she won the fortune, a much younger man came along and she left you. You never thought or cared about me during that time, refusing to meet me or answer my calls and now because it suits, you want to come home. I don't know where we stand with each other Eric, you hurt me." He agreed to adhere to her rules. "I'll pack up my belongings and move home next week." He didn't know what else to say to her and ended the call, she took her phone down from her ear and saw that he hung up hastily. She wasn't sure how to feel after the call, she thought that she would be happy if he asked to come home but now that he had, she felt confused and conflicted.

The week passed quickly and as Eric approached the house, he could see smoke from the chimney of the living room and an amount of caravans parked along in a line close to the mature yew trees. Even though it was only mid-March, people were already vacating the city to enjoy the breath-taking glory of the Connemara Mountain's with the arrival of spring and to watch the sunset at dusk spreading a violet glow across the valleys and hills. He drove around for a short while before he went in through the gates trying to gather his thoughts. He drove up outside the front door and parked his car. Julie wasn't expecting him until later in the week even though there was no certain day planned for him to return she didn't think it would be today. He walked to the front door and he heard his wife's laughter and another man's laughter echoing through the house. He didn't like to have to ring the bell to get into his own house but to get inside he had to. He rang three times to no avail. He was about to go round to the back of the house when Julie opened the door slowly and cautiously. Her dark eyes stared at him. "I wasn't expecting you today." "Sorry if I disturbed you" he said smartly. Her eyes narrowed a fraction and her face which had gone pale whitened further. She stood back and in a rather austere voice told him to come in. He looked over at Sam Weston sitting in his spot at the table, 'what was he doing here this time of day, surely his wife wasn't cooking dinner for him regularly?' Eric felt like saying to him this is a Bed and Breakfast facility not a restaurant but he refrained as he had to be careful not to throw his weight around yet, he was only in the door and didn't want to ruffle his wife's feathers, he knew he had to win his way back slowly but surely.

Julie introduced her husband to Sam and left down a mug of tea to both of them sitting at opposite ends of the table. Eric was grinding his teeth at Sam's familiarity with his wife and indeed his house. The days that followed created a silence that swelled the strain between husband and wife and Julie felt choked. They lived under the same roof, passing each other like ships in the night. Eric then realised that everything had changed so much since he was last here. Conor and Sam became friends quickly and they spent many evenings playing pool in the local pub. Eric wasn't happy with the friendship. One night, Conor asked his father to join them but he declined.

When Pierre announced he was going to France for a longer period than normal, Eve became curious why. She questioned if he could take the time off work and for how long he envisaged he would be gone. "When are you leaving?" she asked. "Next Friday, look Eve I know it is a longer time but I'll make it up to you when I come back, I promise." She knew his parents hadn't been well, so she didn't question him too much. It seemed like a very short week before Pierre had to leave. She had loved spending time with him and thinking of how things would be once they married. She drove him to the airport mid-day and they said goodbye for the umpteenth time.

One evening after dinner Eve went home to visit her parents, the house was quiet so she dug out the mysterious phone number in her tweed purse, she flattened out the piece of paper on the coffee table and after checking the signal on her phone she carefully dialled the number. It was ringing out for the fifth time and she was just about to hang up when suddenly a lady with a French accent said "Did I miss a call?" she had broken English. "Hello, may I speak with the owners of the house?" The lady explained, "It is an apartment and they are away." There was silence and the phone went dead. Eve checked the signal. She had four bars on her phone, which meant the lady on the other end cut her off. She stood up puzzled and walked over to where there was an open window, allowing a warm breeze to flutter the petals of the roses and lilies which stood in vases on the tables and filled the air with a heavy sent. She wondered where her mother was.

When she arrived home, her mother's car was missing from the back of the house. She went to switch on the kettle and just at that moment, her father walked in he looked tired and withdrawn but brightened up when he saw his daughter. "I wasn't expecting you today," he said. "Thought I'd drop over and give Conor an hour off. Where's Mum gone?" he wavered "I don't know at the moment, she didn't tell me and I didn't ask her. That's the way it is now between us." He looked sullen when he said "By the way, I'll soon be able to give back part of the money you loaned me from your savings." "There is no rush with it Dad, whenever you can afford it." He was grateful, and the tension on his face eased. Julie came back from town just as Eric went out to do some repairs on one of the caravan parking spots and just nodded in Julie's direction as he left. Eve felt a deep sadness creep over her. How could her parents have got to this point in their lives? She hoped that would never happen to her? She'd make sure it didn't.

Eve was busy making preparations for the Easter fashion show in France. She had been putting in long hours, and had a reputation and a standard that she had spent many years curating and she needed to maintain this. Even though it was hard work, she loved it. Pierre had to stay away for longer than intended, but she knew had he been with her she wouldn't have seen much of him because of her own work. She had booked into a lovely modern four-star hotel for the duration of her stay; she had stayed there before; it was ideally located for her. After booking in and having a shower to refresh after the flight, she sat on her bed and scrolled down through her phone and decided to try the unknown number again out of curiosity. She didn't give it a second thought and just clicked on the call button. To her surprise, a child answered and spoke in broken English. Eve stalled, not sure what to say. She asks "Is Mammy there?" The child answered "No." Then after a second the child says "But Daddy is here do you want to speak with him?" "Yes, please."

Eve thought she had better explain why she was on the phone in case the parents wondered who the child was talking to. Eve had to think quickly. Tell your dad, "I'm an IT consultant doing a survey." The next few seconds turned into a living nightmare. "Hello, Pierre Rolf speaking." She felt her heart race in her body and suddenly felt sick. Not knowing how she found the inner strength, she managed to change her accent. She continued to pretend she was doing a survey, and thought he might recognise her voice because there was a long pause until he said, "Sorry I cannot take part in that survey today I am otherwise taken up." Quickly she asked "Are you on holiday or resident in

France?" he was slow to respond. But when he did, she was flabbergasted. "I'm not a resident, actually I live and work in Ireland but am spending a month here to be with my daughter and partner."

She was shattered and didn't reply but cut off the call. She screamed and threw the phone from her. It went in through the bathroom door and landed on the white marble tiles. She cried out, trying to make sense of what had just happened. How could he do that to her? They were supposed to be getting married. Was this all just a sick game to him? 'Why had he done this to her? Why?' She stood frozen, stuck in the moment as she tried to piece the information together. She needed to be sick. She just couldn't comprehend it. 'My God, how could I have been a so stupid? Now the constant travelling made sense to her. He was a liar and a cheat. What about the wedding? Was it all a sham? Was he ever going to marry her and the ring? It was probably fake. She pulled it off her finger. She didn't want it anywhere near her. Eve found it almost impossible to calm down and decided on the spur of the moment to go down to the bar and have a gin and tonic. She went back up to her room in the lift with a double gin and tonic in one hand and her key card in the other. After turning on the television, she sat up on her bed against the pillows and stayed there until she had her drink finished. Suddenly, the black cloud that was invading her being, came to the forefront once more and she let herself fall sideways on the bed and screamed, crying until she fell into a broken sleep.

When she woke the next morning, her head felt like lead, her stomach churned and her eyes stung from crying. She crawled out of the bed and just about made it to the bathroom before being very sick. Her throat ached and it felt like her heart was fragmented. She tried to steady herself, telling herself she was there to promote her fashions. There were people in the business depending on her and she couldn't let them down. No matter what, she would have to struggle through the week. After a cool shower and strong coffee, she pulled herself together and after a few hours was ready to contact her agents and carry on her business. She tried to put Pierre to the back of her mind. She managed better during the day as she was busy and surrounded by people, but when she returned to the hotel to the quietness of her room, she really struggled with her thoughts and with her emotions, going from complete sadness to rage. She had decided not to tell her family, as she didn't feel ready to cope with the questions they would ask.

On her return home, Eve's parents knew she wasn't her usual self and were worried that the fashion shows had not gone as well as she hoped. In a wobbly voice she told them about Pierre. It was no secret that her mother was not convinced that Pierre was the most suitable choice for Eve. She waved her hands in the air "I never cared too much for him, there always seemed to be something not quite right about him." Eric was more measured in his response and said that he was sorry it hadn't worked out but that she was better to learn this now than after the wedding. He gave his daughter a hug and telling her he was there for her. He decided it was best to leave Eve and her mother talk it through. Her mother's voice was high pitched when she said "Go over to the house while he's away, pack up your belongings and walk out of his life for good." Eve walked over towards the big window and looked towards the hills. Since she was a child, she couldn't imagine herself living anywhere else except this beautiful part of the country, but now her dreams were shattered. Her plan of her house overlooking the Connemara Mountains was well and truly over. She bit her lip and turned around. Her father had disappeared probably gone down to tell her brother the hurtful news. Eve looked at her mother with an anger in her eyes. "I have a plan when Pierre returns home and it will leave him reeling." She told her what she was going to do. "Don't tell dad," she asked. "Don't worry I won't." Eve was getting into her car when Sam drove up to the house. He was well settled in the place. She didn't know him well but what she saw she didn't like. She hopped in her car and drove off, acknowledging him with a nod. Sam looked her way and smiled. The sooner he was finished in the bed-and-breakfast the better. Sam was too attentive to her mother and Eve knew Julie was flattered by the attention. If only she had been able to see it in her own relationship.

Pierre was flying home tonight and Eve was ready to confront him. She drove to the airport as planned. She looked in the mirror before leaving and without a doubt she knew she was not looking her best. Her hair was pulled back in a ponytail, she applied some concealer and bronzing powder to her face to add some colour to her skin but she concluded it didn't matter, anyway. The jeans and top she wore were only fit for lying around the house in. She placed a smile on her lips and hoped it would stay there until she spotted Pierre. She wanted to lead him on and pretend all was ok with them.

Next thing she saw him wheeling his luggage across the platform her face was aching from the false smile she had plonked on her lips in the hope of keep the pretence up. He rushed over and threw his arms around her, "How is my favourite girl you are looking beautiful as always." That was his first untruth because she was anything but beautiful at this moment. He caught her by the hands and pulled her close to him and kissed her passionately. He noticed she wasn't wearing her ring "I have it in my bag. In the rush to get out, I forgot to put it on" she said. As they drove back from the airport, traffic was heavy and Eve was feeling uneasy. Pierre was chatting as if all was normal. Of course, it was for him. He wasn't aware of the drama that was about to unfold when they reached his cottage. He lifted his hand and started caressing the back of her neck slowly. After what seemed like an eternity, she couldn't tolerate it anymore the pretence was overpowering. She snapped "Please stop, take your hand away from my neck it is making it impossible to concentrate on driving especially in heavy traffic." He wondered why she was so ratty today. "I brought you some presents from France, I think you will be impressed," he was smiling at her and he rubbed his hands together. Eve didn't seem to be over the moon as she usually would be with presents. "What's wrong?" he asked rather irritability. "I'm just tired. I didn't sleep well last night." He left his hand on her thigh "Maybe you won't sleep well tonight either," he said smiling from ear to ear. He continued talking, to her disgust. "I also brought your favourite wine from the duty free. Now, wasn't I thinking of my favourite girl when I was away?" "Very nice," she said out loud and inside she finished the sentence 'you cheating, lying rat.' Next, he enquired for her brother and parents. "Good form," she said. She connected her Bluetooth to the radio unit and listened to soft music to calm her nerves. She prayed to all the gods there were, to shut him up before she exploded with rage.

Conor drove up home from the caravan park. His mother wondered why he didn't go straight back to his house in Galway after he'd finished work. She was having dinner with Sam who was sitting at the head of the table and Eric was sitting by his side with Julie opposite him. "Will you have dinner before you go Conor?" He looked at her oddly. "I will if you have some to spare, I'm not going into Galway tonight." She suspected there was something wrong because her son was quiet within himself. Sam kept talking throughout dinner,

Conor or his father didn't have time to get a word in edgeways. Conor noted his mother was all bright and bubbly, in fact the conversation was a two way between herself and Sam as they were comparing the latest films and books topping the market. Eric was fuming but had to remain tight-lipped because he was only edging his way back into her life. Sam brought up the most popular holiday destinations he had been on and went as far as saying to Julie "Maybe you'll join me some time for a weekend," and as an afterthought he said, "And of course you too Eric." "I'd love to Sam," she said gazing at him. Eric intervened, "My wife was never one for sun holidays" he looked at her "Were you?" She made no comment and stood up and walked out of the dining room into the kitchen to get a pot of tea, Conor got up and gathered the glasses and walked out after her, he heard the plates been stacked on the table and turned back at the kitchen door "You can leave them there for now Sam, I want a private chat with my mother," he reddened up and sat back down irritated.

Conor stood behind his mother as she poured the water from the kettle into the teapot. "Leave the teapot there for a second I have something serious to tell you, she was shocked at what her son had just revealed. Within a few minutes, they were in the dining room and Julie was pouring tea into mugs with shaky hands, she was certainly knocked back with what her son told her in the kitchen. Sam kept joking and laughing. Eric said the odd word but Julie had suddenly become voiceless. After they were finished dinner, Sam got up from the table excused himself and went to his room, Eric went to his usual card game, Julie and Conor stayed put and discussed the alarming situation Julie was in, they refrained from telling Eric for now.

Pierre and Eve arrived back at the cottage late evening. Pierre noticed the house cold and the fridge almost empty and wondered what was going on with Eve? She always had plenty of food in the house when he'd return from his journey and a roaring fire in the stove. "Did you not come up to the house today?" he asked. She was being cantankerous and replied, "I didn't bother." He raised his head from the travel bag where he was searching for the presents he brought home to her.

CHAPTER 7

Pierre is Left Pondering

"Why are you giving me grief after arriving home? I'm hungry and hoped for something nice to eat and a little bit of heat in the house. Was that too much to expect after my long journey?" Then he calmed down, he didn't want to fight on his first night back. He smiled at her saying, "Never mind I'll order a takeaway." Pierre looked back into the bag and pulled out a white box from under his clothes and handed it to her, hoping it would change her mood. "You can get comfortable in that tonight after we have eaten," he smiled. "I know it will make my favourite girl look amazing." He wanted to keep her sweet and put on the extra charm. She left the box on the table without opening it. Eve knew Pierre's games and would not give him the satisfaction of admiring the lace nightwear she knew very well was in the pretty box. But at the same time, she played along.

"Let's eat first," she said and she went about tidying away two weeks' papers that had accumulated on the end of the couch and armchair. Pierre ordered for both of them and when the doorbell rang, Eve took it in from the delivery man. She walked in and left it on the table and waited for Pierre to come down from the shower. They sat each end of the table, Pierre got up, "I forgot to bring in the wine I got in the duty free. I'll go out and get it from the car." She said nothing. He came back and poured two glasses of white wine. He lifted his glass, "To us and our future together." Eve gave him the evil eye. She couldn't hold her anger any longer, "What are you talking about?" she glared at him. Pierre was startled at what she had just said. "I'm toasting to our future together." Something twisted in Eve's gut. She took a deep breath, banged the glass on the table almost cracking the stem. "What future are you talking about?" she shouted. Pierre was unnerved when she jumped up and went out to the hallway to get her leather bag, she walked back in, went over to where he was sitting and emptied the contents of the bag on the table beside him.

The old tweed purse was the last item to fall out. She snapped it open and took out the note she found when tidying the sitting room all those months ago and shoved it up under his nose. "Worm your way out of this," she said in a disturbed voice. Pierre stared at the note numb and dazed. That was the note he misplaced. He desperately searched his brain for excuses to cover his tracks. "Is this your mother's or father's mobile number?" she asked. She knew the number was his partner's phone, but wanted to see if he would carry on being deceptive. He didn't reply he stood looking at her like a mouse caught in a trap. "I know the answer Pierre because I rang it when I was in France and your daughter answered it. She handed it to you, but you didn't recognise my voice. I, however, knew yours. I was the representative carrying out the survey you didn't have time to take part in."

He still didn't speak but stood up and walked across to the big window and looked out into the moonlit night. He tried desperately to get his head around words but found it impossible to plan them with his tongue. "I asked you a question," she said, trying to breathe slowly and collect her scattered wits. Looking at him, as she noted his mouth was set in a firm hard line. He knew he was found out. Letting out a long sigh, he clasped his hands behind his back and paced the floor for several seconds before stopping and facing her again. Eve's eyes stared straight into his, searching for the truth. "My parents died when I was young. The phone number belongs to Destiny." Eve was livid she shouted "Who is she?" "I met her in France when you and I had broken up. Remember when I left college and went back to France you had nothing more to do with me because I didn't complete my law degree? I was staying with my aunt and uncle where I had lived after my parents died within a year of one another. I met Destiny one night at a house party. We were both lonely, her boyfriend was away in America and I had nobody. We became inseparable for a time. Then one day she informed me her boyfriend was coming back soon and she finished the relationship. Three months later, she contacted me and told me she was pregnant." "How could you be sure the baby was yours?" "Her parents made sure there was a DNA test carried out to prove it was my baby. That was when I promised to care for her financially. After our daughter was born I came back to Ireland and we started going out again, you and I."

Eve stared at him she could feel her face contort then crumble as a fresh flood of tears ran down her cheeks. "This can't be true Pierre, it can't, it can't," she cried. Pierre responded "I was head over heels in love with you before I went back to France, and still am. It was you who broke up with me remember Eve? Please don't let this get between us. I love you with all my heart," he cried. She shouted, "Obviously you didn't care about me when you went out with Destiny." "It was only a short time. I never meant for any of this to happen. Don't leave me I'll make it up to you" Pierre begged. Her voice rose almost to a scream, "Why didn't you tell me?" "We were just getting back on track. Again and I thought if I told you, you would never have allowed us to develop." He continued "I wanted to give my daughter the very best and Destiny was struggling to make ends meet I had to get the money some place, I'll keep my promise and pay back every euro." Eve was crying and sobbed, "You were with me just for my money. I was foolish enough to think I was helping your parents who were getting on in years and in poor health. We're finished it's over and you can take your ring." She threw it at him hitting his forehead as it fell to the ground. She could see by the set of his jaw line he was in shock. He bent down and retrieved the ring.

Ripples of sweat trickled down his cheekbones. He didn't want to lose her and was beside himself with grief. He knew the mistake he had made not coming clean with her all those years ago before they got back together. He shouldn't have taken advantage of her, constantly asking her for money. He fell on one knee and caught her hands, looking at her with pleading eyes. "Please, Eve let's make a fresh start. Let me put this ring back on your finger." He stayed kneeling on the floor pleading with her. She kept her expression neutral. He continued begging, "I'll do anything you want to, I'll make it up to you, but don't leave me I would be lost without you." He was numb as he looked up at her and desperately searched for words. Eve pulled her hands away. "We're finished" and she walked into the bedroom and gathered up the last of her bags, which were already packed. When she walked back out she stood and looked at him with a motionless stare. "By the way, if I hadn't found the note I would still be in the dark, of course, that would have suited. It would have given you the liberty to carry on your charade." "I was intending on telling you before we got married" he whined. She shouted, "But you kept putting it off like the marriage." He walked over to her again and caught her by the hands "Please Eve listen to me." "No, I'm finished listening, you can go now and wallow in your own misery" she replied and walked out the door and drove away leaving him standing there rejected. When she was long gone, Pierre couldn't take it in or believe it. He couldn't even begin to imagine his life without her. He walked out into the cold night and started walking with just the light of the full moon going down the hill towards the cliff's edge until he came to the big rock. He sat there until almost morning looking out over the sea with his mind tormented with regrets. Pierre pondered, 'was life worth living at all?'

Eve told her parents what had unfolded at Pierre's. "I need to go away for a while to be on my own and sort out my head. I have already booked into a hotel in Wexford for six nights" Eve said. Julie recommended her staying at home instead for a short period and considering her options. She thanked her mother but explained that she needed to get as far away from Pierre as possible to try to make sense of it all. She was adamant not to be in the same village as that 'cheater'.

The following weekend, she travelled to Wexford for a six-night stay. She lied to her parents and her brother when they seemed concerned that she was going alone and said that Michelle, one executive in the company, was meeting her there for a couple of nights. As she drove away from home, it was a crisp bright afternoon, with clear blue skies, and she noted the honey-coloured sunlight fizzing through the branches of the tree, as if it was giving her a message of hope that eventually the sun would break through, and all would be well again for her. She remained low-spirited as she drove towards her destination. By the time she reached the hotel she was fatigued and went straight to her room. Her travel bag was heavy with the bottles of wine she had hidden in there. This was where she intended to hide away until she came to terms with her heartbreak. First, she decided she would go to the bar for a glass or two of vodka to drown her sorrows.

That's all she remembered until late into the night and the consequences were horrendous. She drank so much that it plunged her into an alcohol-induced semi-coma. She woke up and scrabbled for the phone to check the time. It was half-past three. Her mind was blank all she could remember was being in the bar sitting at the counter listening to people chatting and laughing around her. How did she make it up the lift to her room? She did not know? She rummaged around until she found the bedside lamp and switched it on, pushed the duvet aside and hauled herself out of bed. Her head was swimming and she was nauseous. It took her quite a while to orient herself. She lay back on the bed and looked up at the ceiling and the spotlights, which came on when she pushed another switch. The lights were strong as she stared up at them trying to keep awake and think. Slowly, as though she was struggling through a misty landscape, some events of the evening and past few days came back with a jolt.

She got up and eventually made her way to the window. Opening it she noted a thick fog had fallen. She stood there gazing at the silent hypnotic fall of thick white curls drifting down from the sky. The outline of the car park outside the hotel was hardly distinguishable, everything obliterated by a thick white coating of fog much like her brain at this moment. When she turned around her head throbbed severely with a bizarre dizziness. She glanced at the empty wine bottles on the bedside locker and cringed tightening her hands around her head. She lay down and slept until morning.

The following days brought with it anger, heartbreak, and a period of craziness and indulging that almost left her in a senseless state that might have ended her career. It was Conor, her brother, who hauled her out of the abyss. He rescued her and helped her sober up. Once she came through that initial madness, she decided to try to come to terms with the sequence of events over the past week and try to move forward. Conor convinced her to come back home. He explained to her what was happening with the lodger and the danger his parents were in. It was that which shocked her out of her own dark place. He also let her know he moved home to be with his parents and Diana his girlfriend moved with him for the duration. She said "I wondered why you moved home so hastily because you were settled in Galway." "You know Diana's father, Pat who is a detective? Well, he told me to stay with my parents because Sam was acting suspicious in the area. Mum cannot put him out for no reason until his lease is up. Our parents cannot be left on their own with him." Sam was acting as normal and being the same sweet man he was the first day he came to the door but Pat had informed them he had robbed before and there was nothing to say he wouldn't do it again. Evidently, the last robbery was carried out at knife point. Eve remarked, "I knew there was something ugly about him but Mum had fallen for his charm, and didn't see the hidden side of him." Eve promised her brother she would be home the following evening.

Morning was here at last and after a good night's sleep she got out of bed went over and opened the curtains, the room flooded with brightness and she blinked. The sun was peering through the lifting fog and there was a glimpse of blue sky far in the distance. After a hot shower, she dressed and packed her bag. She had a hot breakfast and started for home. Her only concern now was her parent's safety. She decided without hesitation to stay at home until the lodger came to the end of his lease and they could ask him to leave. As Eve turned into the driveway of her home place and drove up the wide avenue flanked on either side by proportioned shrubs and neatly clipped hedges, in the distance she could see the deep blue sea rippling continually. At that moment, she realised her life was so busy she hardly ever noticed them before. Now she was so jubilant to be home and was going to take time out 'to smell the roses' and take it easy for a while.

Rachael was arranging champagne glasses and nibbles carefully on the coffee table in the sitting room of their new apartment. Benjamin finalised the sale recently and her parents were coming to stay for three nights. Rachael was over the moon as she was going to announce the date of their forth coming fairy tale wedding next year. Rachael felt lucky to have Benjamin in her life. She knew she caught him on the rebound when things hadn't worked out with himself and Eve. She offered him what he didn't get from Eve, attention, consideration, companionship and love. She reassured him they were meant to be together and eventually won him over and now they were planning their wedding.

Julie put Eric in the picture about Sam's past, warning him not to indicate that he knew that Sam was dangerous, because he was never caught in the criminal act he could not be accused without proof. Unfortunately, he had signed a six-month contract which brought his stay to the end of August. Julie regretted drawing up the contract but couldn't back out of it without getting into trouble with the law, as he had legal rights. Diana's father, Pat, was keeping a very close eye on his every move.

It was a beautiful summer's afternoon, the caravan park was packed, Conor had gone into Galway to collect Diana and bring her home after work. It would be late when he got back. Eve's friend, Majella took her out for the day to revive her spirits and Julie had guests coming in the morning. Eric finished mowing the lawns and trimming the hedges at the back of the caravan park. Sam announced he would be away for a few days on business and Julie felt relieved not to have to keep the pretence up, while he was gone. She went about preparing for the guests at her ease. Her phone ran out of battery so she plugged it in before going up stairs. The afternoon turned into evening and before she realised; the evening began to turn into dusk. She went to her office and looked out the window, but there was no sign of Eric. Conor must have been delayed in traffic but it made no difference Sam was away.

As darkness fell Julie wondered why Conor wasn't back she shivered but didn't know why. She stood up and was about to go downstairs to get her phone when she thought she heard the patio door at the back open slowly. "Is that you, Eric?" she called but there was no reply. She wished she had her phone but convinced herself it was only the breeze that was blowing in from the sea. She was almost halfway down the stairs when she heard footsteps. She turned around quickly and ran back up to her office. Going swiftly to the window, she looked out, but there was no car outside. She went back out onto the landing of the stairs and that was when she saw a shadow in the hall below. She was frantic, 'where were Conor and Diana? Why were they not here yet?' She wanted to phone Eric but was afraid to go get the phone. She called out, "Hello who's that?" Then she saw his face in the dim hall light smiling up at her with his gleaming white teeth. "Hello, Julie all on your own I see." "Sam, you gave me a fright, I wasn't expecting you back for a few days, where is your car?" she asked. "Never mind my car, go back into your office now" he replied with menace. Julie continued to walk towards him as she wanted to get her phone. He shouted to go back up into the office. She was petrified when she looked at him, brandishing a knife in his hand. She turned around and ran to try to get the door locked, but he caught up with her, being too fast and jumped close to her. He pushed her into the office, "Get out your bank details." She stalled. "Do exactly as I say" he demanded. Julie thought quickly even though she was scared. "I have to go down to get my folder I forget the pin number." "Shut up, don't annoy me, a business person never forgets their bank details. Do as I say open up your laptop now. Open your banking on line and get into the account. Hurry" he barked. She shivered when he shoved the knife to her back. "I don't have all evening to wait." Her hands shook and she said again, "I cannot remember the pin number." He shoved the knife closer and she could feel the sharpness of it running along her spine." "Of course you remember, open it up or you will be sorry. I'm warning you." Julie shouted out for Conor and Eric and looking at Sam she asked, "Why are you doing this to us Sam, we have never been anything but friendly and kind to you. I thought we were friends?" "Nobody will hear you. I know where your men are and they can't hear a thing, especially with the machinery working." He ran the knife all the way up her back until she felt the point of it on her neck. Julie knew she couldn't argue she was in terrible danger and entered the details of the account, revealing a substantial amount of money.

He rubbed his hands across the back of her neck saying, "This will be our little secret. You'll keep quiet and I will be watching your every move until my lease is up, then I will vanish. Now transfer twenty thousand euro into this account." He handed her a piece of paper with his details. She hesitated and cried, "I can only transfer a thousand euro to a new account number it will take a few days to transfer the rest." He shouted, "Shut your mouth and transfer what you can and we will continue with the rest tomorrow evening and I'm warning you not a word or you will suffer the consequences. I hope you take heed, because I mean every word I say." She could hear Eric working the chainsaw and wished he would stop and she could scream louder. What she didn't know was that Diana's father was collecting his daughter after he was finished duty and dropping her out to be with Conor. She also didn't know her son was back down at the park. Neither her son nor husband knew the danger she was in at that very moment.

"It's getting late," Eric said to Conor. "I called your mother but got no reply." "She's probably upstairs and didn't hear it." "Probably, so we'll work for another while until this is finished." Diana's father, was late collecting his daughter from work they were almost at Conor's house when he mentioned he must go in and book his friends in to the bed-and-breakfast next month. Diana was surprised he hadn't booked it before now and said, "I hope Julie has free rooms, they are fairly busy at the moment." Pat drove up to the guesthouse door, Diana and her father opened it and walked in and Pat heard Julie shout. Sam had caught her by the hair. Then he heard a loud voice "Transfer the money, this is your last chance." Julie was crying out and was about to click the button to complete the transaction when Pat ran up the stairs. He could see immediately into the office, a man holding a knife to Julie's back and his other hand gripping her hair. He managed to grab Sam in an arm lock and roared for Diana to phone the station immediately and to get Conor and Eric. The patrol car arrived within minutes as Conor and Eric helped to detain Sam, who was then arrested. It had been a hugely traumatic evening for Julie. Diana had given her a hot mug of coffee with a shot of whiskey just as Eve arrived back to hear the disturbing turn of events. Julie sat huddled on the couch for a long while and the family stayed together for the night. Pat came back the next evening and took statements and let them know Sam was being charged with attempted robbery and assault. Julie, who was suffering from shock, spent the following few days trying to pull herself together and come to terms with the trauma she had just experienced. It was the worst nightmare Julie had ever endured in her life.

She worked in the kitchen and tried not to think about the harrowing event. She found herself clattering pans and cutlery about as if every single piece frustrated her. Eric noticed she was putting on a show, her smile was too brilliant and sharp-edged like broken glass. They worked side by side for a few days but he felt they were still somehow apart like two planets revolving in their separate orbits. Eric was trying his best to support her in her anguish, as he was aware she was still in shock. He loved being at home, he loved the business, he loved Julie, this had made him realise just how much, but he wasn't sure how she felt about him. He intended to make things right he realised how much he regretted his mistakes.

Conor and Diana had returned to their home in Galway, Eve was getting ready to go on a work trip to Germany, so early one evening Julie decided she was going up to bed. She was overcome with tiredness but after hours of twisting and turning sleep refused to come. It started to rain heavily she could hear it lash against the bedroom window and could almost feel the wind which had started up, suddenly her body shook uncontrollably. She imagined she could still hear Sam's voice as he crept up the stairs. She was scared. She called out to Eric who was still sitting watching TV. He came up the stairs swiftly. She was standing at the edge of the bed. "I'm afraid in the room on my own." He didn't quite know what to say. She continued on, "I can hear Sam's voice all around me." He looked down "What can I do?" he asked. There was a slight shake in her voice, "Will you come back into the bedroom with me?" He nodded. Eric realised that night, that sometimes things happen for a reason even though the event with Sam was horrendous. Eric hoped that there may still be a future for himself and Julie.

Eve was getting on with her life, time was passing quickly since her break up with Pierre and she was doing her utmost to move forward. Her parents were still coming to terms with the shock of Sam being arrested on their doorstep, Julie was still nervous to go out on her own even though Sam was locked up for a few years. Eve was preparing for her flight to Germany where she was going to spend a few weeks opening another boutique before returning home. Julie and Eric were attending marriage counselling and were finding the sessions beneficial and they had gone out together for an evening meal or a walk on the promenade in Salthill.

One evening, Julie heard sobbing from Eve's room and found her crying cross-legged on the bed, her laptop perched on her knees, her phone clenched in her hand, tears streaming down her red face. "Do you feel like telling me what's going on?" Julie softly asked. She looked up with swollen eyes and told her about Pierre's phone call. Julie had little pity for him when Eve said he was depressed, not eating or sleeping, her lips quivered, "He wants us to talk." She could hear the emotion in her daughter's voice. Julie tried to talk it out with her, "I do understand how hard this is for you and it's not a simple thing to do. I think it's the secrecy and lack of trust that are two fundamental issues that have been part of your relationship from the start with Pierre. You can't build a future on that. Look at your father and I trying to work through what he did." Eve shrugged her shoulders, "You're right, but it is so hard because I loved him and I miss him. I saw my future with him and now that's all gone." Her mother nodded, understanding her daughter's pain. The tears continued rolling down her cheeks as Julie hugged her. Julie felt sad because there was nothing she could say that would sort this out for Eve or help lighten her mood, not even reminding her of the trip to Germany. She left for Germany a week later, but before she left home, she promised to bring her mother on a luxury break next year, feeling that they both could do with something to look forward to. Julie was ecstatic when she heard they would be heading for the Greek island of Kos then on to Kardamena.

Eve was familiar with this holiday destination and its waterfront bars and restaurants. Nearby, they would visit Helona beach and also take a trip to the Castle of the Knights of St John, and explore the ruins. In the evenings, they could sit out under a bright moon and starry sky listening to the waves break on the shore, sipping glasses of wine, enjoying the quietness of the evenings and letting the turbulent time of the past melt away. She brought herself back down to earth and turned off her computer, she thought about the work she'd done that morning, and felt really guilty because she had accomplished little at all. She told herself when she got back from lunch that she was going to knuckle down, and get stuck into the backlog. For the past week, she hadn't been able to concentrate because she had turned her thoughts to Benjamin. Her colleagues in the fashion industry were constantly talking about how successful he was. She thought about looking him up on this trip.

The following day, while Eve was in a boutique in the city looking for something to wear for the launch night of her autumn collections, he appeared from nowhere. She was standing there gazing at the dresses when he walked up behind her, "Hello Eve." She swung around, recognising the familiar voice. "Benjamin, what a coincidence." She felt her face getting warm, she looked into his eyes. In fact, she was staring at him in sheer excitement while, at the same time she tried to appear completely calm. Eve explained about being in Germany for a few weeks as Benjamin continued to tell her about his latest venture. She listened to him for ages. She would happily hear him talk forever. He had a deep and sexy voice and she loved it. Then he apologised profusely for having to leave. All the while she hoped and prayed that he would suggest meeting up again. But he simply said, "Good bye and lovely to see you again."

When she got back to her office and turned on the computer, she sat and stared at the screen, seeing Benjamin's perfect face instead of the rows of figures which were really there. Three weeks left in Germany seemed such a short time if she wanted to meet up with him and see if there was still a spark between them. She regretted ignoring his advances all those months ago. She was totally unaware that Rachael and Benjamin had amalgamated companies and were going from strength to strength. It only seemed the proper thing to do before they tied the knot next year. Rachael was already having her dress designed by Benjamin's top dress designer. He told Rachael that evening about running into Eve. "We must invite her to dinner before she returns to Ireland," Rachael said rather hesitatingly. Benjamin agreed, thinking next week perhaps when they would both be free. He was surprised to see Eve in Germany, thinking she would be in the height of her plans organising her wedding to her French man. Benjamin wasn't aware she was due to open a boutique in the middle of the city. It didn't concern him anyway now that he was with Rachael. Eve was definitely in the friend zone in his eyes. Benjamin contacted her and asked her to dinner with Rachael and himself in his apartment. She had heard that he was seeing someone and wondered if it was it serious. When she arrived, Rachael was ready to serve up the meal all bright and bubbly. She looked at her and hoped their relationship was casual.

While Rachael was preparing dessert, Eve was taken aback when Benjamin began singing Rachael's praises. "She is a designer with a difference. She's amazing, talented and has just amalgamated her company with mine. I wanted to tell you, Eve, that we are getting married next June." The impact of his words hit her like an electric shock. Then he asked, "When is your big day, or is it a secret?" She looked at him with a cheerless face, "We actually broke up a few months ago," as she filled him in on what had happened. Benjamin hesitated for a moment and then nodded "I see," his heart missed a beat as he stared at her open-mouthed. So many questions began buzzing in his head. "It must have been an enormous shock for you Eve." "It really was. I did not know at all. I was clueless to it all," said Eve. Suddenly, it clicked with him. Eve was single.

Rachael overheard the conversation and walked into the dining room carrying a tray with a selection of desserts, she placed the tray carefully in the middle of the table and gently put her arm around Benjamin's shoulders saying,

"If any man deceived me like I would do the same, I'd walk away." She continued to serve the desserts and to Benjamin's relief changed the subject, and the rest of the evening was accompanied by smiles and laughter. They didn't talk about anything in particular, but they wined and dined into the early hours of the morning and Rachael insisted Eve stay over and have an early breakfast before going to work. Reluctantly, she accepted.

The following morning, Eve sat at the table and sipped her tea in silence and witnessed the body language between Rachael and Benjamin, which was electric. The way he acted around Rachael made her remember just how wonderful it felt to be with him. Eve could feel his eyes fixed on her for a moment, before glancing away. This left her distracted and she decided suddenly to go, leaving her toast and half a cup of tea unfinished. They both walked her to the door, and Rachael invited her to call again on her next visit to Germany. Eve thanked them both for their hospitality and left. Benjamin noted Rachael was off form. She commented, "Eve still likes you." "No Rachael, whatever there was or wasn't between us is long over. I told you about it when we met, there are no secrets between us." Rachael said "She's a beautiful woman," he wasn't thinking and responded, "She is, isn't she." Immediately, he regretted saying that. He didn't want her to know that he found Eve extremely attractive. Rachael's voice cut into his wandering thoughts "What shall we do for the rest of the day?" "How about going into the city and doing some shopping and you could book in for some treatments and relax and unwind," he said. "Sounds good to me," Rachael ran upstairs and was ready in a jiffy and they were on their way. Benjamin felt relieved that Eve was gone and she wouldn't be back for a few months, and that would give him a chance to think how he really felt about her now, was he really over her, did he just fall for Rachael on the rebound, he needed time to think straight. The following week, Eve opened her boutique in the middle of the city.

That night, she hosted a party in a five-star hotel just next door. She invited her friends and a group of business clients; they arrived early and were shown to the party suite on the top floor and were provided with refreshments. Eve said a few words thanking them for the continued support, while saying the last few words..."The appearance of commercial success is as important to a business as the balance sheets," she was distracted by a middle- aged man, who had just walked in. When she finished talking and walked down off the platform, she could see him through the crowds moving towards her. He walked right up to where she was standing. "I was impressed with your speech," he held out his hand and she left hers into it. He said rather quickly, "I'm Louis Stapleton." She was aware of the strong lines of his brow and his defined jaw, his long black lashes emphasised the roundness of his eyes. He continued to make conversation with her. "My parents are from Birr, Co. Offaly, but I haven't been over there for the past two years. I hope to visit next year. My brother and his partner are running a photography business in the town." Eve wondered why so much information she only met him and here he was almost telling his life story. She declined to give any information about herself. "I feel like a fish out of water here," he said. She wondered what brought him to the party. "Are you in this business?' she asked. "No, I'm chief executive of a car company and unfortunately walked into the wrong meeting and didn't realise until you mentioned dress designing I'm so sorry." He was about to walk off when she said, "Wait, join us for some refreshments." She introduced him to her friends and he mingled.

Eventually, he joined Eve and some of her business associates at the sidebar. He touched her arm, "It was considerate of you to make me feel so welcome and at ease." He found her very elegant. She looked both smart and feminine in the tailored suit she was wearing. He wanted to get to know more about her. He started chatting with a group of women who obviously all knew each other. They quizzed him about why he was at the opening, thinking he was in the business himself. He explained what had happened and how he had arrived at the wrong room. Louis fitted in with everybody and could join in any conversation, so much so that the girls didn't believe him as they thought Eve had Louis hidden away. "I swear he is a complete stranger to me. Like he said he wandered into the room mistakenly and I invited him to join us. That is how it is." Eve didn't intend to fall for any man's charm ever again. She was sworn off them. She noticed though, that he took his every chance to get her alone. She went up to the bar to get herself a drink and there he was right behind her. He pointed to the armchairs by the window. "Sit here and have a quiet drink with me, please." During the conversation, it was apparent that it flowed easily between them and without effort, they both discovered that they were single, but Benjamin flashed through her mind. Louis left his hand on hers. Eve glanced round to see if anybody had noticed this man being too familiar with her. A perfect stranger was flirting with her. Deep down, she was flattered. It had boosted her confidence and she felt desirable. The flirting continued through the rest of the evening until Eve went up on the platform once more and thanked all who had made the night successful. She asked Jane and Lily, two of her colleagues to wait for her so they could take a taxi together. She said good night to Louis, but before he said good night, he suggested bringing her to dinner at the weekend. "I'm rather busy," she said, but he insisted "It's my way of saying thanks for making me feel welcome." The following weekend, they met at a small bistro in the middle of the city. Eve was cautious. She hoped he didn't get the wrong impression this was only a friendship dinner, nothing more. He looked at her with delight while she kept studying the menu. "Are you ready to order?" he asked. She looked over at him his deep blue eyes seemed paler tonight or perhaps it was the pink shirt that was a little pale for his complexion.

She hoped he didn't notice her hands tremble while she read the menu. Eve tried to sound like the calm, sophisticated woman of the world that she ought to be at thirty-eight. Even though she was adamant not to develop feelings for this man, she couldn't help watching his expression as he ordered for both of them. His eyes were one of his best features. There was a certainty to them. She realised with some surprise that her body was responding automatically to his presence. He reached his hand across the table and touched hers. "I'm wondering if you would like to meet tomorrow afternoon?" Eve declined, "Sorry, but I have a full work schedule for the coming week, and tomorrow is my only chance to prepare." She noticed his face darkened then grew crimson. He pursed his lips, "What about meeting up the following week before you go back home" he suggested. "I'm really very busy but I'll call you on my next trip over" she replied. Louis was rather cautious for the rest of the evening and they ate their meal with mostly shop talk. Eve's phone rang twice during dinner. She could hear it bleeping in her bag she knew who it was because he rang earlier and she let it ring out, she wasn't prepared to talk to Pierre. Before they parted company that night, Louis pulled a card from his shirt pocked "It's my phone number." He was gazing at her with serious eyes, as they talked for another half hour then went their separate ways.

The following Sunday evening Pierre rang again. She let it ring out. Eve called him back after she had plugged in her laptop and switched it on. She hadn't the slightest bit of interest in what he had to say. Sitting close to the table she clicked on his number while scrolling down through Facebook. At least it would break the boredom of listening to his tale of woe. He answered momentarily. She noted his voice high pitched and excited. His voice wobbled slightly, "I'm truly regretful, please listen to me; we can build that house of your dreams, I promise." She retorted "With what?" It was her first time to speak. "I'm working two jobs. Please listen to me Eve, I'm sorry I was so awful to you. I was stupid not to tell to you. I was afraid I would lose you." She spoke again, "I'm sorry too Pierre that our relationship didn't work out. Relationships need to be built on trust and if we don't have that we have nothing. I just can't do it, We're finished as far as I'm concerned, I won't be seeing you again, we both need to move on." He panicked, his heart thumped widely in his chest. "Eve, please don't say that, let's try, just give me one more chance. We can work this out. I will never lie to you again." He kept on pleading with her. "You're the love of my life. I want to wake up beside you every morning. I want to spend the rest of my life with you living happily together." "Pierre you are not hearing me. It's over, we are not getting back together. You need to move on." She ended the phone call and didn't hear his reply. She was visibly upset after the call and could feel her body trembling, she loved Pierre but knew that she could never trust him again, it would never work. When she heard his voice, she yearned for him, his voice, his touch, his closeness. She missed him terribly.

Later in the week, Eve had to contact Benjamin regarding a work issue that she knew he could help her with. Rather than discuss it over the phone, Eve asked if it would be possible for them to meet up. It was agreed that they would meet in the bistro beside his offices, as he had little free time in his weekly work schedule. Eve arrived at the bistro the next day and went upstairs, where she hoped it would be quieter. Benjamin came out of his office at the exact time and ran up to meet her. He leaned over and kissed her on the cheek. They ordered light lunches and Eve explained her issue with work, and with Benjamin's help she could tease out the issue and come to a resolution. Eve hadn't planned to discuss what had happened between them previously but knew it was now or never. "Benjamin, did you feel we could have been good together you know as a couple?" she asked. He smiled at her gently. "Yes, I felt that way too, but it didn't really work out for us, did it?" He said no more. He hated when Eve closed her eyes, tilted her head back, and her lips took that twisted, tortured look of someone who was fighting tears. A couple of big drops escaped and she wiped them away quickly. He reached out and put a comforting hand on her forearm. She continued, "Could we try again before it's too late?" He spoke with a voice that was strong and kind. "For you and me, it's been good. We had a chance, but it wasn't meant to be. I think we reached the end of our road when you went back to Pierre to marry him." She didn't reply. The silence went on so long Benjamin eventually had to break it. "You're my friend and always will be, but Rachael and I are going to be married." Her mouth dropped open as she looked at him directly in the eyes. She slowly got to her feet and felt the colour rising in her neck. She turned to go "Wait a second," he said. "Can we talk?" Softly, she responded, "I don't think there is anything left to say Benjamin, I understand what you are saying and respect your decision." "I need you to listen to me Eve." She shook her head and turned and walked away. He called to her. She heard him but she didn't turn around and just walked out onto the street and back to her apartment with tears as her companion. Downhearted, the following weekend, she returned home. Even though her business was booming, it didn't lift her mood and she once again felt like a lost soul.

CHAPTER 8

The house was locked when Eve arrived home from Germany. She was exhausted; the month had been a stressful one and all that was needed now was to get inside and make a hot cup of tea. Her parents were gone to town. She found a note under the flower pot. It was for Conor, telling him they would be back before dinner. The key of the door was in the usual spot. On the very bottom of the note, as if it was an afterthought, her mother let him know she was collecting a takeaway on the way back.

Eve walked down the lane towards the caravan park. She listened to the gentle trickle of the stream that ran through the woodland right at the back of the park where it eventually joined to the sea. As she walked along, she admired the peaceful tranquillity of this place she called home. It was good to be back again. It gave her the space she needed to think and to get her life in order.

Conor spotted his sister walking slowly down towards his office. He groaned to himself. She was the last person he needed now; he was too taken up with his own problems. Conor sent a text to his mother to bring extra food for Eve. As she walked closer "Hi Sis," he said smiling and leaned over to kiss her on the cheek. She looked at him questioning "Now tell me why you looked so grumpy when you spotted me?" "Sorry, was I that obvious? It's nothing to do with you, it's just that Diana and I broke up" he replied. "When and why did that happen?" Eve asked shocked. "Did Mum not tell you?" he asked with surprise. "She never mentioned it, what is going on? Why is nobody telling me anything!" "I moved back home last week," he said rather glumly. "What happened? I thought you two were inseparable?" He made no comment. She didn't question him further because he was acting like somebody entering the eye of an emotional storm. She knew he was pretty keen and she felt annoyed with Diana for letting her brother down like that. "Move on Conor, there is plenty more fish in the sea." Conor clamped his hands over his ears "I can't believe you just said that, of all people you know what it is like," he roared. Sighing heavily, Eve reckoned there was no point in trying to talk to him when he was in a foul mood. She felt bad for having upset him even more. She turned and called back over her shoulder, "I'll pop on the kettle come up for a cuppa." "Okay" he muttered.

They were sitting down in the living room. Eve tried to cheer her brother up as her parents arrived home with the food. After Eve's parents welcomed her home, they all sat to the table and tucked into their meal. Eve told them how thrilled she was after opening the new boutique in Germany and about the success of the launch. Eric inquired jokingly, "Did you meet anyone interesting on your travels?" It was a raw subject with her right now. Julie was enraged at his tactlessness. Heat flooded Eve's cheeks and she bent her head as she tried to hide the telltale blush. Louis was sweet, talented and good-looking, but she wasn't looking for a man to heal her emotional self unless it was Benjamin and that would not happen. Conor looked at the clock. He stood up from the table, deciding to go to the office to prepare the end-of-year accounts. Eve sat with her parents and chatted for a long while, but tiredness took over and what she really needed now was a good sleep. She knew in her heart she had come to the right place to heal herself. She woke full of hope and decided she was entering a new chapter in her life.

She wandered downstairs and through to the kitchen, pausing to flick the kettle on for her first coffee of the day and slotted some bread into the toaster. Her mother, who was in the next room, sensed the exciting new aura about her daughter. "I'm going down by the shore after breakfast for a walk. Will you join me?" she asked Julie. "I'll pass on it today I'm meeting Kay in town for coffee we'll go together another day." Eve was pleased to get away on her own it would give her time to think.

She drove down to the grass margin, parked her car and walked down the lane to the shore front where there was a stiff breeze blowing. Eventually, she stopped to watch a sailboat far out. She could see the shining sails gently pushing the boat along, rippling the blue sea. Here and there was a chalk mark of white foam where a wave had broken. She wondered how a person had the nerve for winter sailing. She watched it until it came ashore. In the time she stood there concentrating on the movements of the sails, she was also deep in thought and like the sails, she too hoped her life was about to change direction for the better. With a breeze on her cheeks, her lips felt cold and her body shivered. It was time to start back home. While walking back to her car, she heard a jeep approaching from behind. She stepped up on the grassy margin to let it pass. She didn't recognise it and was startled when it slowed to a snail's pace. She gazed sharply at the driver who was staring out at her, and by the look on his face he was surprised. Pierre didn't expect to see her there. He thought she was still in Germany.

Eve felt as though she was under water and could only hear a distant noise of an engine running. She didn't know what to do at that moment, so she walked on. He drove up close beside her. He was scrutinizing her face to detect her mood. He rolled down the window. "This is a surprise. Hello Eve," he said. "Hi there." She didn't speak his name. He spoke cautiously. "How have you been?" She said crossly, "How do you think I have been?" His next words provoked her. "Will you come for a coffee and a chat with me?" "No I won't," she snapped. "You ruined our relationship and our future together. My life, the life we had planned together has been turned upside down. We're finished go back to your family in France." He pleaded, "I want you to be my family, I love you Eve." She avoided his eyes and ignored his pleas. She continued on walking towards her car. He felt a wave of guilt wash over him. It was his fault their relationship had ended. He was the one who had caused so much pain to Eve. He followed her until she reached her car. Eve clicked the car door open and quickly turned on the ignition. He continued on pleading with her. She was agitated and drove off at high speed, spinning the tyres and showering gravel all around. Pierre sat in his jeep devastated, thinking about what had just transpired. Eventually, he returned home broken-hearted and knew that their relationship was well and truly over.

In the following months Eve buried herself in her work. She only saw Pierre in the distance occasionally and never allowed herself to cross paths with him. She had moved on with her life, but was getting frustrated with being at home with her parents. She needed her own place so she started scanning the market for a suitable house near to Galway city. Eventually, her dream house was on the market for a reasonable price and the location was perfect. Living in Oranmore would be near home yet far enough away to have her privacy. She could have the best of both worlds, living there and visiting her home place in Connemara. She contacted her friend Majella and trusted she would steer her right. They arranged to meet in the middle of the village and after a light lunch they met the auctioneer and drove up to the house in the outskirts of the village. He opened the door and brought them through, then left them for an hour to browse around.

Eve's budget was six hundred thousand euro, but the seller was looking for six hundred and fifty thousand euro. She hoped if she held out they might see eye to eye with her. She explained to the agent that there was quite a considerable amount of work to be done inside, obviously it was closed up for some time. When the agent contacted her again, he advised her that the owners were prepared to let it go for six hundred and thirty thousand euro but no less. Eve went back to the bank, had a meeting with the manager and secured a further thirty thousand euros. After an amount of paperwork the money came through, and she couldn't believe that she was now the proud owner of her very first home. Her parents and Conor helped her move her stuff. She surprised herself by settling in so quickly, it felt good to be independent. She would not dwell on the phone call she got yesterday while at work. It was from Louis letting her know he had moved back home to Birr and hopefully she would meet up with him sometime soon for a drink. She intended to spend every free moment decorating the house and had no intention of falling into another relationship. That was the last thing on her list of things to do. She had tried her best to move on from her failed relationship with Pierre and from Benjamin who was now married to Rachael and apparently was very happy. She replied saying she would contact him when she was settled in the house. He was insistent and didn't take no for an answer so she decided to meet up with him on Sunday, being a bit pushy, which agitated her. But she decided that there was no harm in meeting for a drink with no strings attached. Living on her own seemed the best kind of life and having to answer to nobody was empowering.

The house-warming took place on Saturday night in Eve's new home. It was a quiet affair with just a few close friends, her parents and brother. Her friend Majella helped her prepare the house and they ordered a buffet and drinks. On Sunday afternoon, Louis contacted her as she was leaving home to meet up with him for the drink that they had arranged. While she was driving, her phone rang again it was Louis for the second time, telling her he was after getting a flat tyre and was going to be late. When he eventually arrived, she got into his car and they drove towards Galway. Louis was flustered. This was not the start he had hoped for. An uncomfortable silence fell between them. She glanced over at him and had forgotten how handsome and dangerously masculine he looked. He glanced over at her with a smile that caught her off guard. "Are you alright, Eve?" he asked in a voice that was throatier than anything she'd ever heard. She nodded. The ensuing silence gave Louis the impression Eve was annoyed with him. Deciding he didn't like the silence he reached out and connected the Bluetooth and Mick Denver from Portumna came across loud and clear with one of his tracks 'Boston Rose' she was relieved with the distraction, she was a fan of his for years and really enjoyed his sweet voice. She was relieved when they reached the pub and even though the place was packed, they found chairs to sit down. Louis took off his jacket. She got distracted, watching him slide his jacket off his shoulders. His shoulders were even more broad and powerful than she'd remembered. He looked at her warmly "I was looking forward to this date with you," he said. Eve smiled. It was obvious Louis was making more out meeting up than her.

After they ordered food and drinks, he started asking her about her designing business. She explained about the amount of travelling involved. She felt he was about to delve into her life, but she didn't intend going there. Her love life was a disaster as far as she was concerned and she wouldn't be sharing it with him. She found him to be a fine specimen of a man, definitely a threat to the peace she was trying to find living alone. There was something about his voice, the way he looked at her. His entire presence made her feel desirable. She enquired, "Were you a sales representative all your life?" "No. I trained as a vet but wanted to travel so I became a rep." "Wow, that was some career change" she said. "Yeah, I know, but unfortunately I got tired going from place to place always catching flights, sitting in airports waiting and waiting so that's why I returned home and took part in a refresher course with a view to opening a veterinary practice in Birr."

She was surprised when he began to confide in her and wondered why he felt it necessary to tell her about his private life especially as they didn't know each other that well yet. "I was engaged in my twenties," he noticed her expression change. "We split up after four years together. The relationship started to go downhill steadily after she changed her job and insisted in staying in Cork five nights a week. Eventually, we ended it amicably. I think we had simply outgrown each other." Louis surprised himself as usually the last thing he'd talk about was his private life but he felt comfortable talking to her. They continued with their meal and chit-chat. As they were finishing, he looked over at her, "I would like to see you again." She looked at him and noted the smile that touched his lips extended from one corner of his mouth to the other and was simply breath-taking. There was something inviting about him. She nodded "Yes I'd like that too." Let's meet again same time in one month from now," he touched her hand "I'll be looking forward to it," he said.

They parted company and after he dropped her to her car, she decided to go over and visit her parents. Her mother was busy as usual, so she stayed and lent a helping hand. While they were having a rest sitting down and Eric was gone outside, Eve told her mother about meeting Louis, but told her they were just friends. Eve knew it was something that had to be taken slowly. "A new someone is the only way to mend a broken heart," her mum said delighted for her daughter. Eve's lips quivered "I want someone to love and someone to love me back. I want my heart to leap at the sight of him." "Be patient Eve, he'll come along, wait and see." Eve said, changing the subject "That's enough about me. How is Conor coping since he opened the coffee shop?" Julie told her that business was booming and that she and Eric were doing their best to help him, and that they were enjoying it. That night, Eve curled up on the couch and turned on the television. It was amazing to be in her own place at last. Looking across at the big window as dusk was falling, she could see the castle and an outlet to the sea as a backdrop to the area, which was quite serene and quaint.

The month passed speedily. Louis was on his way to Galway to meet Eve, even though at times it felt it had been the longest month of his entire life. Finally, the evening had come to see her again. More than once, he had been tempted to come up with an excuse to pick up the phone and say he was on business and maybe they could meet for an afternoon. He decided against his impulse and stuck to what they had planned originally. Eve was up bright and early. Louis was coming over to Oranmore this evening. She was excited to see him. She had been to the hairdresser's yesterday morning to have her hair cut and styled, and it still looked as if it had just been done. The new outfit she bought last week was hanging on the outside of the wardrobe ready to be worn. It was classy, fun, and it gave her a feminine look.

When he arrived, she was ready and waiting and when she sat in the car beside him; she smiled to herself as he had a new haircut cut too. He looked at her "You look absolutely gorgeous. I love the hairstyle." Eve was pleased and smiled. Laughing, she retorted, "You don't look too bad yourself." He caught her hand tightly and continued on holding it until they reached the hotel. Louis had booked dinner for two overlooking Galway Bay as a surprise. "I thought we were going to the same place again as last month." He looked at her "Thought I'd surprise you," he said. They enjoyed dinner and sat and talked for hours. Louis suggested a walk on the promenade. As they walked along, they looked out at the sea, calm and bright with an orange sun illuminating the sky, until finally it dipped below the horizon. They reluctantly walked back to the car and drove back to Oranmore.

When they reached Eve's house, he wanted her to ask him to stay over until morning. It didn't happen, as she wanted to take things slowly. She didn't want to jeopardise the relationship. But she asked if he would like coffee before he went on his journey home. It was mid-night when he stood up to leave. As she stood beside him, he brought her into his arms and they shared a long, lingering kiss. He stood back from her, gazing into her eyes she met his gaze and held it, "See you next week," she knew at that moment that she was pretty attracted to this man. "I look forward to that Louis," they kissed again and she walked him to the front door and stood there until he drove out the gate.

Louis continued calling for months and taking Eve out every week and then twice and three times a week. Eve was home after her latest trip to France. Louis was away on a course and she had the week off work. She spent two days at home with her parents and helped Conor with some paper work bringing him up to date with his accounts. On the third day, she was up early to hear the wind howling off the sea and by mid-day, temperatures plummeted and a storm raged. Gale force winds swirled and echoed around the coast, the sea thundered on the sand and torrential rain battered the windows of the house. After two solid days of rain she was glad to see at last that as this morning dawned, though not exactly brighter it definitely was clearer. After breakfast, she drove into Galway and out towards the coast so she could walk down to the shore. She always loved the first trip down to the sea shore after a storm. It looked so calm and serene as the tiny waves lapped, and the mellow breeze blew on her face, She felt invigorated and happier than she did in a long time, Louis was a ray of sunshine he made her feel good about herself.

CHAPTER 9

Pierre was watching Eve, he wanted her now more than ever and intended to woo her back into his life. She strolled down the path to the water's edge where she stopped and admired the birds flying high in the sky, gathering together to glide away. He stood a short distance from her with his eyes moving around her body and realising how exquisitely lovely she looked even with the wind blowing her hair. He moved over to where she was standing. She heard the footsteps and turned around and when she saw him so close behind she walked briskly. He followed her and caught her by the shoulders, swinging her around to face him. He gripped her hand tightly and smiled at her warmly. His grip tightened fractionally "Eve, please come back to me I love you. Please talk to me." She freed herself from his grip and turned away from him. "Pierre, we have been through this. I am with Louis now and nothing will change that." He persevered "There is still a powerful chemistry between us, you can't deny that." "You're mistaken," she said. She twisted away from him, heading towards the car. She stopped and turned towards him shouting, "Keep away from me. We are well and truly finished for good." Pierre stood motionless. This was rejection at its utmost. Anger began to grow within him. 'Why wouldn't she at least talk it over?' Eventually, he made his way back to his home, feeling emotionally fraught. All he could see ahead of him was a lonely, heartbroken future. The following day, Eve went to visit her parents and stayed overnight before travelling to Cork on business. Her mother was overjoyed. She was after getting a call from her old friend Matthew Walsh, whom she knew in her youth when they were both fancy free and ready to take on the world. They shared many a kiss and promise of love forever, then that all changed when he moved to America and Julie stayed behind.

He was now in his seventies and hadn't been in contact with her for years. He retired last year and the last time he came to Ireland he stayed with Julie and Eric, so he decided to come back to Ireland while he was in good health and able to travel. He told her he sold all his properties, which were department stores but held on to his house. He booked two bedrooms in the bed-and-breakfast for six weeks from mid-December to the end of January. Eve asked if he was bringing a partner but was told it was Grayson Tracey, one of the executives in his company who would be travelling with him. "He is in his forties and has worked alongside Mathew all his business life. Grayson intended to come to Ireland a few years ago, but his marriage was on the rocks and he didn't have the heart to travel under those circumstances. When he heard Mathew was coming over this year, he decided it was an opportunity to join him. Seemingly, Matthew told him a lot about the old days when he was at home in Mayo. Grayson split up with his wife three years ago, life changed for him and having no children of his own, he was now thinking of buying property in Ireland maybe in Mayo where his great-grandmother and great-grandfather lived and farmed all their lives. He is now eager to trace his roots and see the old homestead, which is more than likely in ruins. His grandfather made no will and the proceeds of the farm were divided up among his mother and her eight siblings all living abroad." Eve said "Wow, you got quite the chat." "He is easy to talk to. He was a kind and fun loving man. We were friends in our teenage years before I met your father." Eve noted a little nostalgia flash across her mother's face. "He had a cousin living in Ireland and if my memory serves me right she had a baby boy named Hugh. Her surname was Black, she was a single mother and Matthew was the baby's godfather. They intend to travel around for the first fortnight and spend Christmas week with us. Will you come and stay for Christmas I could do with a helping hand obviously it would be lovely to have you as well?" "I will if I am not away myself." Julie looked at her daughter "Surely, you won't be working. That will be your holiday period. Eve looked distracted and replied, "It is far too early now to make plans, Mum, but I will definitely be here for part of the time, anyway."

Eve's parents always enjoyed her visits even though she lived the far side of Galway it was nice having her home for a few nights. "We'll miss you tomorrow," Eric said. "Oranmore isn't a million miles away. Ye could drop over to see me once in a while," she looked at her mother and gave a smirk. Her father knew she was being sarcastic. Julie was sitting, scrolling through the news on her laptop. Suddenly, she called out to Eve who was watching television in the sitting room. "Eve come here a second and read this for yourself." She stood behind her mother and began reading. "Benjamin has split up from his wife after a brief marriage and she is filing for divorce and suing for half of his entire estate and assets." Eve was shocked when she read it and wondered if Rachael had used Benjamin to get to his money and properties, seeing as the marriage hadn't lasted very long,

It was a beautiful day in the middle of October and after a frosty start; the sun shone with not a cloud in sight. Aside from the lovely sunshine and the brightness of the sky, Eve was happy because Louis had a party planned for the following night in a hotel in Birr. They were staying there for the three nights and she was looking forward to the spa treatments which she heard were amazing. She was also going to be meeting his family and friends. Louis had a younger brother and sister living in his home place where they were running a photography business. She enjoyed the way he brought her partying and away for weekends. He was definitely fun to be with. She noticed that he still had an eye for the ladies even though he was with her. Eve knew she could get jealous easily. Last month, when they were out socialising she went to the bathroom. When she returned, he was over with a group of young women enjoying a hen night. When he spotted her coming back, he moved away from them quickly. Eve was annoyed. "Do you know the girls?" "No, I never saw them before in my life." "Why did you go over to them then?" He passed it off, "I was getting drinks for us and one of them spoke to me. What was the harm in that?" he said rather bluntly. "Nothing," she said irked.

She arrived in Birr late afternoon after meeting Louis and booking into the hotel where they had bar food before meeting his family. She was a little nervous about the meeting but luckily found them to be very friendly and welcoming and all looking forward to the party the next night. Louis brought her for a walk down by the river and suggested an early night. Eve agreed. They spent the following day walking the Slieve Bloom Mountains and the Kinnitty Castle loop, which made her dream about a big wedding maybe in this very castle. Even though it was cold and crisp Eve enjoyed it thoroughly. They got back to the hotel early and Eve enjoyed the spa treatment. Later than expected the party got off to a great start, plenty of drinks and delicious finger food and everybody mingling and enjoying each other's company. The music was loud and lively and they danced all night. Eve noticed the more Louis drank, the less time he spent with her. She didn't want him to stick by her side all night and she understood he was having a good time with his friends whom he hadn't been in contact for a while. But he brought her here to introduce her to his family and she hadn't met half the people and now she was on her own. She began to mingle and let them know who she was. Louis was filling his plate with food and flirting with a group of women. One of them was practically all over him and as far as she could see he was enjoying the attention. Eve was raging and walked over and stood by his side. "Aren't you going to introduce me to your friends?" she asked? She didn't wait for him to reply and just stretched out her hand. "I'm Eve Wallace, Louis' girlfriend." "Nice to meet you," they said. The girl that was giving him the most attention blurted out, "You kept that silent Louis." He looked rather startled. "I never had time to tell you. It must be a year and a half ago since we met last Connie."

Then he caught Eve by the hand "Come over here with me I want you to meet my sister's boyfriend. He is just after coming in the door." The party went on into the late hours of the night and Louis wandered off again. When they got back to the bedroom, it was early morning. Eve had too much drink consumed and she tore into Louis. "Why were you hanging around all night with that group of women wearing sexy stuff? Was it because they were young and paying you attention?" "I was only having a laugh with them," Louis said with his speech slurred. Louis kept on laughing and joking and as far as Eve was concerned he was talking utter rubbish. She got into the bed by the window and fell into a deep sleep. Louis fell into the double bed next to hers. They both woke up with headaches. Louis sat up and wondered what happened last night. Not much, he thought to himself by the looks of it. He saw the single bed was slept in and Eve was in the shower. He got out of bed and switched on the kettle as he needed a strong coffee. He lay back on the pillow and tried to work through his muddled brain and see if he could remember how the party went? He didn't have to wonder for long because as soon as Eve came out from the shower she let him know bluntly what happened. He got out of bed and put on his clothes without showering. He went over to the shelf and emptied a packet of coffee into Eve's cup and two in his own he filled them with water and handed her the light one with a little milk. They sat and sipped the coffee for a few minutes then Louis asked, "Are you mad with me I didn't mean to ruin your night after asking you to come down for the weekend and meet my friends?"

She told him she was never so embarrassed in all her life. "Half of the crowd didn't even know who I was or what I was doing there. I had to put them in the picture myself and the reply from most of them was you have a right party animal there." He said he was sorry for the way he acted around his friends last night, drinking far too much and flirting with the women but intended to make it up to her on the double. He moved closer to her. "Let's go down for breakfast before we visit the castle."

She was looking forward to seeing the grounds of Birr Castle for years but found it difficult to react to Louis' sudden enthusiasm. "Will you forgive me and it won't happen again?" he asked coyly. She shook her head and tried to step back. But he lunged forward and caught her hands with just the very tips of her fingers. She blinked "Last night I felt like going back home." Louis was losing patience feeling that she was overreacting. "I was only having a bit of fun and meant no harm I'm going for breakfast now." He took up one of the key cards and made for the door. Eve told herself don't spoil the rest of the weekend and give him a chance as it was probably the drink. She rushed out after him and caught his hand "You're forgiven," she said and they walked down to the dining room and the rest of the weekend was spent in harmony. Louis continued to visit Eve twice a week, but she decided not to go to Birr again until after Christmas. He was disappointed with her decision because he had a special surprise party planned for her.

At last, Christmas Eve arrived and before they knew it so did Matthew and Grayson. After introductions, Julie went to the kitchen and poured strongly brewed coffee, where they chatted for a while before Eve brought them to their bedrooms. They were very impressed and Eve was pleased for her mother who had put tiring work into the preparations. After coming back down to the sitting room, Eve sat with them and Julie and Eric joined them a little later where they sat for a couple of hours comparing life in each of the countries. Eve continued to talk to Grayson after Eric brought Matthew down to the caravan park to meet Conor. Grayson decided to stay and have a second coffee. He gestured with his hand "I'll catch up with you later. I need another coffee." Julie went back to the kitchen to prepare dinner. Eve sat with Grayson and they compared notes for a long while, she was intrigued with this interesting American. He was tall and leanly built though not scrawny and had the look of a man who was very wealthy. She liked his strong-featured face, his deep-set grey-blue eyes crinkled at the corners, framed by dark lashes. His hair was dark brown streaked with grey at the temples. He was very interesting to talk to and she noted he was a good listener.

CHAPTER 10

At six o'clock on Christmas morning, Eve's parents were woken by Matthew knocking on their bedroom door. "Would you like some freshly brewed coffee?" he asked. "Ok, thank you," Julie said, thinking I would have much preferred been left to sleep until seven. She nudged Eric "Matthew's bringing up coffee." "Tell him I'm sleeping. Why did you give him permission to use the kitchen, anyway?" "Because he is a guest in the house and Americans love their early morning coffee. I didn't think it would be this early, though." Ten minutes later he knocked again. "Sorry Julie I can't find the sugar." Eric turned round in the bed and grumbled. Julie sighed 'I'll be right down.' she had to count to ten to calm her nerves it was Christmas morning she didn't want to get into a bad mood.

She went into the kitchen and showed Matthew where everything was. They sat and sipped coffee until it was time to cook breakfast. Eric wandered down from the room no length after and set the table for the Christmas morning fry-up. Eve and Conor were having a lie in and would no doubt get out of bed when they smelt the aroma of the fried bacon. Grayson arrived just in time after a brisk walk as feathery flakes fell from the sky. Matthew was sitting looking out on the garden and remarked how glorious it was in the winter snow. The carpet of pink and purple heathers that formed around the borders, and the Christmas rose with a background of white reminded him of the story his mother used to read to him from the book 'Christmas Carol,' being in the garden at this time of year building a snowman.

Later on, Eve and her mother listened to carol singing on Galway Bay while preparing dinner. The men got lost until almost dinner time, when they appeared in the kitchen to see the windows steamed up from the pudding bubbling away on the hob. They relished the aroma of the garnished turkey cooking crisp and brown in the oven. After a delicious dinner with all the Christmas trimmings, Eve directed them to the dining room where they spent the evening eating too much, exchanging presents and sitting in front of the television until late into the night.

When going to bed the thought of the call Eve received from Louis by video link earlier in the evening came to the forefront of her mind. He had said it would be nice to spend New Year's Eve together. She was delighted and asked him to join her and her family for the celebrations at her parent's home. St. Stephen's morning Eve was delighted to be back in Oranmore, looking forward to a leisurely day to herself away from all the chatting and activity at home. She turned on the heat and lit the stove as she didn't intend to go outside; the day was baltic and she was looking forward to a day of having to do very little. Julie had given her enough food to take with her, which meant she didn't have to do any cooking today. The wind howling in from the sea was carrying needles of freezing rain and snow that would cut into the skin of anyone foolhardy enough to brave the elements. Waves battered at the shore throwing top sheets of ghostlike spray all around. It made a lovely picture with Oranmore Castle to the forefront of the setting. She sat down by the stove with her dinner and was about to put the fork to her mouth when her phone rang. Eve looked at the number but didn't recognise it. Letting it ring for a second she wondered 'Who the hell was ringing her today.' She lifted the phone to her ear "Hello, Eve speaking." "Hello Eve," she recognised his voice immediately. A slight frown creased her brow as she wondered what he wanted. "Hello Benjamin," is all she said, curiously she waited to hear what he was going to say in the next breath. "Thought I'd phone and wish you a happy Christmas, and New Year." "Thank you. Are you having a nice one?" she asked. "Not really I'm on my own now, Rachael and I split up" she thought to herself for God' sake why contact me today to let me know about this. She said rather carelessly, "I'm sorry to hear that. You both seemed so happy together." Benjamin felt his heart beat uncomfortably it wasn't why he had rung and he was unsure of what to expect from Eve, she seemed preoccupied. She waited for him to continue on talking but there was silence, then she realised her phone was dead she forgotten to charge it last night. She plugged it in quickly, but he didn't ring back. Her dinner was cold and anyway her appetite was gone. Her chilling out day had changed within a few minutes and now her mind wandered back to when she first met Benjamin and how she had feelings for him back then. When she found out Pierre was lying to her, Benjamin was the first person she thought about, only to find out he was going to marry Rachael. More memories stirred, those secret ones she tried to bury. Louis was in her life now and she intended to see where their relationship brought them. Eve went to the fridge and poured herself a glass of wine and sat in front of the warm fire sipping it while she watched 'Home Alone' as a complete distraction.

January always seemed like a slow month for Eve, but this year it passed so quickly, before she knew it, it was the end of January and time for the American guests to leave. Eve was home to her parent's house bright and early. Matthew was going back to America today and Grayson was moving to Mayo in the morning where he had purchased a cottage. He needed to view it to see what work was required to do on it. Julie had enjoyed having Mathew in the house. She knew she was going to miss him. She reflected on what might have been all those years ago as she looked at Mathew. He was a broadly built man with receding hair, almost six and a half feet tall. He was a powerful man, distinguished looking and full of life and laughter. After Matthew put his cases into Grayson's car to go to the airport, he asked Julie to come outside for a moment. He walked over and leaned against the timber gate that led into the back garden. Julie wondered what he wanted to say to her as he spoke in a low voice. "I told you I sold my entire empire last year. The only asset I have now is my mansion, and that will be yours when I pass on. You can do with it as you will when the time comes. When I get settled back home, I will go see my lawyer and leave him your details." Julie stood there spellbound, she remained speechless. "I loved you all those years ago. You were so beautiful and full of life. I wish you could have gone to America with me back then. Nobody else stole my heart like you. There were lots of love affairs, but I could never get you out of my mind." She threw her arms around him and they stayed locked in a warm hug for a long while. He took out a notepad and wrote her details and they parted company. Julie watched as Matthew got into Grayson's car and waited until they drove out of sight. She wondered secretly what would life have been like with him and hoped their paths would cross again in the future.

CHAPTER 11

Grayson arrived back from the airport just as Julie and Eve drove in the gate from town. He continued on to his room and walked down into the kitchen within a few minutes. "Well, I had better make headway myself. It's getting late and I have a two-hour journey before I reach my hotel in Westport" he said. Eve asked him, was he looking forward to viewing the country cottage tomorrow? "I can't wait. It looks quite modern and airy inside and the decor bright but sympathetic to its era. Maybe you and Eric will come to visit me sometime? You too, Eve." She smiled "I'd love to." "I really enjoyed my stay with you all. I'll be up in Galway in March and might drop out for a visit if that is ok." Eric left his hand on Grayson's shoulder saying, "Of course, you are welcome anytime." Grayson then kissed Julie on the cheek. He turned to Eve and looked at her. She'd thought at first she was imagining it, the hint of interest in his eyes, but as she captured that look she was sure now that it was for real. She stretched out her hand "It was lovely meeting you Grayson and good luck with your house viewing."

As Eve walked into the dining area of the hotel, it was very warm inside. She was meeting up with her work colleagues for dinner. She peeled off her hat scarf and gloves. It was a typical mid-February day, bitterly cold outside with a biting frost and cutting wind. She was looking forward to catching up with the girls. They ordered drinks while they viewed the menu. When waiting to be served, they nattered away comparing how they spent Christmas. "How's the romance going?" Stella asked. Eve breathed in heavily, "To be honest I'm not sure. I've noticed when I'm with Louis unless we go out clubbing, or go away for exciting weekends, or end up in a bar he is not full of life. He has no interest in sitting in for a night and relaxing. Like, when I went to his place before Christmas and he arranged a party to introduce me to his family and friends halfway through the night, he forgot I was there and went flirting with any good-looking woman in sight." Siobhan was loud, "I don't think he's a keeper!" A moment of reflection fell as they sipped their drinks. Eve sank back in her chair, agitated. She was usually quite talkative, but this evening she had gone the opposite, reserved. The girls were enjoying their meal, joking and laughter, then Lisa said something funny and Eve burst out laughing and joined in the fun for the duration of the evening.

The weeks moved on it was now March. Louis visited twice a week and Eve got caught up in the high life of partying and unexpected weekends away accompanied by lavish gifts but there was something missing. She asked him to sit at home with her to try to book an Airbnb, but he replied that there was no fun in sitting in for a weekend when they could be out having a ball. She was realising her scepticism was for real. It didn't seem to her he was the settling down type. Eve had cut down on her travelling time since she started marketing her clothing on line. She worked mostly from her office in Galway. It was outstanding having weekends off. She had worked hard to build her business to the stage that demand on line was crazy busy; she knew this was because of the hours she had worked in Europe over the years, creating a high end brand name for herself. Settling down was to the forefront of her mind this past year. She loved nothing more than when Friday evening came, locking the office door behind her, hopping in her car, going to the shop for a bottle of wine and a good book and nothing was different this evening. Once home, she'd stick something in the oven or order a takeaway, change into comfy clothes and slippers and throw herself down on the couch. After she'd eaten, she would pour a glass of chardonnay and sit back with her book.

Conor sent a text to remind her that Grayson was coming to visit her parents tomorrow afternoon. Eve and her mother were home to greet Grayson, Conor and Eric were out cleaning up the garden and getting it ready for spring. As darkness began to fall, they came in and they started chatting. Grayson told them how happy he was with the country cottage. He added his belongings were being shipped across and that once he set them up in his place, it would begin to feel like home. Grayson described the cottage while showing them the pictures, starting with the cosy little sitting room with a wood-burning stove. They could hear the excitement in his voice as he continued, "The kitchen is a good size, with a breakfast bar in the middle. When I'm sitting on the high stool, I'm looking out at the long narrow back garden, which is an overgrown jungle at the moment, but eventually, I'll get garden designers to help me develop it."

It was Sunday evening and Eve was on social media catching up with the latest trends in the fashion world when the door-bell rang. When she opened it, she was surprised to see Grayson and Conor standing there. "While we were in Galway, we decided to call out to see you" Conor said. Grayson looked around "Lovely place you have here, that view down to the castle and inlet to the sea is beautiful." They stayed almost two hours before they left. Grayson followed Eve into the kitchen when she went out to get her phone. He was looking down at the ground before inviting her for a cup of coffee in the morning before going back to Mayo. It was the bluntest invitation she'd ever received but felt somehow that didn't make it any less attractive to her. "Why don't we meet down in the village at twelve?" They met for coffee at the Poppy Seed restaurant. He chatted about his new job in IT and she found him to be probably the most direct person she had ever met. He was refreshing and she got the feeling that his life was never dull.

It was a beautiful bright June evening and Eve was mowing the grass on the front lawn when Louis drove in unexpectedly. She was surprised to see him. "Are you not excited to see me?" he asked. "Of course I am Louis, but look at the state of me and my hair is all over the place" she replied. "Yeah, but you still look beautiful to me" he noted. He stepped out of the car and walked over to her and threw his arms around her and kissed her passionately. He finished cutting the lawn for her, then wheeled the lawnmower back into the shed and suggested staying overnight and going to a club in Galway. She declined and clarified that she wanted to spend a night at home with him. Later on in the evening, they ordered takeaway, but she noticed he was slightly quieter than normal and wondered was he upset with her? After a couple of large glasses of wine, he mellowed out but she couldn't figure out what was annoying him.

They were up and out bright and early the next morning. The sun was just beginning to creep over the shore and shine on the castle in front of them. They walked briskly along the water's edge with the early morning dew touching their faces, listening to the burst of birds singing, with a grey blue sky and the hint of orange from the rising sun casting a peachy glow right over the rooftops of this quaint little village. Louis ran. Eve ran past him, showing him how fit she was. She could see his shadow keeping up with her pace, then it disappeared. She kept on going for a minute until she stopped and looked back. "What's wrong Louis?" Her voice was tense and tight, she felt her heart starting to hammer in her chest after running. She walked back to where he was standing. She willed him to stop talking while he continued to ask her to move in with him. He was staring into her eyes and she could see he was emotional. "Eve, will you move into my house with me?" Her eyes were holding his, yet suddenly they were unreadable. He saw her take a deep breath heavy and controlled. She spoke, her shoulders flexing with a heaviness in her voice that made no sense to him. He was still waiting for her reply. He shifted uncomfortably as he read the seriousness of her expression. She slowly shook her head "I can't move in with you." He stood still, looking at her in disbelief his hands fell down by his side. She continued to say, "I'm sorry, Louis, but I think we want different things from life. I want to settle down and have a family, but I don't think that is where you see yourself. I have tried to convince myself that we can make it work, but I think we are just too different in what we both want. I think it is better for us to go our separate ways. I wouldn't want you to change your life for me. I'm very settled in my ways and you're a free spirit. Somebody will come along for you that will enjoy the high life, but that life is not for me." He felt a stab of bitter disappointment wash over him, but he knew when he reflected Eve was probably right. Louis had an inkling there was no changing her mind as her rejection finally sank in. He began walking. She followed on behind, torn in different directions. He walked into the house and up to the bedroom, he shoved his belongings into a travel bag, walked back down and passed Eve in the hallway where they said their tearful goodbyes. She watched him get into his car start it up and drive off. Eve was devastated but knew it was for the best.

CHAPTER 12

Eve had always dreamt of having her own brand of cosmetics and was delighted when she could partner with a company with the same ethics as herself and after much hard work 'Flawless,' was unveiled. The business thrived as soon as she launched her website, and it grew from strength to strength. She was lucky that she could divide her hours between being at home part time and the rest of her working week in her office in Galway. She was already successful in the fashion world and had built a reputation which brought in a substantial turnover each year. She ground the coffee beans and filled the filter basket of the Moka pot with cold tap water and let it heat. She turned on her laptop and searched for the latest orders placed online. Since breaking up with Louis, she had met a few men along the way but nothing serious. There was George who was unreliable, then Austin a divorcee who talked about his ex-wife three quarters of the time and the Australian Nick, who was handsome, kind and fun loving but didn't tick all her boxes. He was eager for a long distance relationship, but she said that wouldn't work for her. She was thinking she would never find a partner.

She woke up and began thinking about getting older and as she reflected on her life, she was very aware of how the days passed into weeks, months and years. Her life was passing her by far too quickly. Grayson asked her out a few times. They enjoyed each other's company, but he wasn't coming up to visit her parents as regularly as before and didn't make any arrangements to meet her again. Benjamin kept in contact with her through social media, WhatsApp, and

Snap Chat, but he only seemed to be interested in the amount of money she had turned over in the year.

This evening she was meeting up with her work friends for a meal and a catch up. After showering, she went to her walk-in wardrobe and decided on a blue dress. It felt a little tighter than the last time she wore it. She promised herself to go back to the gym next week and also to cut down on the 'wine o'clock times.' She scanned herself in the long mirror on the landing of the stairs to see her own face reflecting at her as she ran her hand through her newly coloured hair. She talked to herself 'I'm a woman who owns her own power. I am strong, vital and beautiful, but I'm tired emotional and lonely.' A gusty sigh rose from somewhere deep inside her. Perhaps it was time to take stock of her life. This week was shaping up to be quiet and perhaps it could provide her with enough time to think and maybe reach a few decisions about her future and where she could see herself heading. If she faced facts, she wasn't really heading anywhere fast. She seemed to be forever caught up in her work and failing relationships.

Conor called to the house as he often did when in Galway. He rang the bell three times before she answered. He laughed "Thought you were in bed." "No, I was getting ready, I'm going into Galway to meet up with the girls from work" she said. "Sounds like fun, by the way Grayson rang earlier says he is coming up to visit in September and hopes to stay for a few nights. Did he contact you?" Eve put on a jaw-dropping face, "No he didn't, sure why would he?" Conor cheekily responded "I thought you two were getting on well and that you fancied him." "Have some sense, I don't particularly want to go out with him, anyway he is a little boring for me" she laughed. "How about coming to a jazz club tomorrow night, my friends are playing the music?" Conor suggested. Eve sighed deeply. The last thing she felt like doing was listening to an amateur jazz group and making conversation with her brother's mates. Seldom he asked her to go with him so she agreed and tried to be cheerful about it. Conor was delighted, "Great Sis I'll collect you about six."

The night out with the girls turned out to be just what she needed, fun, light heartedness with loads of chat. The following evening, Conor collected her on the dot of six. The jazz club was what she thought it would be, dark, stuffy and noisy but very atmospheric. As her eyes became accustomed to the muted light, she saw six lads and a girl waving at them from a table near the stage area. They went over and Conor introduced his sister to the group after they took their places at the round table. Eve sat between a chatty girl called Niamh and a good-looking guy called Justin who looked much older than the others. He had chiselled features, his hair was jet black he was softly spoken and seemed rather shy. She was surprised to discover he was part of the jazz group called Trio. He was wearing a light blue linen shirt and black jeans which made him look laid back and trendy. Eve was charmed to feel included in their conversation and admitted to herself she was wrong about Conor's friends as they weren't dull at all. Even though she was older than most of them, she felt part of the group. Several times while conversing with them she found Justin studying her. His warm brown eyes were intense but sincere, she felt herself blush. Eventually, the Trio went up on stage where Justin picked up an electric guitar, the younger man of the group joined him on the saxophone, and the girl was on the double bass. Eve swayed to the beat of the velvety music finding it mesmerizing. She turned to Conor and said, "I thought you said they were amateurs they sound more like professionals." When the night ended and the music stopped, there was silence for a few seconds, then the crowd that had gathered realised the band were finished, people got to their feet and the room erupted with cheers and applause. Eve heard her mobile ring but she didn't answer it when it stopped she turned it down to silent and didn't bother to look to see who rang her. Justin walked over to where Eve was standing and asked if she would attend the jazz festival in Galway in a month's time? "Conor will be coming." She smiled "I might just do that." The call she missed was from Benjamin. She didn't call him back and he didn't ring her either. She wondered what he wanted and brought up his number several times but refrained from pressing the call button. The weeks passed by quickly and Eve was looking forward to the festival in Galway.

Eve woke early and smiled in anticipation, the festival weekend had arrived finally and instead of her usual cleaning shopping and sitting around the house she was off to Galway. Going downstairs, she prepared breakfast and went to the dining table chewing her well browned toast. She sat there reflecting 'was she was too old in joining Conor and his friends at a jazz festival?' Then she concluded Justin was of similar age. When she had finished eating, she went upstairs and showered quickly, then dressed. She loved her beautiful tranquil bedroom which was a haven of creams, powder blue and navy echoing the colours of the nearby sea. She pulled on a fresh white cotton top, a pair of skinny jeans, leather jacket and her boots and was ready to go. As Conor drove her towards the city, she felt a tiny bubble of hope that Justin would look forward to seeing her, as much as she was to seeing him.

Galway was packed, the sun was shining, people were ready for a weekend of music and fun. Every place you turned to had music playing, the city was electric. Eve hung around with Conor until he met his friends she then browsed around the shops and enjoyed the festival buzz. They planned to meet up at mid-day and go for a bite to eat and then go to the venue where Trio were performing. Eve was walking towards the Spanish Arch when she heard music and recognized it as Justin and his friends. She felt her heart leap as she went towards the spot where the sound of their music echoed through the surrounding streets, there was a crowd of young people gathered around them all clapping and cheering. She walked by slowly hoping Justin would spot her. She thought he looked her way but didn't acknowledge her. She continued on walking feeling deflated.

She joined Conor and his friends for lunch before they made their way to the bar venue where Trio were performing for the evening. When Justin walked in with the others, she put on her most seductive smile and kept looking towards him. He lifted his hand and waved to her then he turned away and started talking to a group of young girls. Eve looked around the bar slightly embarrassed and flustered. She walked up to where he was standing talking to the girls and stood there for a few seconds then tapped him on the arm. He turned around smiling and then to her dismay his smile froze on his lips. He caught her by the elbow "Excuse me for a moment," he said and strode away. Eve stared after him confused, not sure what had happened. She could have sunk through the floor. Then she saw them setting up on the stage where they played soft music. Eve had a lump in her throat she looked around for her brother, but he was surrounded by the same group that Justin was talking to a while ago, they were laughing and having the craic. She didn't know where to turn, luckily Niamh must have noticed because she walked over and got her to join the group. Conor had to leave relatively early as he had an important

114

meeting tomorrow afternoon. He was going to put in for planning to extend the existing coffee shop. Conor was all chat about his friends and the music on the way home and presumed Eve had enjoyed herself. She couldn't get Justin out of her head but obviously he had interests elsewhere. She lay awake for hours that night wishing she was in her twenties again, foot loose and fancy free. The next morning she went straight home to her parents she hoped they would be there because usually they went shopping on Monday. She was delighted when her mother was inside. When she walked into the living room, her mother was glad to see her.

"You look exhausted," Julie carried in two mugs of tea and set them down on the coffee table. "So what's wrong? Come on, Eve I can tell when something is troubling you. Spit it out I'm all ears." Eve took a deep breath and told her the story about the festival and Justin. "I really liked him and I thought he found me attractive, maybe now that I'm getting older, I'm losing my touch and reading signals that aren't even there." Julie listened, upset for her daughter. She stayed on until late in the evening and when she got home took an early night hoping to feel better in the morning.

The following Wednesday, Grayson rang to book in for a weekend. He informed Julie that he was coming to Galway for three days and with excitement said that he had met an English girl that he liked and wanted to show her around. "That's fine, I'll reserve a double room so." While Julie was happy for Grayson, she was concerned how Eve would feel when she heard this. All of her friends were settled or settling down with partners and she knew Eve wanted to find her Mr. Right but it wasn't happening for her.

It felt like another groundhog day for Eve, at first she had a hectic schedule at work but by the end of the day she had decided to go to Barbados with one of her friends next week. Outside the sun was shining and at last she was on her way home as she sat into her car and was relieved to feel she could finally relax. Her phone rang it was her mother telling her about Grayson. "I'll be away in Barbados that week, myself and Kathy are doing a promotional tour and incorporating a holiday as well. Conor will be there to talk to Grayson and sure you and Dad will get on well with his girlfriend."

Eve and Kathy arrived in Barbados late Sunday night and slept until lunch time Monday. When Eve woke, she wondered if Kathy was awake yet, as they had decided on separate rooms. They met for lunch and then retired to their rooms to prepare for a conference later that day. When evening closed in, Eve opened the windows in her room and the lightly scented breeze drifted in. She watched as the sky changed from blue to grey and red as the sun set. The conference was to promote the latest product in the makeup collection. If it was successful and there were orders placed, they could relax and unwind for most of the week ahead. The night was profitable for them and many orders were placed.

A boat trip awaited them the next morning and they were up early to make the most of their free day, cruising along to a most beautiful inlet, which was quiet and picture perfect, the only movement was the palm trees swaying gently in the wonderfully refreshing off-shore breeze. The crew from the boat slung hammocks between neighbouring trees and Eve was the first to claim one. They enjoyed the picnic Kathy prepared that morning and even though it was early they had brought drinks to get into the holiday spirit. The holiday was a mixed bag; it incorporated work and leisure, but they thoroughly enjoyed it and Eve felt refreshed going back home. When they were back in the airport waiting to hear their flight announced, Eve's phone rang. It was her mother; she sounded extremely upset. She slowly told her that Matthew had died suddenly yesterday morning. Grayson had informed her. Apparently, Mathew's partner had told him he had died peacefully in his sleep. They think he had a heart attack. Eve was sad for her mother. "I didn't know he had a partner though," Eve said. "Neither did I she was much younger than he. Grayson tells me she was only in her early forties." Later that night, Eve arrived home and stayed overnight with her parents. They talked about Matthew's death and Eve's mother mentioned that Grayson was travelling over to America for the funeral with his girlfriend.

Eve had another week off work and after spending the first two days de-cluttering the house, she decided it was time to take a day away from the house and go hill walking. She dressed in her leggings, trainers and a light navy fleece. The day was warm and sunny with only a scattering of clouds across the sky. She walked high on the hill looking down over the sea and inhaled the intoxicating salt-scented air; it was invigorating. Her phone rang she pulled it out of her pocket and complained to herself that she had forgotten to turn it off, she answered it anyway. The signal was poor it was a man's voice. It was impossible to hear who it was, so she cut him off saying "I'll call you later I'm way up the hills walking." She could only vaguely hear him through the broken signal but heard him say "I know where you are, I'm right behind you." She swung around and was unaware of the dip in the long damp grass, her foot slipped and she fell forward head first down over the steep drop and down towards the sea landing in deep water. She quickly realised she was being pulled strongly in the deadly current of the water rendering her powerless and increasingly desperate as her strokes were useless against such force. She tired quickly, her arms laden with the effort of fighting the sea. A wave came sideways at her and she was pulled under. She took a mouthful of water in and was pushed back up coughing and disoriented, barely able to draw her breath. Another wave sent her under again, her strength was gone.

Suddenly out of nowhere she felt something grab her hair and yank her roughly and painfully to the surface. "Grab on," a loud male voice commanded. He shouted at her again transferring his grip from her hair to her wrist, she clambered on to the jet-ski. With her scalp stinging she was gasping, coughing and sobbing with relief. She rested against him and held on tight. He saved her, he literary saved her life. She couldn't see his face, her eyes were blurred then she passed out. She remembered nothing else until she woke up in an unfamiliar bed. "You're awake," she heard a woman say quietly "How do you feel?" She lifted her head but felt dizzy and lifeless, her neck and back felt stiff. She closed her eyes and had a flash back to dark freezing water, then she remembered a smack when she hit the surface and the speed with which she sank. She was drowsy so she was being kept in hospital where the nurses continued to observe her condition.

She opened her eyes and looked up at the nurse "What happened?" she asked sleeplessly. "You've had a terrible shock, do you remember anything?" "I remember being in freezing water." "You were lucky, a man on a jet-ski saw you and hauled you out of the water into the jet ski, he saved your life. He dialled 999 and when you got back to shore the ambulance arrived within a very short time." "I have no recollection of any man," she closed her eyes. "Don't worry about that now just rest we'll take good care of you." After a night's rest Eve woke up the next morning a little brighter and could give her parent's phone number to the nurses. The following day Eve was up and walking around even though she was still stiff and sore. She was trying desperately to piece together what had happened but her memory just wouldn't allow it, which worried her. When she was discharged, the first thing she planned on doing was to replace her phone, it had been lost when she had fallen into the sea. She didn't know how she was going to recover all her numbers, but that was incidental when she thought about what might have happened to her if she had not been rescued. She was still concerned who had rung her whilst out walking but she just couldn't piece together who it could have been.

Grayson and Emily flew back from America two weeks after Matthew's funeral. They headed straight to Galway and booked into a hotel for the night. The following morning, he contacted Julie to meet up, Grayson was nervous because he had unexpected news for her. She invited them to dinner that evening and shortly after dinner Grayson asked if he could have a private chat with Julie. She got up and walked towards the office. Grayson followed her and closed the door behind him, she could tell by the acute look on his face he had something alarming to say. She sat on her office chair. He leaned against the window, "Matthew had told me of the promise he made to you when he was home." Running his hand through his hair he said "There is no easy way of telling you this he got married last month and the mansion will go to his wife." She looked at him shocked, all her dreams and plans fell apart like a cardboard castle in just one second. She looked at Grayson with watery eyes. "But I had plans for the mansion he promised it to me and he didn't mention having a partner when he was in Ireland." "He met her four months ago when he went for physiotherapy. Seemingly, she fell for him overnight! I believe he was besotted with her and asked her to move in with him. She refused unless he married her first so he did last month." Julie pondered 'no guesses why she insisted on that!' Grayson continued, "His lifelong friend Jonathon who I met after the funeral filled me in on the past few months of Matthew's life. Before I left for home, he met me again and gave me the name of his attorney who I went to see before I flew back." She sniffed back the tears that threatened to escape. He reached over and touched her hand. "I'm sorry with the way it turned out for you it is a terrible blow." Then Grayson smiled 'He left you a locked box though, the attorney gave it to me for you, seemingly Matthew gave him written instructions to get it to you safely. The attorney also gave me a form to ask you to sign as soon as I delivered the box safely to you. I'll go out to the car and bring in the box and form." Julie went into the kitchen and looked at Eric with a wayward look on her face. He wondered what had happened but didn't ask in front of Emily. Grayson came back in carrying a heavy dark-coloured timber chest it was almost the size of a small suitcase. It was decorated with leaves and many flowers and it had two gold coloured locks on either end. There was a sealed leather type wallet connected to the lid which contained the keys. Conor whispered to his father "What good is that box to her?" After Grayson and his girlfriend were gone, Eric placed the box on the counter. Julie beckoned her husband to open it while she looked on with her son. "God, the locks are tight and rusty, the keys don't work. It reminds me of something that you would find at an auction or car boot sale" he said. "Open it dad and never mind where it could be seen, it's what's inside that matters." He tried to ease it open with a wrench but to no avail. Conor went out to the shed and fetched his tool bag and took out the small hammer.

His father hit at the locks with strength and that didn't work so Conor took the hammer and gave it one sharp thump and it knocked off the lid and it fell to pieces on the floor tiles. To their dismay, the box was empty. Julie was still holding the wallet. "Was there nothing inside the wallet only the keys?" Eric asked. She pulled it open and there at the very bottom of one compartment was a tiny note rolled up. She unrolled it and read the few words inside which looked like as if they were written quickly. 'Julie, forgive me for breaking my promise, but the money is in this box. Matthew.' She read the note over and over "But there is nothing in it!" she said, "It's nothing, get it out of here." Eric gathered it up "What will I do with it now?" he asked Julie. "Take it out and throw it down into the bottom of the skip that arrived to clear the yard for the new building and never mention Mathew's name around me again." Conor gathered it up and went outside with it. Julie chatted with Eve over the phone later that night about the disappointment. Eve understood her mother's disappointment but tried to remind her she was upset over something she never had and that she had managed without it, so she would come to terms with it. Julie cried I was hoping to sell it and make money for us. Forget about it now. It doesn't exist.

Back at work, Eve's phone rang. She grabbed it up off the desk "Hello, Eve, it's me Benjamin." As if he had to tell her, she thought to herself. "I'm going to be spending a few days in Galway towards the end of September. Maybe we could meet up?" Eve wasn't sure if she had any interest in meeting him but suggested, "Text me the evening before and if I'm free, I'll meet you in the city centre." She wondered what was bringing him over to Galway, was it business or leisure time but didn't have to wait long as he added "I'm meeting a business executive of a clothing enterprise in the west of Ireland, he's helping me find a suitable location to open up a few branches of my stores." She was more than surprised. He had never showed any interest in trading in Ireland in the past.

The end of September came all too quickly. Eve didn't want the summer to end because the bright evenings would be a thing of the past and the long nights would creep in and with them darkness. Sure enough, Benjamin sent her a text before he arrived and they met the following day for coffee. He talked continually, but Eve was preoccupied and barely heard half of what he said. Then she suggested showing him around before it got too late. He had a meeting at four and she didn't intend to stick around waiting for that to finish. When they stepped outside, there was a cold, stiff breeze and with the look of the sky it felt like it might rain shortly. They were walking around for a short while when his phone rang. She heard him say, "I'll be there in ten minutes." He stood and faced her "I have to go now, the others are waiting for me." Eve suggested, "I'll walk a part of the way with you my car is parked in the underground park." When they reached the entrance to the car park, Eve said, "This is where we say goodbye for now." She found him looking at her as if it was for the first time. He smiled and reached for her hand "Thanks for meeting up with me maybe we could meet tomorrow and go for a drive to your favourite place on the hills." "Why don't we see what happens tomorrow" she responded. He squeezed her hand. She actually thought he was going to kiss her but he let her hand go and said goodbye. The only thought in her mind at that moment was 'How did he know about her favourite hills for walking?' There was something unnerving about the way he said it. It had an air of familiarity about it but not in a good way. Eve convinced herself that she was just jumping to conclusions and that Benjamin had nothing to do with her fall, 'how could he?' she asked herself. She had tried so many times to jog her memory to make herself remember but to no avail. She quickly moved on from her thoughts but decided that night that it was best that she would limit her time with Benjamin from now on. In fact, she let him down and didn't meet him at all because she had an insight that it was him on the hills that day and she intended to cut ties with him from now on.

CHAPTER 13

Eve was sympathetic towards her mother receiving an empty box from Matthew. It made little sense, why write the note and not put anything in the box? Julie now regretted telling the lads to dump it in the skip. She was crying while explaining to Eve, "I went down to the yard to take it out but the skip had been collected early the next morning. I'll just have to forget about this entire episode it wasn't meant to be."

Autumn had crept in which was clear by the leaves falling from the trees. Colder wetter weather swept in across the country, it was time for warm fires and cosy nights in with a good book to read. Eve went down to Charlie Byrne's bookshop where she knew she would be spoilt for choice from the multitude of books on offer there. After spending an hour browsing, she picked up a few good recommendations from Vinny in the shop.

It was St. Patrick's day in a week's time and Conor asked Eve if she would like to go to another jazz session during the holidays. She declined because at the Jazz festival in October when she felt Justin ignored her. "I wouldn't know anybody there anyway and would sit on my own." "My friends don't mind you joining them in fact they enjoyed your company the last time you met them.' She said, "I'll think about it," as she dished up a stir-fried beef and rice for the two of them. Conor had come over for a late dinner.

After she finished work the following day she was talking to Pearl one girl clerking in the County Council offices. "Are you going out St. Patrick's night, Pearl?" She told her about the jazz session and her brother wanting her to go with him. "Let's go," Pearl said excitedly "It might be a bit of fun, we could do with the distraction in our lives." Eve didn't want to be a spoilsport and it would fill in Patrick's night, anything was better than sitting at home looking at the four walls so she went. She ran around town in search of an outfit with a hint of green to wear the following day. A couple of hours later she was laden down with bags that contained an olive green dress, a jacket, new shoes, tights, shape wear and makeup even though she had her own brand the shopping experience in Brown Thomas always excited her. She decided she must have a bag to suit at home and wasn't sure if that thought was guilt for spending so much, or tiredness at the thought of having to face another store.

On the way back to the car parking area, she wandered across the street to the cafe where she and Pierre sometimes went on Friday evenings back in the day. She instinctively went to the table by the window and looked out at the rain-soaked view. She stirred her latte and looking across the table wished there was somebody there to share her time with. Eve knew she was getting on in years and thoughts like these came thick and fast over the previous few months. She knew well that not so long ago she'd have loved the chance to dress up, revelling in the occasion of it rather than inventing reasons not to go. Patrick's evening, Pearl and Eve met at the venue at seven o'clock. In high spirits, they went over and sat at the round table with Conor's friends. Eve relaxed she looked at Pearl and smiled. Half way through the evening Eve's eyes darted to Justin's and his to hers like as if they were observing each other. Eve's glowing cheeks were accompanied by an embarrassing smile. As the night was ending, the music stopped, laughter was loud, and voices high. Lights were dimming, letting the crowd know it was almost closing time. Justin strolled over to where the girls were sitting. He spoke to both of them as Eve introduced Pearl to him. She noted they hit it off straight away she only got a word in edge ways, in fact Justin was standoffish and it saddened her. Eventually, they were getting up to leave. Eve noticed Justin and her friend exchanging phone numbers, then he said good night to both of them. Eve didn't pretend to her friend that she fancied Justin. Pearl talked about him nonstop all the way home in the taxi. Eve was furious. Pearl continued talking with a slurred voice "He's handsome, talkative, and loves the craic. We're meeting up next month." "You can't be," Eve said upset. Then Pearl dosed off for a few minutes but wakened up just before the taxi came to a halt to let her out at her house. She turned her head to face Eve "Justin said you were a very attractive lady but out of reach for him." Eve didn't understand what was meant by the comment. "When did he say that to you?" Eve asked. The taxi came to a halt and Pearl got out and didn't wait to reply. The next stop was Eve's place and she went in with a spinning head from over indulgence of mixed drinks and she fell into bed.

She woke late the next morning, got out of bed and looked out the window. It was a rainy chilly morning. Her head ached, and her clouded brain felt like it had been hit with a thump from a heavyweight boxer. She thought about Justin and maybe they were like strangers who'd shared a moment but now he seemed to be moving on with somebody else. She went straight down to the kitchen switched on the kettle then went to take her phone off charge; she was in a depressed mood and hoped nobody would come near her house or call her on the phone today. She slid the phone across the countertop and grabbed a mug out of the dishwasher; she pulled open the jar of coffee and loaded two teaspoons of instant coffee into the mug, then poured in the boiling water. Just as she took the first sip, her phone rang. She snapped it up "Hello," she said in an abrupt voice. "Hi Eve, Pearl here I want to apologise for anything I said out of the way last night, actually I don't remember the half of it. I must admit I drank too much Prosecco and it clouded my brain. Go on remind me what I said." Then Eve said, "So do you remember meeting Justin from the Trio, then?" Pearl retraced her words "Well I remember him alright, he asked me to meet him next month." Eve continued, "So is that all you recall?" She paused and asked Eve, "Were you and Justin an item?" "No not at all." Pearl changed the subject. "How about coming for a game of tennis?" she asked. "I'm useless at it," Eve said. "I haven't played tennis since I was in school." "Neither have I," said Pearl. "It'll be fun." She decided to go it would give her a chance to question her about Justin. They went the following afternoon.

It was brilliant fun and Eve went to Pearl's for a cup of tea afterwards. They were chatting about the fun they had today and decided they needed more practice. Eve quizzed her up about Justin and asked if she was really going out with him next month. "Yeah I am, just as friends, though." Eve looked at her friend with a cold, glassy stare. Suddenly, tears sprung to her eyes. Pearl left her hand over on Eve's "What's wrong?" "I thought he was into me the first night we met." "But obviously not if he thought of me as out of reach, I never gave him that impression, why would he say that?" Pearl tried to retrace her words but it didn't work. Eve couldn't understand why he had ignored her so suddenly with no reason or explanation. She thought that she was unlovable and destined to be on her own.

"Wake up Julie" Eric waved a small piece of paper under her nose. "Sit up and read this. I found it under the press. It was over near the wall.| She sat up and grabbed the paper and began reading the message. It was from Matthew, "Julie I hope you receive this box safely. I had it in the vault in the American bank I had to keep it a secret. If anything happens to me it's yours to sell. It's worth a small fortune there is only a few of them in circulation, I bought it at an auction some time ago and invested thousands of dollars in it. I think it could be worth around one hundred and fifty thousand euro in Ireland to the right buyer. Fetch as much as you can for it." Julie was flustered, "My God, this note was in the box and we missed it." Eric reckoned it must have slid under the press when the lid smashed. She jumped out of bed while she continued on reading.

Conor heard the commotion and joined them in the kitchen. They were spellbound at the news. Eve had dropped over to visit and was standing, watching the three of them tear into each other one blaming the other for losing the note and her mother's sharp voice was so shrill that it could have cracked concrete. Eve barked, "Stop fighting over a stupid box." Julie kept shouting "But it wasn't just a stupid box read this note. Eve read it over and over again open-mouthed, she blinked in shock, surely it couldn't have been worth that much, Matthew must have been mistaken or maybe confused" she said. "How dare you say he was confused he had a perfectly sound mind?"

Conor was grinning from ear to ear and then laughed. "I didn't throw it in the skip that day, instead I researched and found a repair shop in the UK, shipped it over to get it back to its original state, I thought I'd keep it for myself seeing you didn't want it around," he was looking at his mother amused. They emailed me after and said it was worth very little and asked me to sell it to them. With sheer expectation she asked what he said. "I told them to repair it first then I would be prepared to negotiate a price." Julie jumped for joy but wished she had held her tongue quiet. After they calmed down and were sitting around the table having a late breakfast Eve dropped another bombshell. "I'm thinking of selling my company and talking up a different job." Nobody commented.

"I've spent so many years as a fashion designer, it was rewarding and I will admit challenging but I'm not getting any younger and want a change in lifestyle." She knew her mother was only listening with one ear as she was completely distracted by the box. Her father questioned her what she intended to do from now on? "I've been called for an interview with a tour bus company next week, the job starts at the end of the month" she replied. Her father wasn't encouraging her either and looked at her in total disbelief. He knew how hard she had worked to get the top of her profession and couldn't fathom why she would want to give it up now. Conor responded "If that's what you want, go ahead, don't let anybody stop you. It sounds very interesting and a change might be just what you need. If your heart isn't in fashion design any more, change while you are still young enough. You can always go back to fashion if it doesn't work out for you, so go for it." Before she left for home both her parents wished her luck and hoped she wouldn't regret her decision. Little did Eve know that her life was about to transform soon.

She was successful in the interview and was just about to start on her first voyage of being a tour guide. The coach and its party were heading to Seattle for ten days. Her business was still operating, but up for sale. There was a lot of interest in it so she was hopeful it would soon be off the market. With all loans and taxes cleared she would be left with a tidy sum to keep as savings for a rainy day. She travelled to the bus depot where the group was assembled; they were travelling to Dublin airport to board a flight to Seattle where they would stay for ten days. There would be a coach waiting for them on the other side for the duration of their stay.

As the bus was about to pull out for the airport after checking boarding passes and names, Eve took up the microphone and was about to welcome all aboard and go through the itinerary when she was interrupted by a man running up and hammering on the door of the bus. Eve felt a twinge of annoyance. He must have mistaken the bus for another but because there was nobody missing from the list. She went to have a word with Donald the bus driver. At this stage, the man was hanging on to the door handle shouting to open the door. Donald said "I'll open the door and send him on his way," but as soon as the door slid open he jumped on board. "I'm sorry, you seem to have caught the wrong bus," Donald said calmly. He fumbled in his pocket while insisting he was travelling with them to Seattle. "I'm Hugh Black and this is my booking confirmation." Eve took it and scanned it. "Your name is not on my list" she said. She also kept very calm, "Hold on one moment until I contact the travel agents." A few moments later she told Donald the bus driver, that apparently it was a misunderstanding not to have added Mr. Black's name to the list. He was a late booker and they accommodated him because he was travelling alone and there was an empty seat available. He was standing there with two suitcases.

Donald looked at his watch and said to Hugh Black "I've got a schedule to keep, I'm not opening the hatch now, put your cases in at the back until we make the half-way stop for coffee." He walked towards the middle of the bus and lifted his cases and shoved them overhead on the top racks. He stood outside the single seat where there was a man sitting beside the window. Eve sat down and the bus moved off. Hugh Black then walked up to where Eve was sitting on the front double seat. He leaned over the back of her seat "Sorry to bother you again but I asked for a window seat." She sighed, "Unfortunately, Mr. Black we can't guarantee specific seats with late bookings." "I could sit next to you," he said. Eve just replied, "I'm afraid that's not possible, this seat is strictly for the tour guide only. Sit on the seat left." He went back and sat down. It took her some time to collect her wits before she could address the party. She stood up after some time, and as she did, she gave the driver a beaming smile that probably made her look more confident than she really was. Then she faced the crowded bus and with microphone in hand, she introduced herself and welcomed all aboard. She invited them to call her by her first name. She continued on to say she hoped their time with the 'Blue Ocean Travel Agency' would be enjoyable.

She ran through the safety regulations and the itinerary for the ten-day trip. "We will land in Seattle tonight and there will be a coach to meet us and take us directly to the hotel in the middle of the city. We will spend the next ten days touring the scenic area, which will include experiencing Seattle from a top sky view observatory, it being the tallest public observatory in the Pacific Northwest and the perfect place to begin the Seattle experience. It will allow us to take in the breath-taking 360 degrees views from Mount Rainier to Mount Baker, the Olympics to the Cascades, and everything in between. We will also travel to the Olympic Peninsula where you will view magnificent mountains, rugged coastline, and temperate rain forest, combined with charming small towns with culinary delights. We will also visit coastal beaches and other Olympic national park destinations during our stay. On the last afternoon, we'll experience a delightful cruise on the waterfront next to the city itself. Thank you for your attention and ask me if there is anything you are unsure about."

The group clapped and Hugh Black raised his voice above the applause "Well done, I can see we are in expert hands," and he smiled at her warmly. They arrived at the airport shortly after. When they had gone through the check-in desks and in the waiting area, Eve walked away from the group and over to the window looking out over the runway. She needed to ring her parents to let them know she had gotten over the nerves of the morning and was excited for the trip to come. Before she hung up, she told her mother "The group are very pleasant, except for one smart ass who was late arriving for the journey to the airport whose name wasn't added to the list. The tour operator seem to know about him but must have forgotten to place his name on my list." Suddenly, they called over the intercom, "Boarding call for flight 377 for Seattle," she said goodbye to her mother and at that moment she was ecstatic and felt so excited about the trip ahead.

CHAPTER 14

When they finally reached their destination, the coach parked directly outside the hotel door. As they made their way into the reception area, the manager welcomed each person individually. After signing in and keys distributed, the group dispersed, going to their rooms to refresh before the evening meal. After Eve had rested a while, she went down to the foyer to unwind with a quiet drink before the group began coming down for the meal.

Eventually, small groups wandered down slowly until the group was fully assembled. At this stage, the foyer was full of chatter and laughter. Just as the bell rang to announce dinner, Hugh Black came banging out of the lift with a face like thunder. He whizzed over to reception. "I want a room change. There's no view of the mountains where I am and the Wi-Fi is non-existent in that room." He continued on ranting, "I like to open the window and breathe in fresh mountain air in the early morning when I'm on vacation." People were moving towards the dining room. Eve was listening to the conversation taking place at the main reception desk and recognised that the receptionist was confused. Eve walked over to where Hugh was standing. She tried to remain calm "Is there a problem Mr. Black?" Even though she had heard the conversation already, she listened to him tell her the whole saga again. She remained cool, "I'm sorry but a late booker won't get a choice of room actually you were lucky that there was a free place at all." The receptionist said very politely, "Leave it with me and I will see what can be done I'll talk to the manager later." After all were seated and studying the menu, Eve took her place

129

at the table for two. She was engrossed in deciding what to order when Hugh Black sat opposite her at the table. She looked at him with a rash stare. "Unfortunately, Mr. Black company policy says tour guide and driver must share a table." He gave her a seductive smile, "Surely you can bend the rules a little." "I'm afraid not, sorry" she replied with frustration. He got up and walked down to the far end of the dining room where he took his place beside an elderly couple. The days flew by and Eve was really enjoying her new role. She felt a new sense of invigoration. Today, they were visiting the rain forest and after the visit had pulled in to a tourist shopping centre with a restaurant to one side.

Eve spoke over the intercom and let the group know they had one hour to browse around and to please be back in the coach promptly. Most of them headed for the main shopping area but Eve wandered off on her own and found a small café, she ordered some food then sat back and took a breather. She had just begun to enjoy her soup when Hugh Black spoke above her head. She jumped out of her thoughts. "Do you mind if I join you he asked?" Those blue eyes of his were staring at her most disconcertingly. She felt him a little too familiar, but she adapted a neutral tone when she spoke again. He thought to himself, 'If only she knew who I was.' "By the way, call me Hugh drop the Mr." He was definitely odd and she wondered for the umpteenth time why he was travelling alone. He was testing her patience to the limits, but she'd coped with far worse situations. He had a takeaway mug of coffee in his hand "Sure, sit down," Eve said "I'll be off as soon as I finish my soup. I want to browse around the shops for a quick look. The time is tight." They made small talk and when she was finished eating, she got up "Excuse me Mr. Black, I'll see you back at the coach." "Ok then," he said and she went out the door and left him sipping his coffee alone. The hour ended shortly after, and she strolled back to the coach and counted each one of the group as they took their seats, 'one missing Mr Black is not back yet.' Fifteen minutes later, he came jogging towards the coach with not a care in the world. He lifted his hand up "Sorry. I lost track of time." Eve was furious, "Mr. Black, the driver is on a tight schedule and it is vital we all respect that, go and take your seat immediately."

The next week was most enjoyable, the weather was radiant, and the scenery and walks were breath-taking as were the beaches, giving a magical holiday atmosphere. Even though Mr. Black was making a nuisance of himself, he entertained the group each night, telling jokes and singing, as they assembled on the last evening for a special gourmet dinner, he announced he had organised a dance afterwards to an instrumental eighties band. The meal was splendid and afterwards, as the tables and chairs were cleared away, the band began to set up on the stage. Some people went to their rooms to freshen up while others went to the bar for after-dinner drinks. Eve noticed Mr. Black wasn't anywhere to be seen. She stayed in the bar with Donald who was going to retire for the night after one drink as he felt he needed his sleep to be ready for the early morning drive to the airport. The music started up lively and eventually the bar was empty and all were sitting inside in the ballroom. A few couples got out on the floor and danced to the beat of the music. An hour after the music started Mr. Black walked into the ballroom. She felt her heart leap when she saw him immaculately dressed. 'Wow,' she said under her breath, which only served to amplify her unwanted feelings for the man. He stood at the door for a while, then a young good looking brunette joined him and a sharp pang stuck in Eve's chest and she saw them move on to the dance floor laughing and talking continually while they whirled around. Eve chatted to the people around the table and tried not to look his way. When the night ended and she was going into the lift, she felt slightly jealous when she spotted Hugh and the young girl in a brief but passionate looking embrace.

She didn't look his way the next morning, but found refuge in her role as tour guide. She reminded the group that their luggage needed to be in the foyer by ten thirty ready for departure at eleven. The return journey was uneventful, with only a little hum of chatter among the group she presumed they were tired and a little deflated going back home. She sat in silence herself, except to reply to the odd remark Donald made along the way. The following evening, Eve reported to the office as requested. She hoped she had been successful on her first tour. She was nervous because the questionnaire the group would have found in their package on the last morning would reflect on her performance. The questionnaires would now be examined in front of the manager of the travel agency and it would tell a lot about how she got on or if she was successful on the trip, or indeed if people were satisfied with her guiding the tour. Of course, she wouldn't mention Mr. Black it was all part of the tour and that was now over.

When she arrived at the travel agent's office, the boss was waiting inside the desk. He was smiling from ear to ear and she got a good vibe from him immediately. "Good evening Mr. Gorman." "Hello Ms. Wallace. First, I must congratulate you on the excellent way you guided the tour and for your courtesy to all aboard. The feedback from all on the tour has been extremely positive, and we would like to offer you the position with the tour company." Eve was delighted with the praise and looked forward to her new career change. "My son will draw up the contract, and when you sign the paperwork, you can head home and we will contact you during the week with your roster." Mr. Gorman stood up and so did Eve. He shook hands with her then said, 'You may sit down and Hugh will be down in a few seconds. I believe you have already met." Eve was confused but didn't dare ask. She thought 'no it couldn't be him.'

Suddenly, the office door opened she turned around and to her amazement there he was, Mr. Black, she stood up to face him her legs were like jelly. He stepped towards the chair and offered her to sit down. Mr. Gorman went out and closed the office door. "That was my stepfather." Eve was surprised and he noted the confused look on her face. "My father left my mother when I was young, so that explains my surname, Black. Mr. Gorman married my mother ten years ago. They met in this very office when she became, a tour guide. She worked here for a short while after their marriage." Eve said, "No need to explain to me Mr. Black." "Please call me Hugh. I'm sorry I gave you a challenging time on our travels, but it is my job to observe new employees and find out if they have the stamina to deal with all kinds of customers when on tour." Then she realised Donald, the bus driver, was also in on the pretence' He smiled at her brightly, "You passed well done." "Thank you Hugh," she said. He then produced the contracts and after reading through them she signed all the necessary documents. When she stood up to go he opened the door for her. She went into the corridor and he followed close behind. She was still in a daze when he caught her by the arm she turned around to face him he gave her a teasing grin "Would you allow me to take you to dinner as a peace offering for being so annoying on tour?" As she graciously accepted his invitation, she sensed that a special rapport was already building between them.

Julie rang her daughter the following evening and asked her to call home. She spent the night at home with her parents and she explained all that happened on the tour and about Hugh Black. Her father came up from the caravan park and he was no sooner in the door when he asked" Did your mother tell you, Grayson and Emily are getting married next year." Julie said "I didn't get a chance with all we had to catch up on since she came in." Eve explained she was happy for them even though he flirted with her when he came to the house first she knew that there wasn't a real connection between them.

Eve buried herself in the new job and enjoyed every second of the travelling. After her evening out with Hugh they met in the office regularly and had the banter, but then seemed to be always travelling in opposite directions. Christmas came and went and Hugh was back in the office after a two-week break. His stepfather had left him in charge for the next month. He was going through upcoming winter bookings mostly skiing holidays but his mind kept drifting to somebody he hadn't been out with for a long while. He thought about the way she'd walk across the floor, the gentle sway of her hips, the bounce of her hair, and the way she was a joy to be round.

Eve was in contact with Hugh's stepfather Mr. Gorman mostly and Hugh seemed to be scarcely in the office. He wondered if Eve had even noticed that he was missing from the office regularly or that he seemed always to be in a hurry when he met her. But Hugh had a secret and wasn't sure if any woman would ever want to stay in a relationship with him, anyway. His last two relationships came to an abrupt end when he mentioned his commitments. He liked Eve and would love to get to know her on a personnel basis rather than just an employee. Without giving it any more thought he grabbed his phone and went out the door locking it behind him. 'A man is entitled to a lunch break,' he convinced himself even though it was only twelve o'clock. Hopefully, his stepfather wouldn't decide to ring him yet. He was constantly checking in with him.

Today his stepfather was flying out to the United Kingdom to attend a wedding with Hugh's mother Victoria. Hugh ran down the steps of the building and round to the back to where his car was parked he hopped in and drove the short distance to the nearest flower shop. When he opened the shop door, an aroma of unfamiliar scents hit his nostrils. He wanted to surprise Eve with a bunch of flowers and let her know she was appreciated as a diligent worker in the business. The assistant inside the counter suggested a bouquet of lemon coloured lilies imbedded in green fern leaves. Even though it was a working day, he decided to throw caution to the wind and head out to Oranmore to surprise Eve. He knew she was off work for the week and hoped she was at home today. When he pulled up outside her door, he was thrilled to see her car there. Then his stomach gave a quiver he hoped she wouldn't be upset with him for calling on her unannounced. He got out of the car and opened the boot and lifted out the flowers with sweating palms. He touched the doorbell once and it sounded like an orchestra in his ears it seemed to vibrate through the house with force. She opened the door slowly and she looked at him with surprise. "Hello Hugh," her gaze landed on the flowers she smiled up at him. He smiled back at her and handed her the bunch of flowers. She was flattered, "They're beautiful, actually they're my favourite flowers thank you so much." "Come in" she gestured "Can I offer you a coffee?" He nodded even though caffeine was the last thing his galloping heart needed right now. They talked for a short while each feeling bashful. Then his stepfather rang, wondering if he was in the office. "I'm on an early lunch break I'll be back in the office soon," Simon Gorman said to Hugh "Hurry back the girls are overrun with calls." Hugh said rather perturbed, "Yeah, ok" and he hung up. He got up to leave, spontaneously they both leant closer until their hands were touching, she was gazing into his eyes a faint smile curving her lips, without a thought they kissed and it felt like the most natural thing in the world. He asked her out on a date and she accepted.

The more time he spent with her, the fonder he got of her. And she felt the same way. They never ran out of conversation. One evening, while they were exchanging family information he mentioned his godfather who lived in America and had died a while back. Eve asked his name. "Matthew Walsh. He was my mother's cousin and he was in Ireland after I was born and my mother asked him to stand for me. He was so good to me when I was growing up and looked after me financially. Unfortunately, we lost contact a few years ago." Eve thought, 'surely it couldn't be the same Mathew Walsh my mother knew.' She questioned him further about Matthew. She found it unbelievable that he was the same man and when she filled him on the story, he was gobsmacked.

Julie twisted and turned for the first half of the night. The wind had howled around the house and the rain lashed down so hard it sounded as if someone was throwing stones at the upper window. They were travelling down to Mayo in the morning for Grayson's and Emily's wedding. Julie hardly slept a wink, not fully to do with the breeze but because of the outfit she was wearing. Tomorrow was supposed to be a sunny day but it didn't look like that now. The purple floral dress she had spent a fortune on in an elite boutique in town now seemed too flimsy for the damp, miserable day that would no doubt follow. But her prediction was wrong the sun shone, and a warm breeze blew and the wedding went perfectly. They arrived home late into the night and slept late the following morning. In the afternoon Conor dashed into the hallway, he was carrying a large parcel. He left the parcel on the table and said to his mother "Open it." She got a sharp knife and slit the tough tape all along the side and each end of the parcel, when the brown paper fell open there was a cellophane bubble wrap taped tightly to the box inside. She pulled it off with her hands and there it was, her precious box all intact as new. She stood with her hands clasped to her face. "It's magnificent, look at the shine on the mahogany timber and the lid is perfect, one would never know it was smashed to pieces at all." She opened the clasps and lifted the lid then she closed the lid again. Rubbing her hands on the clasps, she looked over at Conor who had not spoken since he asked her to open the parcel. "Are you pleased with it?" he asked "I'm over the moon, it must have cost you a small fortune, but I'll pay you back when I sell it."

Her son knew by her reaction she had taken back ownership of it right away. "Thank you so much for saving it for me." "The owner of the repair shop in London also has an antique store and wondered if you would consider selling it to him." Eric walked in, he was in awe with the sight of the box. "What's this about selling it, sure it only arrived today give your mother a chance to consider what she wants to do with it." Julie was overcome with excitement. "I'll hold on to it for a while then I'll consider selling it. But I want to make sure it goes to somebody who will appreciate it. Her thoughts wandered back to what Grayson told her yesterday at the wedding before she left for home. He brought her aside and she was astonished at the news he had for her. Matthew had a godson in Ireland he mentioned him to me and I know he meant to look after him in his will." Julie reflected that this probably changed once he married.

CHAPTER 15

The conversation and the wine flowed. Eve found Hugh funny, interesting and easy to talk to. They were going out almost six months today. He brought her to the Riverside restaurant and they sat out on the balcony enjoying the lights of the city reflecting on the water. He talked about taking her on a trip to Paris to attend a concert there next year. She told him she loved André Rieu, the Dutch violinist, and it was her dream to attend one of his concerts but hadn't got to see him yet. He'd make it happen for her next year. None of the men she knew had touched her heart the way Hugh had. He was uneasy and knew he needed to tell Eve his secret before somebody else did but he feared her reaction when he told her. Eve was thrilled she had met Hugh, what made it so special was that she hadn't expected to meet anyone. If she didn't change jobs, she wouldn't have met him. She looked forward to the times they spent together and they were growing closer, she couldn't remember being happier. But she had noticed on occasions he would check the time and would seem to be uneasy, as if he had a commitment or had to answer to somebody, on these occasions he would almost always have to go away early. Like last month when they were out for an evening dinner and relaxing, alarm bells rang when halfway through the dinner his mobile rang and he immediately dashed out the front door with the phone to his ear. She felt something wasn't right because when he came back he sat down and was somewhat subdued. Eve didn't ask who was on the phone she ignored it and kept eating. After dessert, he mentioned it was his mother on the phone "I must take you out to Barna to meet her one of these days" he offered. There was something secretive about him and she didn't want to fall deeply in love just to find out she was wasting precious time again. She had her share of secrets with Pierre and would not allow that to happen to her again. She was quite aware the spark between them was definitely flaring up but she was being cautious.

It was early morning with dawn just breaking. Eve heard a song thrush singing its bitter sweet song. She took a deep breath and stared over at it in the tree directly outside her bedroom window. She turned on her side and closed her eyes and wondered was it an omen of something significant to come? She was delighted to have two days off just to do nothing. Being a tour guide was tiring even though she enjoyed the travel to different countries, it entailed having loads of energy, keeping up with information on every country and dealing with many people from all walks of life.

Hugh rang Eve to tell her he would be over later. The first step he took inside the door she noted the serious look on his face. In fact, he looked stern. She wondered what was troubling him? He came in to the kitchen where she was preparing food. He was giddy and talked non-stop about, this, that, and the other. After a moment of silence, he said, "Eve, there are things you don't know about me." She looked at him over her shoulder and said, "Like what?" He tilted his head slightly and she noticed his foot shaking "It is difficult to tell you this," and with that the doorbell rang he jumped "I'll get that for you." She heard him say in a high-pitched voice, "Hello Conor." Her brother came in full of the joys of life. Eve greeted him with the thought, 'of all evenings, what a time to turn up.' Her mind went blank what was Hugh about to divulge. Conor noticed a tense atmosphere in the kitchen. "Did I call at bad time if so I can come back?" "No, not at all," Hugh said "In fact, I'm in a bit of a hurry," he walked over and gave Eve a peck on the cheek "Call you later," and he was gone out the door. Conor walked over to the cooker where there was spaghetti bolognaise simmering in a pot "Looks like there's enough there for two," he said laughing. "Were you passing or have you some news for me?" she asked. "I have news for you. Mum is going over to London next week to meet up with the owner of the repair shop and hopefully they will make her an offer on the box I'm going with her and Dad is staying to look after the business, will you come with us?" "I doubt if I will get holidays, Hugh is going to Germany tomorrow evening with a tour and he will be away for ten days. Anyway, you are well capable of looking after her. Just make sure she gets the value of the box." Later that night Hugh rang "Are you on your own?" she said. "Yes, Conor went home after he enjoyed your portion of dinner. Why did you take off when he came in? It looked so obvious that you had no interest in talking to him?" "That's because I have something on my mind and I want you to know before I go on tour." She sighed worriedly, "Come over now. I'm not working in the morning, anyway." "See you in a bit" and he rang off.

It was eleven o'clock when Hugh arrived and despite being very anxious she was ready to hear what he had to say. She pointed towards the couch to sit down and sat beside him. Half afraid of what he was going to say she asked "Well, what's the big secret that couldn't wait until you came back from Germany?" He stuttered while he said, "I am the father to ten-year-old twin girls, Josephine and Patricia." For what seemed like an age but surely only seconds, Eve could only stare at him. Shock was making her pulse race. She wanted to scream at him but couldn't sound her voice.

He continued to say with a flush that tinged his cheeks, and she knew with certainty he was under pressure. "Their mother was from Switzerland, we split up after two years and she went back and left me with the girls. I have full custody of them now. My aunt Esther helps me care for them and I live with her and her husband Jake they have two teenage girls of their own. But it is a constant battle to be there for them, and be on tour but I have to earn a living. Their mother refused to pay child support and I never brought her to court over it. I had hoped to get married after they were born but we grew apart fairly quickly and she went back home, promising that she would be involved in the girls lives but since then she hasn't been in contact. It's as if they never existed to her and I haven't been able to reach her at all." Eve said almost silently "I don't understand how she could walk away from her own children." "Neither do I," he said. He waited for her to say something else but she couldn't find the right words for the way she felt at that moment. "Maybe I should go it is late!" "It would be better if you did I have a lot process." He asked if they could meet in the morning before the trip to Germany. "I think not, it's best if you just go on the trip and we can talk when you get back." He was disappointed. She opened the front door and stood inside as he walked out and into his car then she closed and locked the door and there was a striking silence. She spent the

138

night and all next day in semi-shock. Back at work, she found it hard to concentrate, her duty was to man the phones and take bookings for the autumn season. In the evening she drove over to her parent's place which was buzzing with campers, caravans and guests in residence in the bed-and-breakfast. Even though Julie was busy, she got time to sit and listen to her daughter when she told her about Hugh and the twins. Her mother said with concern it would be an enormous responsibility to take on a family overnight if you were to stay with him.

Julie and Conor were travelling over to London for three days hoping to sell her precious box; she was excited and nervous all at the same time. Eve was expecting Hugh back mid-week and was so confused about their situation. Julie and Conor arrived at their hotel late afternoon after resting for a while, they made their way to the repair shop which was directly across the busy street they were staying on. Conor had already made an appointment with the owner last week and he was expecting them this evening. As they went through the door, a tall man in his seventies approached them, he stretched out his hand to greet them "I'm Robert Brown, pleased to meet you." Then he said "Well I suppose it's down to business, if you both come through to my office we will negotiate a price. He addressed Julie. What price had you in mind?" "What is it worth?" she asked. "I had it valued last week he said there are only a few of those left in the country." Then Julie spoke up, "When I thought about what Matthew said about the box I carried out my research and I'll sell it for no less than one hundred and thirty thousand sterling."

Conor was flabbergasted with his mother's assertiveness, Robert responded "We were thinking more like one hundred thousand." Julie argued, "No way." Robert suggested they could meet some place in the middle. "I'm afraid not Robert, if we can't come to an agreement then I will take it home and wait for the next person who will see the value of it." Robert then offered one hundred and twenty thousand, he knew Julie meant what she said. Julie quickly said "One hundred and twenty-five and nothing less, take it or leave it." So the deal was made, Julie sold the box and went home, one hundred and twenty-five thousand sterling richer.

After arriving home, Julie poured herself a glass of wine and sat in her comfortable leather chair by the fire, waiting for Eric to come up from the park. She was happy to be home with a nice stash of cash in her own bank account which she opened last month. After letting him know how she got on, he joined her for a drink to celebrate and he filled her in what happened while she was away, with more tourists bookings for August and September. "The contractors came yesterday and have said that they will start building the extension to the coffee shop next month." "I thought ye had forgotten about building that, sure we didn't discuss it in years and I didn't see any paper work coming in about the grant so why are contractors arriving suddenly, unless there is a grant it won't be built." He didn't tell her the grant wasn't approved because of a late application and they would have to pay for the building themselves. It would cost about forty thousand euros and he knew that was not available in their account, and there was no hope of a loan as they were already paying back the last one. She wondered why he said very little about her money. She didn't elaborate because she intended to hold on to the money she had just received for a rainy day and not to spend it straight away. Conor came in and was all excited about her fortune. "I presume a foreign holiday to the sun is on the cards Mum and maybe a new car" as he winked at his father. She got up and walked over to the sink with her glass, saying at the same time "No, I think I'll hold on to it for a rainy day." Then Conor blurted out that they had got word while they were away that the grant was refused for the building because of a late application. She looked at Eric and Conor unable to digest what she was hearing "I left the applying to you both, and now look what has happened. I just don't believe this." Eric beckoned at his son to come outside. "Leave it for now give her some time to think about it," and they went back to work. Julie couldn't believe it. Had neither of them learnt anything from what had happened before with money issues?

Eve was just home from work when her phone rang, it was Hugh back from tour and eager to meet up with her tomorrow evening. She agreed to meet him in town for coffee because she was out of the office for the next few days. In fact, she was going on a tour to Kerry for five nights with a group of older adults the day after tomorrow. Eve and Hugh meet the next day and talked at length. Hugh asked her if she gave some thought to his situation 'of having twins.' "Kids don't scare me." she said. He felt a glimmer of hope. "But I need time to think it through properly." "Take all the time you need I would really like to have you in our lives though" he said. She knew he meant it and she wanted to be with him, but she worried about so many different scenarios that were going round in her head.

The Gleneagles Hotel in Killarney was booked out with tourists from France, America, United Kingdom and of course all parts of Ireland. After getting booked in and distributing the keys, the guests went to their rooms to refresh before dinner. Eve opened the door of her room and left her case on the shelf and lay on the bed to unwind, she closed her eyes and thought about Hugh. She was falling for him but a ready-made family was an overpowering responsibility to take on over -night. The time away in Killarney gave Eve time to reflect on where she stood with Hugh and his twins. Hugh rang her the last night of the tour. He knew she needed time, but he wanted to understand what she was thinking and answer questions she must have. Eve headed home after Killarney and spent the day with her parents. She stared out the window; it was a beautiful day the sun shone from a turquoise sky, and roses bobbled beneath the sill. She could hear the hum of Conor mowing the lawn, and a blackbird singing in the hedge. She told herself that she really must cheer up and stop moping; she needed to decide and talk to Hugh.

Hugh was planning on bringing the twins away for a holiday to the seaside. He was looking forward to the morning when he would be alone in the office with Eve. His stepfather was away on tour with a group from Clare and wouldn't be back for three days. He wasn't sure if she had changed her mind on being in a relationship with him after he told her about the twins. The four other employees were in a separate office. Hugh had coffee ready when she came in. He beckoned towards the chair by the filing cabinet, "I can imagine that you have so many questions Eve, but I think that if you met the girls, it would give you a chance to get to know them. I have booked a five-night stay in a lodge nestled by the seashore it is in an idyllic setting where the twins would enjoy some swimming, horse riding and maybe bike riding. It will be an action packed break I booked time off on the first week of June. Please, will you join us?" he asked. "Please Eve." "This is so unexpected Hugh I haven't met the twins yet and you are asking me to go on holidays with them, they mightn't want me there, it's their holiday with you. It could be a disaster" she said. "Maybe you could come over next week to meet them I'll let my aunt know" he replied. Eve didn't want to lose him but wasn't sure if she was prepared to take on the new family. Hesitantly, she agreed to go over to his aunts, suggesting "Okay then I'll drop over next Wednesday evening after work."

Wednesday arrived a lot quicker than she had expected as she drove out to Barna. Hugh was there before she arrived. He opened the door and introduced her to his aunt Esther and her husband Jake who were very welcoming. The twins were smiling at her. Hugh introduced "This is Josephine and Patricia." "Hi girls, it's great to meet you," Eve said. Esther knew Eve wasn't familiar with kids because she greeted them like new clients. Hugh pointed to the couch for Eve to sit down. The twins plonked themselves on each side of her. She wasn't sure what to say to them. Hugh intervened and eventually she talked to them and they told her stories about school and what games they played. They were laughing and talking as if they knew her always. Eve knew they were smart, friendly kids and used to meeting people. Hugh admired them inwardly the three people he loved most in the world already looked like a family with any luck Eve would hopefully feel the same, but he knew he had to give her time to adjust to noisy kids.

After a little persuasion, Eve agreed to go with them on holidays. Five nights away with Hugh seemed wonderful. It would give them time to relax and unwind and enjoy each other's company and get to know the twins. Of course, the twins would have to be entertained and she was slightly anxious because she knew nothing about looking after children and hoped she would have the patience they needed. She knew she was very set in her ways, which more than lightly came with her age. Early on the morning of the breakaway Hugh collected her before ten o'clock and they arrive at their destination before mid-day with the twins being so elated to be going on holiday they talked non-stop on the journey. Eve was delighted when they reached the lodge and jumped out of the car into the warm sunshine, feeling that this is exactly what she needed as she smiles spreading her arms out and turning towards the beaming sun.

Deep gulps of warm air smelling of sea salt fills her with a sense of wellbeing that she hasn't experienced for months. The lodge was just at the sea's edge, surrounded by all types of shrubs and trees, giving a magical feeling of a

142

hideaway. Eve and Hugh walked towards the reception with the twins walking along happily beside them. When they signed in and collected their key cards, they went down the long corridor to the family room. The twins had a separate compartment divided by a door. Hugh and Eve were in the master room, which contained a double and single bed. As soon as they opened the main door, it hit home with Eve. They weren't really alone with the twins next door. This was so new to her. There were four of them not two. All was going well, and Eve decided she would take a shower before they went out to explore the area. Next she heard Josephine shouting, "Can we go swimming now Daddy?" "Yes, we'll go down after lunch, is that okay with you Eve?" "That's fine with me, sounds good, sunbathing is my favourite relaxation." They spent an enjoyable evening on the white soft sand and in the warm sea water. Eve had great fun with the twins and they stayed there until the tide rolled in and they all started to get hungry. Just as they finished dinner, Hugh noticed the kids were getting tired and beginning to fight, so he decided it was time for bed so they would be ready for horse riding in the morning. He suggested to Eve that she stay in the bar and enjoy the music and he would be back down when the twins were settled in bed and the house baby sitter was ready to take up duty. "I'd rather come up and read for a while and we'll both come down later. I think the band plays until late." They went up and as soon as the card swung the door open Patricia started complaining, "I don't want to sleep in that room it's too small I want to go into the bed in your room Daddy." Josephine yelped, "Me too." He brought them back to their own room and sat them down and explained to them that Eve was sleeping with him in his bed and this was where they had to sleep. The girls were not agreeable to what their father suggested and they continued giving out until Eve said, "Hugh let them into the double bed, and you sleep in the single beside them and I'll take their room." She was now in the twin's room and standing at the end of one of the single beds. They didn't get down to the bar because the twins were unsettled. Eve eventually had an early night and closed her door and turned on the television. She was upset with Hugh because the twins seemed to be setting the itinerary and their father was agreeing with them. She was so used to doing what she wanted, when she wanted, so maybe this would not work out after all. Hugh was all attentive to her the following morning and the twins were on their best behaviour and promised to stay in their own room from now on. She joined in all the fun and each day was action packed. The nights she envisaged as romantic turned out to be non-existent because she never knew when one girl would appear out of their room, even though they made a promise not to, but they would always come up with an excuse of some kind just to get their father's attention. Eve never realised kids were so tiring and full on. As the holiday drew to a close, Eve was arriving home worn out from the five days. Hugh and herself arranged to meet at the weekend before she went on tour to Rome.

She was definitely falling for Hugh and wanted nothing to stand in her way of being with him not even taking on the responsibility of motherhood overnight. She liked children but knew it would take some getting used to. Hugh and Eve continued to go out and get the odd weekend away alone. It was on one of those weekends that he surprised her. They were dining at an exclusive restaurant with the most amazing ambiance. Everything was wonderful. She didn't expect him to propose, suddenly to her amazement he was off his chair and down on one knee. She gasped she couldn't believe this was happening; he was going to pop the question in the restaurant in front of all the diners. He looked up at her, "I love you Eve with all my heart will you make me the happiest man on earth and be my wife?" She was staring at him. She was aware all eyes were on her. Hugh gazed at her adoringly. She knew she loved him. He was fascinating, entertaining, and thoughtful. She loved him without a doubt. She cried, "I'd love to be your wife." He jumped up and swung her around in his arms. Everyone around them started clapping and cheering and the manager came out with a bottle of champagne and they celebrated for the night. When Hugh's stepfather, Simon heard the news, he was over the moon and offered to throw a celebration party in the garden of his lavish home. Hugh's mother, Victoria was elated and made big plans immediately.

CHAPTER 16

E ve's parents were happy for her and hoped when the twins came to live with her she wouldn't feel restricted. She would go from being carefree to caring for two ten-year-olds. They would have to come first and she would have to be willing to adjust and make this work for everyone. Even though they were Hugh's children when they were married half the responsibility would fall on her shoulders. There would be no more going into town at the drop of a hat or going for a night out without arranging her time off. Julie sat her down and talked her through all of this but she said she had her mind made up to marry Hugh and she would adapt to family life with him. She explained to her parents that Hugh and the girls would move in with her eventually, as he was selling his house in Galway and paying off the bank loan leaving him debt free. The following morning she got up early and walked down to the hair salon where she had an early appointment. The summer wind seemed to have a lighter feel to it, blowing across from the sea was the scent of fresh seaweed. She felt she was walking on air after accepting Hugh's proposal. She walked into the saloon and went over and sank into her usual chair. She spun it around, "You seem chirpy today," Wendy said smiling. She lifted her hand and waved it in the air "I couldn't be happier Hugh asked me to marry him." Wendy ran over and hugged her, looking at her sparkling ring. Wendy continued laughing "Lucky you marrying the owner of a travel agency there will be no problem there booking sun holidays."

The following weekend, the happy couple had arrived at Hugh's mother and stepfather's house for a celebration barbeque. The smell of barbecued chicken greeted them as they climbed out of the car and walked around the side of the house into the large exotic garden, which had matured over the years with all kinds of shrubs. It was a hot summer's evening with the sun flooding through the hedges with not a cloud in the brilliant sky. Eve looked towards the wooded area at the end of the garden where there were matured trees, their leaves a wonderful mix of various shades of green. She felt it gave a wonderful backdrop. Hugh's stepfather Simon was in command of the cooking while Victoria was rushing around, setting up places to sit. The twins arrived later with Esther and husband Jake. They were elated to be staying in granny's house for the night and were going in and out of the house. Eve looked at them, delighted that they were happy with her joining their family. Eve's mother, father and brother came over later in the evening. The conversation turned to wedding planning between the mothers. Julie said, "Eve doesn't want an extravagant wedding. I think she intends to keep it simple." Victoria said rather acutely, "Easier said than done my dear." Hugh came across from where the men were sitting "Mother wants the wedding of the century seeing I'm her only son," he said. But Eve spoke up and made her wishes clear. She could see by the way Hugh's mother was planning, it would take some convincing to bring her to see the bride's wishes, but she would eventually get her there. Hugh wished in silence that his godfather Matthew hadn't passed away he would have been thrilled to see him settle down. Hugh remembered when the twins were born how he helped look after him financially. It was a comfort to know he saw them when he was last home and stayed in a Bed and Breakfast in Galway.

Matthew came up in conversation later that night when Victoria remarked that Hugh's godfather would have been thrilled and she told them all about him. Neither Julie nor Eric could believe the connection between the two families and were fascinated to hear more about Mathew and his life. There was nothing said about the box, as Julie was adamant it was never to be mentioned to anybody. She didn't mention to Eve yet that she intended to pay for the wedding. Tonight wasn't the place to mention it anyway, or Victoria would definitely press for an elaborate wedding, pulling out all the stops.

Eve couldn't believe how quickly time seemed to pass. She was busier than she had ever been, organising the wedding, supporting Hugh and the girls and arranging their move into her house. While looking forward to all the changes, she was also feeling a little apprehensive and worried, in case things didn't go according to plan. Eric and Julie decided that as they were getting older and not as well able for the pressure the business brings at certain times of the year, they want to scale back on their workload. After discussing it with Conor, they decide to take a step back and employ a worker in the bed-and-breakfast. Conor text Eve that evening to explain the changes their parents were making. She was over the moon because the help she normally gave her mother would be limited especially when the twins and Hugh moved in. When Hugh sold his house and paid off the bank loan, he intended to help Eve with her mortgage. He wasn't very flush with money, but he would do the very best he could. Julie interviewed about a dozen girls before she met the girl that ticked all the boxes. Her name was Matilda Dowling. Eve had gone home for the day to her parents. They just sat down to dinner as Conor walked in to join them. During the meal, the doorbell rang. Eve went up and opened the door. A few moments later, she came back into the kitchen. "Mum, there's a girl in the living room she said her name is Matilda Dowling she said something about cancelling her interview last week because of sickness." Julie got up and went in to meet her. Even though she came across as having a serious nature, she seemed to be a warm and happy-go-lucky person with a friendly smile and a good work ethic about her. Julie decided there and then to take her on for a month's trial. She told the family when she was gone that she hired her for a month. Matilda came up from the midlands the following week and started work. Julie introduced her to her husband and son. Conor noted the colour of her eyes instantly they were hazel and matched her long brown hair.

As the days turned into weeks, Conor and Matilda became good friends. He was drawn to her sweet manner and her kindness and the way her nose crinkled when she laughed. She had a serious side to her and he felt she was a woman with whom he could develop a connection. He asked her out towards the end of May. She was a full-time employee now and had settled into the business with great ease. Julie noted Conor and she had become good friends and worked well together. One bright evening at the end of May, he came up to the house and asked Julie if Matilda was going home early. "Not tonight we have a group coming in tomorrow at lunch time so we have an early start to give the rooms a once over before they arrive." He went into the kitchen where Matilda was emptying the dish washer and asked if she'd come into Galway and walk the promenade with him. She agreed, with no hesitation. The prom was busy with evening walkers, the air was warm and sweet, the sky was painted with shades of cobalt and sapphire that stretched across to where they entwined with tangerine and amethyst. The sparse clouds were like puffs of pink cotton-candy, dusted with icing sugar, as they floated languidly across the open expanse of the horizon. They walked hand in hand like two people who had known each other all their lives. When they reached home that night, Matilda got out of the car and slipped her bag over her shoulder. Conor walked over beside her and caught her unaware. He gently cupped her cheeks, smoothing his thumbs over her cheek bones. They moved closer and she could feel the heat of his breath on her face. Her heart pounded and he lowered his lips to meet hers and they kissed. She took a step backwards "I'd better go inside, see you tomorrow." Conor touched her arm "Good night." She went in and the place was in darkness. She stood inside the door and left her hand on her heart, savouring the kiss they had just shared. It had been so intense, so wonderful. It was something she'd never experienced before. It was exhilarating and she didn't want it to end. Conor was staying down in the park in the mobile home with his parents. They used this time of year for their private accommodation when the guest house was booked out. Matilda had the spare room in the guest house for when she had an early start rather than travelling home. As Conor drove over to the mobile home, he hoped that their friendship might develop into something more beautiful. Over the next number of weeks, Conor's parents noticed Matilda and their son had become very close.

The day finally arrived when Hugh and the twins were moving in permanently. Eve went out to water the flowers at the front of her house. The sweet scent of the flowers in the window boxes and hanging baskets teased her nostrils, making her experience the expectation of hot summer months before the return of dark winter nights. She took a deep breath, today was the beginning of her new life with a family, she was excited and hopeful that it would be lifelong and happy. She heard the removal van pull up outside the front gate. She opened the side door and told them to leave the contents into the spare room. After they had gone, she went back in to the room and couldn't believe how packed it was with mostly small stuff like books, clothes, desks, a computer and lots of other knickknacks that filled the room. She wasn't too sure where they were going to store all of it. Later that afternoon, Hugh and the twins arrived. After getting out of the car he made the girls stand quietly and asked them to walk into Eve's house mannerly. "This is our new home and we want to show Eve we know how to conduct ourselves reasonably" he said. Hugh stood there for a few moments in deep thought. It was a dream come true, having a proper family with a place of their own. He felt so lucky to have met and fallen in love with a beautiful woman like Eve. He was determined to make this work. His only concern was that Eve wouldn't bond with the girls and to living with a family. She was excited to see them outside and opened the door promptly. "Come in," she said and hugged each one, "Welcome to your new home." She had to remind herself occasionally during the evening that this was going to be the way it would be every day from now on, the house wasn't her own anymore. She was now sharing it with three others. They were her family now and she knew it would take some getting used to. Tomorrow was her day off when she usually had a lie in. She hinted at Hugh after going to bed that night that maybe he would look after the girls in the morning before going into the office. That didn't happen Hugh woke up late. He turned over and left his arm across Eve's waist, "Wake up my love, I'm really sorry, I'm late for work. Could you look after the twins because they will be up as soon as they hear me move?" He got up and showered and dressed. She could hear him in the kitchen rattling dishes and clicking mugs in his rush to get breakfast. He shouted, "I'm off now" just as the twins called out that they were hungry. She heard him say, 'Eve will get breakfast for ye," then the front door pulled shut and he was gone leaving her with her new charges. The day turned out far busier than it would have been in the office Would she ever get used to this new role? She tackled the spare room throwing out a portion of the stuff she knew Hugh would never miss and she found places for the rest. It was summer, the school had closed for holidays that meant the twins would be with her from now. They would go to Hugh's aunt when Eve was working which was four days a week since she finished tour guiding and took up office work instead. Sometimes, she envied

149

Hugh when he went to different countries on tour. It took some time for Eve to acclimatise to her new role but eventually she did and found it both enjoyable and rewarding. They had become a very happy family and Eve felt that their happiness would be completed by the end of next year when they were planning to be married.

Within a short time frame, Conor and Matilda became inseparable. She loved the way his eyes lit up every time he walked into the room. They were out for an evening relaxing in the village pub when he returned with two glasses of wine; he left the white in front of her. She waited for him to sit down before taking a sip. "Are you happy working with my mother? I know she can be full on at times?" She took another sip of the cool crisp wine, enjoying the sensation as it slid down her throat. It was stronger than the usual grape she indulged in. In fact, she could feel the effects of it filtering into her bloodstream, relaxing her instantly. "I'm certainly enjoying the work and especially meeting the people. I get on brilliantly with your mother she is so considerate and a pleasure to work for. If I'm doing anything that would upset the customers, she lets me know in a way that I don't feel that I am being given out to. I'm always learning from her." He was very pleased with what she said about his mother. He went for more wine and while he was waiting to be served, he looked over his shoulder at her back at the table. Deep down in his heart, he knew that he more than liked this girl. They continued talking for a long while.

Matilda was getting tired and knew she had to be up early in the morning as she checked her phone for the time. "Now, how about I get us another glass of wine before we finish up?" Conor suggested. "Go on so, then it will be time for us to call it a night. Don't want to be groggy in the morning when preparing for the English group who have booked in for five nights. By the time the taxi dropped her off near midnight, Matilda's face was aching from laughing as Conor had regaled her with stories about his time working at home in the park. He had met so many people and formed lifelong relationships. He was clearly one of life's likeable characters. She thought secretly he was the type of man a woman could fall in love with. She really liked him. Conor's parents weren't surprised when he announced that Matilda and he were moving in together and it was only a month from Eve's wedding. They rented a house across the road from the park overlooking the sea.

Eve was tiring of the diet she started last year, she was eager to lose weight, but her trouble was snacking especially since the girls came to live with her, she seemed to join them in crisps and chocolate at odd times of the night especially watching films. The wedding dress she bought a year ago was expensive, and it was a case of having to fit into it. She was thrown when Hugh came home in poor form; he had tried to secure money from the bank to keep his house, but it fell through. He decided it would have been an asset if he could hold on to it rather than sell it. "If only he had a way to pay the arrears on the mortgage," as he talked to himself out loud. Eve wondered to herself if Julie would help and they would pay her back. It wasn't easy to mention it to her because Hugh knew nothing about his godfather giving his treasured box to her mother. He might wonder where Julie would get an amount of money like he needed, which was twenty thousand euros.

CHAPTER 17

E ve and her mother made a habit of catching up for a coffee and chat once a week. As soon as the twins were dropped at school Eve headed over to meet her mother. It was a bright October morning, as they sat and chatted while overlooking the water with the sun twinkling ed on it and leaves on the trees moving slowly in a gentle breeze. Julie wondered at her daughter's sombre mood especially as it was only six weeks from her wedding. But what she wasn't aware of was that Hugh had only four days left to find the money to pay the arrears on his house mortgage Julie had a wedge of Victoria sponge and cream but Eve just ordered coffee. "Are you sure you won't have cake this morning?" Julie asked. She laid her hand on her stomach. "I had a big breakfast and I need to be able to fit into my wedding dress. Hugh was up early and he made breakfast for all of us." Julie looked down at the table "Can't remember the last time your father made breakfast for me." Eve laughed "That is probably because it never happened," they both laughed. Then Eve made it known to her mother about Hugh's problem. She didn't say much just listened and after a short time they each went their separate ways. The following evening after discussing the money issue with Eric they both went over to Oranmore and told Hugh all about his godfather and selling the precious box. She decided to give them a wedding present of the amount due leaving him with the chance to hold on to his house. Julie said "I know if Matthew was here that is what he would have done for you." Hugh was emotional and ecstatic all at the same time, "Twenty thousand is too much to take from you, I'll pay back some when I get on my feet." She gestured with her hand "It's from Matthew not me, now you can look forward to the wedding." He gave her a hug to show his appreciation for her thoughtfulness and loyalty to Matthew.

Even though it was almost five months since Hugh and twins moved in with Eve, it felt like the new chapter of her life hadn't fully started, not until the wedding was over and Hugh was her husband. Having being single for so long she was secretly relieved to be settling down at last. She was praying for a dry morning, tomorrow was her wedding day. She loved the little Church in Barna overlooking the sea where she was making her vows to Hugh. The twins were flower girls and Majella her best friend was her only bridesmaid. Hugh asked one of the coach drivers to be his best man. Joe and Hugh were lifelong friends since they started school together. The morning rain had given way to afternoon November sunshine. Eve stepped into her wedding dress and was pleased with how elegant she looked. The low-cut neckline and full skirt with a pearl tiara made her look like a princess, her look was finished with a simple up style in her hair and natural makeup. The twins were dressed in fuchsia coloured lace dresses and the bridesmaid dress was in a complimentary tone, with a fitted bodice and lace sleeves. The bridal bouquet was put together by her mother it was a combination of wild flowers and heather. Gradually, the small church filled. The wedding guests turned around as Eve walked up the aisle linking her father's arm. She looked radiant and walked with her eyes fixed on the man standing in front of the altar. As he turned around his eyes sparkled and there was no doubting the love that flowed between them was eternal. The ceremony was everything she had hoped for and she savoured every minute of it. Once the serious business of the church ceremony was complete, the happy couple walked down the aisle together to the most beautiful sounding music, Eve clutching her husband's hand tightly. From the corner of her eye she could see her parents shed a tear. When they went outside Conor walked over to where they were standing at the church door, "You look gorgeous sis," and gave her a tight hug. She looked at him walk away and wondered would he be standing in this position one day maybe with Matilda. They walked down the beach to the sea's edge and faced the photographer with the ocean directly behind them. Eve's nostrils filled with the scent of salt water and fresh sea weed. She couldn't remember a time in her life that made her this happy and this was the beginning of the rest of her life. The reception was incredible, with tables set looking out to the most stunning and splendid scenery. As evening slipped away and darkness began to fall the view of the bay, all twinkling with lights was entrancing. The happy couple kissed under the terrace lights to a toast from the bride's father. "I love you, Eve," Hugh whispered. Eve gazed into his eyes. "I love you, too." They had decided to spend their honeymoon in Copenhagen. Eve spend her childhood reading Hans Christian Andersen books and it was inspiring to be travelling to the master storyteller's city for her honeymoon. They could enjoy the holiday because the twins were happy to be staying with Hugh's aunt for the ten days.

Eve was thrilled when the twins began to call her Mum soon after they got back from their honeymoon. Eve and Hugh ran the tourist agency diligently with help from Simon. Eve told her parents' life was perfect. Time was moving on, it was now six years since Hugh and Eve got married, Conor and Matilda bought a nice size cottage on the coast near to the bed-and-breakfast and were a couple who were very serious about each other. They decided that they were in no rush to get married, wanting to do things and go places before settling down.

Hugh was heading off to Paris on tour mid-August; it had never occurred to Eve that life could change so dramatically during one week in a hot summer. The twins helped their father with his travel bags. Eve went out to the car just before Hugh went to make sure he had his paperwork in order for travelling. The twins were talking together and even though they were getting older, the last thing they said to him was, "When you come back promise you'll bring us to Center Parcs." He kissed them both on the cheeks "I promise if Eve agrees to come up on the roller coaster with us," she laughed as she leaned in and kissed him a soft sweet kiss on the lips "Maybe I will, let me think about it." He waved to them "I'll be back home in ten days to my beautiful girls" and he drove out the gate and tipped the horn on the car as he drove off. Eve left her arms around the girl's shoulders, "I think we deserve a day out, we'll go to the beach and sun bath, I'll bring the barbeque and we can spend the full day there and go swimming when the tide goes out." They stayed until late evening as they sat and enjoyed the barbeque and quietness of the beach. There were other families still there who had the same idea as themselves. The moon was visible now, a silver crescent high above the sea, casting its glow over the surface of the water, that now turned black, mysterious, wonderful and intimidating. As she drove home, she felt an aura of sadness shadowing her, it was like being followed by a storm cloud and wondering when the storm would break, and she'd be soaked to the skin. But then the girl's loud laughter and chattering revived her and she joined in the fun.

Eve kept busy for the next eight days and was glad of the two months leave she decided to take when the twins were off from school. They tidied up the garden, cut the lawn, clipped hedges and painted the outside furniture and cleaned the windows. "Your father won't know the place when he gets home," Eve said. They talked to him each evening on the phone and couldn't wait for him to be home and have family time together. With the twins getting older, Eve knew they would soon be more independent, going out more and needing herself and Hugh less.

The day before Hugh was due home they decided to go over to Eve's parents and spend the day. Julie and Eric enjoyed the girls' company and they would spend the day chatting to Julie, lying out in the garden, on their phones and eating many goodies. It was evening time and Eve was down in the caravan park with Conor and Matilda when the twins came running frantic towards her. "Granny said something about a touring bus that crashed out in Paris today." Eve turned around, "Stop shouting girls let me go and ask Granny where she saw that." Josephine shouted "It was on the six o'clock news." The all ran up to the house and into the kitchen where Eric and Julie were sitting in silence listening and waiting for the advert break to be over. The news reader had said, "And still to come an Irish touring bus crashes in Paris killing six people and injuring several others." They huddled together and listened in silence. Conor and Matilda stood at the door and waited. The news reader announced there would be no further details until the families were contacted. Eve pulled her phone out of her bag "It's not our bus, Joe is a careful driver, it is probably some other tour operator," she said but at the same time she was dialling Hugh's number. To her horror his phone was not responding. She dialled over and over

155

again but to no avail then she called his stepfather and she knew when he answered that the news was devastating. "I was about to contact you Eve, I have extremely bad news." While she listened to what he was saying she wrapped her arms around herself swaying, her eyes closed trying to take in the enormity of Simon's words. She fell back on to the chair beside her and began wailing. The twins stood there shocked to the core. "What is it?' her parents asked, she said with her voice quivering "Hugh was killed instantly when a truck skidded into the bus putting it on its side." Then there were no more questions to be asked. Eve's parents cancelled all bookings for the next week in order to support her and the twins. Simon and Victoria came over to be with them, they were beyond grief stricken.

After the funeral was over everybody went back home and Eve and the twins went back to Oranmore, the weeks that followed were heart breaking and lonely. The weeks turned into months, but time seemed to pass so slowly, Eve tried to fill every gap with caring for the twins who were now back at school. She tried to get back to some normality but no matter how hard she tried she could find no way back without her husband. All hopes of a baby for her and Hugh had gone and she found it almost impossible to come to terms with the loss of Hugh. She fell into a dark place and continued that way for almost a year when she decided to take a friend's advice and seek a therapist's help.

The twins were now getting older and needed her more than ever to be a mother and father to them. They cried mostly at night and she could hear them trying to comfort each other. They wanted him back. As time passed, she knew they were coming to terms with their bereavement. One night, they went into the garden and as the clouds parted and the stars appeared she spotted them gazing up at the bright sky. Eve stood at the door out of sight and listened. Josephine looked at Patricia, "See that bright star far beyond the castle, that's dad's star." Patricia gazed reflectively at it, "I'm sure, it looks like the last star at the end of the universe." "It is," Josephine agreed and "It's guarding the gateway to beyond, because that's where he's gone on his next great adventure." Eve rubbed her wet cheek with her palm. That was the breaking point for her and she decided to seek out a therapist sooner rather than later so that the three of them could start to enjoy life again. Matilda and Conor were now engaged to be married. The twins spent time over at the park with their grandparents leaving Eve with free time to meet her friends with the hope of rejoining them in the work place. Julie kindly helped out with bills and left her daughter with less financial worries.

After Christmas and coming into the spring, Majella asked Eve to go shopping with her. She knew it would be so easy not to bother going out but didn't think Hugh would have wanted for her to hide away. She agreed to go. Her mind wandered as they drove along the countryside, she noted after a typical winter, the fields and hills looked battered, that just made the sight of the land coming back to life more enjoyable. She noticed daffodils in several front gardens, soon the fields would be dotted with lambs, always a heartening sight. Like nature, her life at the present time was beginning to come to life once again.

It was July and almost a year since Hugh passed away. Eve was up early and wanted to take a long walk on the promenade before the appointment with the therapist. The twins were helping Matilda in the guest house. She parked and stood out of the car; the sea was on her left and she watched as the grey, white-capped waves raced to dash themselves on to the shore, on her right were the amusement arcades and shops. She started to walk the length of the promenade, standing to look across the vast volume of water. Tears blurred her view as she remembered Hugh and their long walks here and it triggered a familiar stab of pain. When she turned back, there was a stiff breeze blowing and the tang of the salt air was invigorating. She stopped every so often and watched families out early with their children watching their dogs playing in the surf. There was the odd couple walking hand in hand, even the birds flocked together. At that moment, she felt so lonely and lost. She reached the car and looked at her watch realising it was almost time to head to the therapist. She reversed out of the car park and turned off at the prom driving along the seafront to where the house was situated. Crawling along and looking for a gold sign on a front door with the name Jack Grimes and some letters after his name, after driving around twice she spotted the little gold sign directly on the wall inside a glass-panelled door. She parked on the street outside, her stomach churned. Here she was seeking professional help for her grieving. He sounded nice on the phone with a kind soft voice, as she tried to reassure herself. She touched the bell once and it played a soft melody then stopped. A man opened the door. "Come in you must be Eve". "Yes," she nodded. He stretched out his hand. He was of medium height and slim build. His rich brown hair was sprinkled with silver. His eyes were bright and his smile highlighted a deep dimple on his chin. "Take a seat," he indicated to an armchair. The room was bright, the curtains moved with the breeze from the sea coming in through the slightly opened window. He sat on the chair opposite her. "How can I help you?" he asked. She was clasping her hands tightly on her lap. She explained about her husband's death and being left with the twins. She noticed he raised his eyebrows, "I will help you through your grief. We'll take it slowly at your pace. I must warn you it won't happen overnight it will be a slow process." He reassured her that anything she told him would be in strictest confidence. She continued to attend one session each week for the following twelve months, each time she left for home she felt the grief diminishing and her life was beginning to take shape once more, the twins had started college, one studying business, the other Arts, they were happy to stay with Eve as she let them have their independence and Julie bought them a car. Eve couldn't be happier to have them in her life, they were the best of friends. One winter's afternoon, Jack asked her to put on her coat "Maybe we could take a walk and breath in some of that fresh crisp sea air." "Why not?" she said as they walked, they chatted easily about the view, the people they saw, the weather, the birds flying overhead, it felt natural like being with a good friend. When they got back to his house, he suggested with his heart beating a little faster "Perhaps we could walk together regularly." "I'd like that very much," she said.

CHAPTER 18

For the following year they walked each week and talked. Eve's life began to take shape once more. It was now the third year attending Jack's practice and she didn't want her visits to end. She knew he had become part of her life. It was a dark April afternoon with a grey sky overhead, the waves on the sea front were lashing against the rocks. She noticed Jack different today he wasn't concentrating on the therapy instead she was aware of him trying to avoid making eye contact with her. He looked like a man that hadn't slept for days. There were frown lines out on his forehead and his eyes were wide and anxious. She tried to find something to say to break the tension between them. "Jack, I think my therapy sessions are coming to an end, you brought back my spirit when I thought it was gone forever. You found a sparkle and vitality within me and brought back a bubble of hope to my life. I can't thank you enough for everything you have done for me." She suddenly realised she wouldn't mind seeing him again next week but there was no excuse anymore. She turned around and picked up her bag. She held out her hand to say goodbye. He caught it in his but it wasn't to say goodbye, instead asking "Eve would you like to come for a drink with me, we could go across to the hotel." "Yes," she said too quickly.

In the lounge bar they sat by a window looking out at the people and traffic going back and forth. "A non-alcoholic wine will be fine for me," she said. It was an odd feeling to be out with a man having a drink. She had grown to trust this man over the past three years. He really was an amazing, lovely, and understanding person and they shared so much time together in chatter and laughter and tears. It was a life-saving experience for her. She could see his eyes focusing on hers over his beer glass. She dropped her gaze she didn't want to look into his eyes. Afterwards, they sat on the rocks and talked to the accompaniment of the waves rolling onto the shore

When Eve was home with her parents the following day they were delighted with their daughters bright outlook. It was proof if they ever needed it she was going to be ok, she'd worked hard on herself during counselling. She walked into her mother's office which she had converted back from a bedroom years ago now. "Have you bookings?" she asked "I always fret the park won't be full for the summer yet here we are again fully booked out for the season, thankfully. Now I can relax, Conor and Matilda will look after the B&B and leave me to look after the guest house. I can take the twins on for the summer, they are great to have around the place, a real energy about them and the money will come in handy for them." Life was looking good for Eve, she knew it would never be the same without Hugh but she was learning to live without him. Eve continued meeting Jack once a week for their walks and coffee break even though their counselling sessions had finished. She took up a part time position with a fashion designer in Galway. She didn't want to go back to work for Simon on account of the letter she received from him months ago about her husband's house, claiming the rights to it because he made some kind of agreement with Hugh to be named as a partner. Hugh had made it quite clear to her occasionally he was leaving it to the twins that was the reason he decided not to sell in it the first place, it was their future he said and Julie had given him that chance when she gave him the money to catch up on his repayments.

Eve was aware the letter she received from Simon wasn't worth the words spoken unless it was signed and sealed in a solicitor's office. Eve intended to go to Hugh's solicitor and sort it out but didn't get around to it yet. 'One day soon' she promised herself.

Eve more than liked Jack but wasn't sure where their friendship was going. One evening he asked her to dinner, after eating good food and drinking fine wine they walked under the sunset over a windswept bay. They kissed and cuddled and held hands and she felt more alive than she had in a very long time. She was hurt when he suddenly apologised for kissing her. She pretended that she felt the same, but a lump formed in her throat, she had wanted him to kiss her but now she felt foolish and believed that maybe he had only done it out of pity for her. He left his hands on his knees and leaned his chin on them and began to tell her more about his past, explaining that he was born in Wexford and that his parents immigrated to Australia when they were young, his younger brother still lives in Perth but he hasn't seen him since he went out to stay for a few months ten years ago. He continued to chat more about his parents and how much he missed them since their passing many years ago. He told her about Priscilla, the girl he met and left behind, because he couldn't settle out in Perth, as he always felt a drawback to Ireland and she wasn't prepared to come back to Ireland with him. He came home on his own and bought the house beside the sea and opened the practice he has today. She listened attentively. There was a sadness to his story which only served to endear her towards him more so, they stayed talking for longer without mentioning the kiss again before parting company.

The twins were nervous about starting in their first jobs; it was on occasions like this that Eve really missed Hugh. He would have been so proud of the girls who were growing up so fast. Eve was so thankful that they were in her life, she knew without them she would have struggled so much more with Hugh's death. Sometimes she felt as if their roles were reversed, that she was the child and they the parents, but without a question she loved them unconditionally. She reflected on when she first met them and her worry that she wouldn't be able to adjust to her new life, little did she know how much they would enrich her life.

Eve was more aware that her parents were getting on in years, not that they would ever admit that to her or themselves but they were slowing down which was expected as they were now in their seventies. Conor and Matilda were running the business exceptionally well with Julie and Eric in the background. They were still engaged and in no hurry to marry anytime soon. The twins had moved out and had secured apartments in Cork where they both worked. They made new friends quickly which didn't surprise Eve as they were very sociable, with Josephine even announcing last week that she met a nice guy and they were spending all their free time together.

Eve loved meeting Jack, they made each other laugh, and had the same interests, like hill walking, going to the theatre and galleries and spending evenings deciding what to watch on Netflix. Eve was falling for him but wondered was she just company for him because he gave no indication of any feelings towards her lately. On one of those days when they had been out walking earlier in the morning, Eve invited him to her house later that evening, she hoped it wasn't a step too far and was delighted when he agreed. She dressed with care in a pastel blue dress. She set a table outside in the shade of the large oak tree. She tried not to let her nerves show because she was excited that he was coming over. The August sun was low in the sky, with the clouds swimming around giving a real summer vibe to the evening. She sat outside waiting for him; the wine was chilling and the cheese and crackers with caviar were in dishes on the counter ready to serve. She had pulled out all the stops to impress him. Jack was an hour late which was out of the character for him. She walked around the garden, then went in and looked in the mirror fixing her hair with her hand and touching up her makeup. She went over to the countertop and lifted the tin foil from over the food and covered it again. She walked up to the window and peeped through the plant on the windowsill. Three hours later she was inside sitting in front of the unlit stove. She tried his phone for the tenth time 'no reply.' 'Where did he go? Why did he not turn up? Did something happen to him? Why was his phone unanswered?' She was sick to her stomach. She contemplated ringing the hospital or Gardaí, but didn't want to panic yet. There could be a perfectly reasonable explanation, maybe she really was only a passing friendship to him, and inviting him over for wine and food scared him away.

Later that night, she was lying in bed looking up at the ceiling deep in thought when her phone bleeped. She sat up sharply and switched on the bedside lamp. She read it over and over. That's unbelievable, she lay back and read the text again, 'So sorry I didn't get there tonight, I should have contacted you sooner, I will explain when we go walking next time' and he signed off 'your friend Jack.' She sat out on the side of the bed annoyed that he hadn't the courtesy of ringing her to inform her. 'That's it, it's obvious I'm only a friend to him, nothing else,' as she spoke out loud to herself. She was upset and wondered would she go walking with him ever again, she felt miserable because she knew she really liked him. Jack regretted having let Eve down, without as much as an explanation. She meant more to him than that and he knew he was acting cowardly. But he was hurt badly once before, and he had to make sure this was what he wanted. He was carrying a spark for Priscilla all those years and wasn't sure if it had fully quenched. He didn't want to hurt this beautiful woman he had gotten to know over the past few years.

His life was moving like a roller coaster but love seemed to be exempt from it. He felt sick to the pit of his stomach, and the familiar feelings of insecurity, rejection, fear and sadness threatened to overwhelm him. He shut his eyes and tried to snooze then he dreamt about Eve and hoped she would understand. She didn't. He chanced texting her but she didn't reply. As the week went by, she began to mellow slightly, he was good company, she liked him but seemingly he only considered their friendship as purely platonic based on the interests they had in common. Obviously, he didn't have romance on his mind. She decided to meet him after he sent her a text for the second time about joining him for their usual walk. They walked in silence for a short time then Eve said, "I don't know why you choose to let me down on the evening we were to spend together without even a text. I felt so confused and hurt that you didn't even phone me to explain. Imagine having food and wine ready and you just not turning up, how do you think that made me feel?" He apologised and went on to tell her of his life so far leaving out the small piece about his feelings for Priscilla. After hearing his insecurities she felt sorry for him and pondered for a moment silently. She said, "It is unbelievable that a therapist who tries to fix everybody else can have issues himself and yet be so professional at his job." They continued to walk on briskly. Before they parted company, she told him she was going on holidays with the twins the following weekend. He didn't make a date but said he would contact her when she returned. He seemed lost and sad as they parted company oblivious to each other's feelings.

CHAPTER 19

The weekend had arrived and Eve and the twins were boarding a flight to Crete to arrive late evening. After a good night's sleep they sat out on the balcony of the cabin they had rented. It was every bit as good as it looked on the website. It had a large living room and kitchen, bathroom, shower and two bedrooms. It was positioned away from other cabins and surrounded by trees. The spa bath was roomy and great to relax in after the day's activities. The balcony was positioned looking down on the hillside across the ochre earth, striped with rows of dark green olive trees. In the distance, it was possible to see the mountains and the sea. In the evening time the twins sipped their drinks and agreed it was a fantastic place to come for a holiday. Eve was thrilled with the companionship of the girls. The peace and beauty gave her time to think, unwind and relax. She enjoyed the village with its pale buildings and tiled roofs. The cobbled square had a fountain in the centre surrounded by cafes and Eve had sampled coffee in almost all of them by the end of the week. The cabin was a short distance from the hotel's amenities and a little further down was the beach. The days took on a routine of sightseeing, exploring historical places and browsing around the many various shops in the village. They returned to the cabin each evening to laze on the deck and spend some time sunbathing. She missed Jack and thought about him and hoped maybe he missed her too.

It was mid-September and Jack hadn't contacted Eve since she came back from holidays, coming up on three weeks tomorrow. She missed his caring and considerate way, listening when she wanted to talk, making her laugh when she was feeling down. It was the last week of September and Matilda and Conor had organised a party for Eric and Julie who were fifty years married. Luckily, the forecast was predicting warm temperatures up to late evening, meaning that they could transform the back garden into the perfect place for an autumn party. There were flowers and balloons everywhere, with candles on all tables ready to be lit. A long table was set up where Matilda was laying out platters of delicious finger food. The twins looked amazing and were enjoying themselves mixing large pitchers of cocktails. Conor was in the background playing an eclectic mix of songs for all ages through a speaker via his phone. The place was buzzing with happy chatter. Eve lifted two glasses of champagne from a tray carried around by Josephine and handed them to her parents. She went over and took one for herself "Here's to our parents," she declared then the sound of glasses clinking together filled the garden. Matilda was watching out for Jack to arrive. She encouraged Eve last week to invite him to the party if she was keen on him. "Go on, it will be an excuse to see him." By midnight everybody had gone home and Jack hadn't appeared. Matilda had a feeling Eve didn't invite him and on reflection maybe it was the absolutely correct thing to do when he made no contact with her over the past while.

One cold October afternoon, Eve went walking along the cliff edge, after a short distance she veered off on to a grassy track which climbed steadily between windswept trees and overgrown bushes. It was a place she came to on occasion when she was at a crossroads and needed time to think. Positioning herself on the wooden bench halfway up, she gazed across at the vast expanse of the Atlantic ocean. She sat there for a long while with her mind in limbo "Hi," a voice said and Eve jumped. "Sorry, I didn't mean to startle you," he added. Eve found herself looking into the cheerful face of a brown-haired man with eyes as blue as the water below. "I sometimes like to take a walk along this path," she said as if trying to justify her actions. "I haven't noticed you walking here before," he said. She wasn't sure how to reply. "The view is something special isn't it?" she remarked. "I grew up not far from here, my parents own the caravan park up the road. I was just about to head home." "Please, don't rush off because of me, you only just arrived," the man said. "What can I call you?" "Eve," she said reluctantly, not knowing what to make of the exchange. He stretched out his hand "And I am Garrett, I'm an artist and live alone, not too far away," as he pointed down the hill. "It's the perfect setting for an artist to

165

live, you must have no problem painting here," she said. He produced a business card 'seascapes and portraits' she read. She was handing it back to him. "Keep it, I've a habit of handing them out to anyone I meet." He didn't ask her anything about herself and she was glad. He stayed for a short time "I should leave, you came up here for solitude and I'm intruding on your precious time." He turned and started to walk away, calling back over his shoulder "Feel free to drop in for a coffee on your way back, if you fancy a hot drink, my rented cottage is at the brow of the hill." "Maybe the next time," she said as she watched him stride away. As he walked away from her, she felt a renewed energy. She sat back on the bench and gazed once more at the trees now blowing in the gentle breeze. Her thoughts and emotions had suddenly stopped tumbling over. Suddenly she sat with a clearer mind and she could feel the tension ebbing from her. The small chat from a stranger had cheered her up and taken her out of her thoughts for a while.

The shrill cry of a seagull reminded her it was getting late and it was time to be heading home. She was walking at a fast pace until she slowed down to look over in the direction of the artist's cottage. 'Would she take him up on his offer for coffee, a perfect stranger; maybe the next time she thought.' The following week as it was nearing early evening Eve decided to go for a walk but wasn't sure what direction she would head towards, eventually she decided to veer towards the cliff walk. After walking for an hour she had a thought, to call over for the coffee Garrett had invited her for the first day they met. She walked over to the house knocked twice and walked into the little hall inside. He heard the door open and walked out to where she was waiting to hear his voice. "Eve, what a surprise to see you, I take it you were you out walking." "I was and decided I'd call to say hello." He brought her into the living room where there was a stack of blank canvases behind the door and paintings hanging on the back wall. She took the opportunity to view them while he poured the coffee. The seascapes were simple but stunning, particularly the way he managed to capture the light through the breaking waves. He came into the room and handed her the coffee with a heart-stopping smile. "You're a very talented artist, these are amazing," she remarked as she continued to admire his work. She stayed a long while with him and chatted over several cups of coffee, it was early afternoon and Eve was afraid she might have outstayed her visit. The time had passed so fast, they got lost in conversation, it was like as if they had known each other for years and were catching up on their lives having not been in contact with each other for some time. Before she left, she was puzzled when he said "Call again, if I'm still here you will be welcome for coffee." "Where else would you be then Garrett?" "I'm hoping to be able to move in with my sister. I won't be able to afford this place for much longer." Eve wondered at that. He mentioned earlier in conversation that he had a younger sister but wasn't in contact with her after he left home, then unfortunately he was homeless for a period and he never heard from her. She didn't pry anymore or ask where his sister lived. She looked at her Fitbit, he laughed, "Are you checking to see if you got your steps in today?" "No, not at all just checking how long I've been here." She could hardly believe that she had been in his company for four hours. As she looked out the window, she realised it was getting dark so Garrett offered to walk her back to her car. The sea that was raging earlier, had calmed down considerably. The waves were gently lapping on the beach as they walked along to the soothing flow of the water. When they reached the car Garrett said, "Stand and watch the copper sun begin its decent, look as it leaves in its wake, a fiery red sky." They watched until it sank below the waterline and the sky turned violet and indigo. Eve went home feeling confused and thought maybe she'd better refrain from going for coffee again but yet she walked each week up the same path but she never saw Garrett. Jack contacted Eve just before Christmas and when he spoke she knew he was finishing their friendship, "It is for the best," he said. She cried all night with disappointment even though she knew that deep down it would probably not work.

Garrett paused on the path and looked towards the sea shimmering in the sunshine thinking, one would imagine it was dancing to the tune of the gulls in full cry, and the whip of the liners going out to sea. It was early spring and Garrett wondered if Eve and Jack had moved in together. She told him all about her marriage to Hugh and meeting Jack. He liked her and wondered why she never called again.

CHAPTER 20

The month of June slipped in like a thief in the night and Eve breathed a sigh of relief as she slid off her shoes and sank into the cushioned depths of her sofa thankful that another long working day was over. She took an appreciative sip of her take away coffee that she had grabbed at the filling station on her way home. Even though the temperatures outside were hitting the early twenties, there was nothing like a mug of hot coffee to revive you. The peace was invigorating and she lay back and closed her eyes. Suddenly her phone rang and her peace was disturbed. She jumped up and went to her jacked pocket and tried to get it out before the caller hung up, it might be one of her parents or even the twins. "Hi Eve, it's me, Jack." It took her a few seconds to register who it was, he sounded so casual she couldn't believe her ears. Her heart sank slightly at the sound of his voice because she was almost over him and she was doing her best to move on. "Hey, didn't expect to hear from you." He noticed Eve's voice was a little sharp with him. "I'm sorry Jack, I've just got in from work, I'm very, very tired and need to put my feet up for a while." "Ok." He continued to say "Would you like to meet for a chat?" "Let me think about it, but not now, maybe contact me next week." He got the message loud and clear, "Ok let's talk next week," he said. She said bye to him and hung up feeling frustrated. She went outside and sat on the back step looking at the garden as she finished her coffee. The evening shadows stretched across the grass and she could hear a couple of blackbirds frolicking around under the overgrown bushes. The whole place could do with a tidying up perhaps she'd bite the bullet and have a go at it next weekend she thought. Finishing her cup of coffee she got up and went back inside, tired from the day's work and annoyed that Jack felt he could play with her emotions like that. After catching up on her favourite soap, Coronation Street she decided to have an early night.

Julie was worried about Conor lately, she noticed he was withdrawn and not taking an interest in the business as usual. Eve was over the following evening and she could see a distressed look on her mother's face. Her parents were under pressure when she arrived as they explained that Conor and Matilda were away all day even though the park and guest house were full. It frustrated Eve to see them in that situation especially as they were getting older. When she asked was there anything wrong her father said "Conor and Matilda take off regularly and leave us in charge." He continued to say, "Friction is starting to build between Conor and Matilda for the past few months." Julie found it hard to swallow with the lump in her throat she managed to say, 'I hope they don't split up." She looked thoughtfully at her daughter, "Maybe we rely on them too much." Eve was raging, "For God sake if they are taking over the business full time, they have to get used to the long working hours that goes with it. When they return leave them at it and take a break." Eric responded "I have no interest in going away I'd prefer to spend time in the garden." He suggested to Eve, "You and Julie could go away for a few nights to a hotel and relax." So that was what they decided to do. When Conor and Matilda returned mother and daughter headed for Galway. They were no sooner gone when Conor let his father know Matilda was away again for a few hours but would be back to look after the guests in the morning. He was annoyed but kept tight-lipped. Julie and Eve shopped, browsed and drank coffee until evening. It rained for most of the day but as they arrive at the Galway Bay hotel, the rain had stopped. The grey clouds have already begun to disappear revealing a brighter sky, the air became significantly warmer and they could get the scent of the seaweed by the ocean. Julie sat in the reception area while Eve went to the desk to book in for two nights. Julie was enjoying her surroundings and delighted to be out and about for three days without having to book in guests, make beds or cook breakfasts. The receptionist frowned slightly and began to tap her computer terminal with her long pillar-boxed-red nails. "I'm so sorry but we are fully booked out." Eve looked at her in disbelief thinking, the receptionist cuts across Eve's thoughts, "We have a group in for a conference," she explains apologetically. "So there is no room vacant. I'm sorry." Eve felt her composure begin to crack. The receptionist detected the disappointment on Eve's face and continued to view the screen in front of her. "Let me see if there is a vacancy in one of the other hotels" she said. After a few seconds, she had located one on the other side of the city. She gave her the name of it. Eve was very thankful and booked it right away. She had no doubt about the hotel being crowded because there were people in all corners chatting, laughing, drinking coffee, all holding folders, brief cases and laptops. She wondered what the conference was about? As they were walking out of the hotel, Eve thought she spotted Matilda, standing among a group of women and men dressed up in suits. She decided against going over to her as she didn't want to distract her if she was attending a work event and she wanted to give her attention to her mother. She also knew that her mother would be concerned and worried that Matilda should be in the guest house with the Conor and Eric helping them and not at a conference.

CHAPTER 21

The following evening after Julie and Eve finished dinner they went to relax in a detoxifying seaweed bath. Julie was more than happy to spend the rest of the night reading. Eve wanted to buy her an iPad last year to be able to access eBooks but her mother insisted she'd rather have a book in her hand. She would miss holding it and the look of the printed pages, she reckoned an electronic gadget could never replace a book for her. Books were 'like a warm embrace of a good friend' she said. Eve chilled out on the balcony of the hotel room. Her phone rang she answered it to Jack saying, "Hi Eve, I know it's late, I hope I didn't alarm you but I'm going to Cork tomorrow morning and even though it is short notice, I'd like if you would come with me. We need to talk." "Jack, I can't because I'm in Galway enjoying a break with my mother." He sounded frustrated. "I'll contact you as soon as I get back." She wondered why now so suddenly after having no contact for the past months. Then she heard him say before he clicked off. "I want us to go walking again like we used to, remember." She sat there staring over the city and began thinking about what Jack wanted, the problem at home with her brother and Matilda before eventually going into bed. Her eyes were getting heavy and beginning to close and she fell into a deep sleep. During breakfast the next morning Eve noted her mother was pale and tired looking, with anxiety etched on her face. Her eyes red and faced flushed. There is something I have to tell you before we go home I can't hide it anymore. Eve was shocked at what she heard, "I find it hard to believe it," she said. "Look mother we'll talk about it when we go home, try to enjoy the time we have left. I'll come over tomorrow evening after I leave the office and maybe Conor and Matilda will be there, don't worry yourself too much it will work itself out wait and see." Eve's stomach was churning as she spoke to herself 'this can't be happening, what is Matilda thinking about, she is engaged to my brother but that doesn't give her to right to do what she is doing, I'll put a stop to that.' Her mind was on what her mother had told her and it troubled her.

Sitting in the office the next morning, sipping her coffee while gazing out the window, Eve had a slender view of Lough Corrib and could see the sparkle of the sun on the water. She found it hard to dislodge her thoughts from Matilda and Conor. As the office filled up with workers, she hauled herself back to the present and took a large sip of coffee and did her best to concentrate on her work in hand. Jack's text came in around noon but she didn't respond to it. Instead, she decided to leave it until the following morning, she wasn't quite ready to meet up with him yet. She was going to her parent's house after work because she had promised her mother she would try to iron out the problems they were having with Matilda. Eve went back to her own house for a warm shower after she finished work hoping it would ease the tension from her tired shoulders and revive her before she called over home, she wanted nothing more than to fall into the couch, but she had to put a stop to what Matilda was planning on doing it was ludicrous.

Just as she reached the hot press to get a clean towel her phone rang again. She groaned and snapped it up and answered it sharply. Her exasperation was heightened ever more when she heard Jack's voice. She didn't have time to talk now because she couldn't think straight. "Hello Jack," she didn't give him time to speak or encourage a conversation instead she said "I'm on my way out." "You say you are going out." "Yes, sorry about that Jack. Was there something you wanted?" "Well, actually I was going to ask...." his voice trailed off. Eve felt a wave of irritation. "Ask me what?" Silence. "Jack I'm sorry but I really do have to go." She took her keys off the shelf in her room and fumbled with them. "I was actually going to invite you to afternoon tea tomorrow and a stroll in the park." "I'm not off tomorrow but I'll meet you the following afternoon."

She arrived home to her mother and father who were sitting out in the conservatory; they looked confused. Conor and Matilda had just joined them and they were no doubt on tender hooks as well. Eve called her mother outside,

"Do you think you misunderstood Matilda, surely Conor would have asked if it would be alright." "I understood everything," she said "Let's go back inside." As they walked in the door Eve noticed her brothers face drawn and tense as if he'd not slept well. Matilda seemed equally on edge. Conor tried to smile. There was an uneasy look between the two of them. Conor spoke first. "Matilda will explain everything." Julie or Eric didn't speak. Matilda spoke up in a very matter-of-fact tone and informed them, "It is like this, I have an older brother whom I lost contact with years ago, he got in touch with me a while back and told me he was searching for me for the past couple of years. Finally, through a friend of his in an art gallery he tracked me down. He has changed so much in the years since I last met him I think if met him on the street I would hardly know him. He is an artist, and lives in a rented cottage, in the woods close by, it is overlooking the sea. She looked at Eve you know the place you go walking there sometimes." Eve was speechless. "What's his name?" Eve was almost afraid to ask. "Garrett Hamilton, he is cash trapped and is being evicted so he has to leave the cottage before the end of the month." Eric said spontaneously, "Let him get a job then he will pay his way." "It's no use, he will still have to leave, the landlord won't rent the house to him under any circumstances after falling behind in rent, he is ten months in arrears." Eve was shocked. Conor still didn't speak. Matilda continued in a high-pitched voice, "I don't want to see him homeless, that is why I offered him one of the apartments Conor built last year." She was explaining with her hands in the air, "He is an artist and will hopefully sell some paintings in the future and pay Conor for the rent of his apartment." Conor was rubbing his hands nervously together and the sweat was visible on his forehead. His parents' faces told their own story. Eve was livid and spouted out, "That's not happening. You had no right to take advantage of my brother's property. Garrett will have to sort himself out but he won't be staying here." She couldn't believe the charming man she met in the cottage was being evicted and about to move into her home place. He was without a doubt taking advantage of his sister's husband to be. She liked him but not the situation that he was forcing them into.

Matilda admitted she knew nothing about him at all. "He can't move in here I'm sorry, we know nothing about him" Eric was stern. Eve caught Matilda's eye and realised she was on the verge of tears. But more noticeable was that Conor looked upset. Eve felt sorry for him knowing that he was feeling caught between his parents and Matilda. No matter who he sided with he was going to upset someone. He knew Matilda's parents separated when she was young and that she had lost contact with her father not long after that. Eventually, her mother met another man, an American and went to live there she didn't keep in contact with her mother either and has no clue where either of them are to this day. She hadn't mentioned she had a brother, only recently when Garrett went looking for her did she tell Conor about him. He was baffled, what else was she keeping from him he wondered?

CHAPTER 22

Eve left work late on a damp Thursday evening, she had arranged to meet Jack after all this time apart. She put the car into gear and headed off through the heavy traffic towards the park down by the sea's edge where she was meeting him. As soon as she caught sight of the sea, she smiled. She loved the way the sunlight breaks up on the water and shatters into a million sparkles, and the sense of infinity the sea brings. She travelled on. She was looking forward to a leisurely walk and perhaps getting back on track with their friendship, she still liked him and he was an excellent listener. She certainly wasn't ready for a brisk walk today. She just needed to clear her lungs and refresh her brain with clean fresh air and get clarity on what exactly Jack wanted.

When she drove into the car park, she spotted him walking down towards her briskly. Eve's energy levels were low because of the worry she was having about home and a long walk was far from her agenda. She looked up at the sky and remarked it had turned an ugly shade of grey. He ignored her remark, "Lock the car and come on it won't rain." They walked slowly then he got faster and faster, Eve found it difficult to keep up with him. As they walked, they talked but she soon noticed he was babbling on about himself and wasn't listening to her at all. She wondered what happened to the Jack that used to listen to her every woe. They were halfway down the trail when the heavens opened and thunder rumbled in the distance. They turned back but the rain pelted down furiously and they were saturated. When they reached her car, she unlocked it and pulled of her jacket and ran her hands through her dripping hair she sat in and banged the door and let down the window. "I need to go home and shower and change." Jack suggested, "I was hoping we could meet later in the evening when you have changed and showered for a bite to eat. It is great to have you back in my life." She looked at him coldly, "Who told you I was back in your life, you haven't discussed anything with me." "I presumed when you agreed to meet and go walking we were good again." "Well you presumed wrong." She was aggravated and declined the invitation. He felt frustrated and wondered what happened or why she was giving him the cold shoulder, he was doing his best to please her. The meeting with Jack didn't go well and she wasn't interested in going out with him again, he had changed and maybe she had too.

Eve was having lunch with clients when she noticed her phone ringing, she had it on silent. She saw Julie's name on the screen and went out and answered it. Eve couldn't hear what she was saying she was inconsolable on the other end and wouldn't calm down but she knew by the tone of her voice it was serious. "I'll get there as soon as possible," and she hung up. She went back in to the table where the meeting was taking place explaining that she needed to go home for a family emergency. Arriving at the house, she drove up to the door and rushed inside. "What has happened?" she asked her father who was standing inside the kitchen window. He pointed over to the apartment "He's moving in, there's the removal van, we saw two men unload his stuff." Eve looked around, "Where is Mum gone?" "She went down to stop them unloading his belongings; she is in an awful state. With that Julie came back in the door and she was frantic. "I want him out now, they can't do this to us. Eve, why didn't you come down and back me up?" "I only just came in, calm down and let me think." Eric said "Conor is afraid he will lose Matilda if he refuses to let Garrett move in, he told me so last night." Eve was maddened and rang Matilda. She could see her through the window of the apartment occupied by her brother. She didn't answer. Her parents were standing beside Eve. "She is probably watching the screen on the phone and ignoring me." She stabbed at the button to end the call then redialled again then she answered. "Hi Eve, I'll hand over to your brother." She waited to hear his voice 'Have you taken leave of your senses letting Garrett move into that apartment?" She did her utmost to get him to listen. "I'm coming over to talk to you Conor, go to the office." She was making sure she didn't have to go near the apartment that Garrett had just occupied; under no circumstances did she want to run into him like this. He would also have discovered at this stage that she was Conor's sister.

She walked over in an aggravated state and into the office where her brother was standing. As she rushed in the door, her brother sat down and began studying the screen of his computer. Eve was fuming. Conor kept studying the screen without acknowledging her. "Talk to Matilda tonight about her brother, he can't stay here indefinitely he should never have moved in." "What am I supposed to do, throw out my fiancée's brother on the street? Come on, Eve surely you have a heart." "Of course I do Conor, but you're upsetting our parents, they built this place up to what it is today and so did you. Matilda is only a short time here, she has no right to let her brother move in. Mum and Dad should have been consulted first. You can't just spring something like this on them." "I didn't want to tell you but now I'm forced to let you and our parents know Matilda put up the money for the apartments so she has every right to let her brother stay indefinitely," he was shouting angrily at her. Eve was shocked "You mean to say Matilda owns those new buildings?" "That's right. So I have to keep my slate clean in case I lose her." "It would be very complicated if you did," Eve continued, "Because the land they are built on is yours. You shouldn't have let her build them in those circumstances. What happens if it does not work out in the long run, what does it mean for us all?" Conor wouldn't listen, "I don't want to talk about that now, all I know is that Garrett is here to stay for a period, anyway."

She realised her brother was refusing to feel the least bit guilty and she left him and went back up to her parents to explain the plight Conor got himself into. They were fuming. Eric got up and was about to go down and cause a terrible row until Julie restrained him advising that it was not the way to deal with the situation. Eve was in a rage, what was Conor thinking, he would have had to sign many amounts of documents for the planning permission to go through, on account of the land being in his name. They sat and talked into the early hours of the morning and could come up with no solution only to accept that Garrett had moved into the apartment and couldn't be evicted for the foreseeable future.

The sunlight that came streaming through giant petals in Eve's garden sent shafts of peach, rose, and ruby on to the white floor tiles and it made her mood lighter. The door was open, Jack walked in cheerfully she was surprised to see him. He walked over to where she was dusting the top of the microwave. "Hope you don't mind me walking in on you unannounced" he quipped. She thought, the impertinence of him to walk in to her home without being invited. She was equally vexed when he said, "Thought I'd surprise you rather than ringing, it's not the same chatting on the phone especially after our last meeting on that windy wet day." Annoyed, Eve replied, "I would have preferred if you had called me first Jack. I don't like anybody surprising me," she was stubborn and fighting the feelings she had for him.

CHAPTER 23

Two days after Jack's surprise visit they met and walked on the Silver Strand, each immersed in their own thoughts. Eve noted huge white and grey clouds, edged with navy and grey, billowing over the sea like the smoke above a volcano, the waves were getting bigger and crashing on to the sand in a jumble of white foam; she gave a shiver as the wind picked up. He took off his jacket and put it over her shoulders as they walked along. Eventually, they turned back. Eve thanked him for the few hours out walking. They didn't arrange to meet again and Jack didn't know where they stood as Eve walked off, got into her car and drove out of the car park.

It was a mild and muggy evening even though it was only mid-August it felt more like the end of September. Eve was on her way over to visit her parents who were doing their utmost to come up with a plan to improve their business which had taken a downturn recently. After Eve and her parents sat down with cups of tea, they looked at each other neither one knowing what to say. Julie started off, "We see little of Conor and Matilda. The guest house is quiet this week but we have bookings for next month. The festival is on in town so hopefully that will bring in some much needed revenue. Your father said Conor seemed to be happy with the park even though it is not fully booked out. I think him and Matilda are planning on coming up with a plan to advertise on social media." She was hesitant to ask about Garrett, but didn't have to because her mother said, "Garrett is fully settled into the apartment, Conor and Matilda are working as usual as if he was part of the place and taking it for granted that everything is hunky dory." Eric was agitated and said, "We don't have a clue how to address the issue without causing a scene and with Conor and Matilda leaving us in limbo, we have to grin and bear it for now."

The back door opened and Conor rushed in and over to where his parents and sister were sitting near the big window. "Look he said," and scrolled down through his phone "What do ye think of these pictures I took today of the place? I was thinking of putting them up on social media to advertise for guests. I also intend to get brochures printed to leave into the tourist office." They were engrossed when the door opened again and in walked Garrett and his sister. Eve wondered how he had the cheek to come up to her parents uninvited when there was a family matter being discussed. She kept studying her brother's phone and didn't look up at all. Then, Conor took his phone from Eve and passed it to Garrett who began studying the images. Eve looked across at him. He had handsome features no doubt. She noted his eyes were intense in their concentration and a muscle twitched across his tanned cheek. "They're wonderful images,' he said. "You might get away with them on the website, but the quality isn't good enough for a brochure. I'll take photos in the morning when the sun is shining." Eve was reluctant but Conor was agreeable and Matilda was chuffed that her brother was taking an interest in the business's advertising. Matilda brightened up and said "Well taken photos give people an insight into what a place is like, Garrett suggested having a promotional day. We could get caterers in, lay tables in the apartments and offer simple refreshments as people walk through." Julie and Eric were in the background listening and saying nothing as they didn't want to spoil Conor's chances of getting the business up and running again. Conor was enthusiastic about the plan. Everything seemed to fall into place for them. Eve said without looking at Garrett, "It could work alright." Julie felt the rug was being pulled out from under her and Eric. Garrett was all business, "Okay, I can have the brochures printed out tomorrow afternoon, we'll meet here tomorrow evening and decide what path to take, all agreed?" Eric and Julie went with it but felt ignored. Eve asked "How would be possible to get brochures printed so quickly?" He smiled one of those wide smiles at her "I have contacts Eve, I promise I will have them on the table by tomorrow evening," he held her gaze until she looked away. The following evening they viewed the brochures. Julie and Eric were impressed but didn't voice their opinions. Conor and Matilda were over the moon. Eve kept in the background away from where Garrett was sitting. "What do you think Eve?" Garrett asked and as he looked at her his eyes lit up. She sensed her colour rise "I really like what you have come up with." Eric agreed the strategy was well thought out, "Fair play to you Garrett." Julie nodded in agreement, then she crossed the kitchen and opened the conservatory door feeling the immediate rush of crisp air refresh her senses.

Today was the open day and it was all hands on deck. The twins stayed overnight with their grandparents so that they could help. The caterers were moving into the park, Conor and Matilda were hanging balloons, signs and bunting all along the buildings, Garrett was opening the doors of each apartment and helping to put tables together to display the food and drinks. Eve had just arrived when Garrett walked over to her and asked would she pass a brochure to each person as they entered through the electric gates. She wasn't impressed being asked by him but didn't want to put a spanner in the works and said "Yeah," but he noticed her being standoffish. An enormous crowd turned up and the day turned out to be very successful with multiple bookings taken for the following year. The family were over the moon with the success. The group of people representing the tourist board were very impressed and one person was designated to speak and thank the owners for the open day. A tall man stood out from the group and started off by saying "Thank you to all concerned for a most enjoyable day, I speak on behalf of the tourist board when I say we will recommend this facility to tourists and clients. There's something really special and welcoming about the place. A big thank you to the family for been so charming and for your hospitality." The man speaking did not know who Garrett was but praised him for his attention to detail. Julie and Eric had to agree they were impressed by Garrett's business skills, he was a real people person, engaging with the crowd and everybody took to his charming ways.

That evening after the place quietened down and the caterers had packed up and left, Julie cooked a light meal for the family and asked Garrett to join them, he declined at first but after some persuasion from his sister he agreed. Eve was in the conservatory when Garrett walked in and up close to her. "Was everything up to scratch for the family?" he asked. She looked out the window saying "They are an impressive bunch, those caterers." She turned and looked at him "You've done immensely well, you know," Garrett moved closer and she

181

was a little disturbed by his proximity. "Thanks," he said, "I hope it's enough to encourage more business in. Letting people see they are welcome and will be looked after is key to making any business successful." Conor and Matilda came just as Eve said to Garrett. "You were really invested in this today weren't you," Eve was scrutinising his expression. His voice was almost a whisper, "I'm just helping in lieu of the apartment." And with that Julie called them all to eat. As they turned to walk into the kitchen Garrett stalled, "I don't suppose you fancy going for a drink later," he asked? Eve took a slight step backwards and replied, "Thank you for the invite but maybe some other time, the twins are staying with me for a few days so I had better go back with them. We haven't been together for a while and I am really looking forward to chilling out and catching up with them." He nodded swiftly saying he understood but his smile was hesitant and disappointed with the reaction. Then, they all had dinner as they analysed the day before going their separate ways.

CHAPTER 24

Despite wearing flat shoes with cushioned insoles to work, Eve's feet were throbbing by three o'clock. It was hard going having to get stock organised in time for the weekend and attend two meetings. Five o'clock came at last and she was making her way towards her car with thoughts of a long soak in a hot bath and a plate of hot buttered pancakes when she heard a voice call her name. She turned and her heart sank when she saw Jack coming towards her. "What are you doing here?" she hoped her voice didn't betray her exasperation. "I was waiting for you." There was a wide smile on his face. "Do you have time for a chat?" he asked. "I'm pretty tired to be honest," she replied. Eve hoped he'd get the message, but he didn't. "Come across to the cafe for a cup of tea." She went with him and he ordered tea for two. They were sitting down for a second when she said. "Is there's something you want to tell me? She prompted, "Yes there is, but first I want to apologise." She was ratty, "For what...?" "For not contacting you after our walk on the Silver strand, to be honest I was in limbo where you and I stood." She looked at him questionably, "What do you mean?" He started to talk "I thought you were giving me the brush off lately, so..." He stopped talking because a woman walked down beside the table close to him. She stopped, he looked blankly at her, "Hello Jack," Eve couldn't fail to notice the warmth in her smile as if they had some kind of connection. The woman was staring at him, waiting for a response. Eve noted a momentary flick of the woman's eyes in her direction and was starting to feel uncomfortable with the situation. Jack stood up and looked directly at the woman. "This is my friend Eve," she noted how he leaned on the friend bit,

"And this is Priscilla Nixon she is home from Australia on holidays as she is studying law and took a few months out." Priscilla and Eve greeted each other. Jack was filled with a mixture of guilt and embarrassment.

Priscilla pondered for a second then asked to be excused and walked off. Jack sat down. Eve leaned over "Now everything makes sense. For a moment when you turned up out of the blue I thought you'd come to see me because you enjoyed my company, but no you wanted to introduce me to your Australian girlfriend." "I wanted you to know that Priscilla the girl I left behind in Australia has come back into my life. I never expected you to learn it like this." Eve remained tight-lipped. She was jealous of Priscilla and didn't feel like holding a conversation with him. "This is the end of the road for us so, I take it Jack." He left his hand on hers she whipped it away. "Keep your hands to yourself," she felt dejected. She stood up, snatched her bag off the back of her chair and walked out leaving him sitting there.

CHAPTER 25

The months had passed since Jack had surprised Eve in Galway. She hadn't been in contact with him since, but no doubt he was happy now that his long-lost girlfriend was back in his arms. The April breeze was blowing lightly with the sun beginning to play on the lily of the valley in their beds. The scent filled the narrow space in the corner of her garden and she inhaled it and smiled. The twins were just gone back to work after a week at home, which they spent lazing around and meeting up with friends. When the boyfriends came to stay for a few nights, she disappeared into the background. Eve enjoyed their company and they kept her young at heart. She missed them when they were gone but knew they would always be there for her if she needed them. Eve asked Matilda to be prepared to meet three guests booking in tomorrow midday because Eric and Julie would be away for the day and Conor would be busy down at the park. Matilda was hesitant "I'm a little nervous because Julie always interviews guests before taking a booking but I'm not familiar with that part of the business yet. I have no experience at all." Eve was serious when she said, "You need to meet and greet the guests because that is the most important part of taking bookings." Eve promised, "I'll be in the background if you need me, but I know you will be great. Vetting the guests will let you know if they are suitable to stay here and always trust your instincts. Start by asking them their name and the reason they are staying. Are they on holiday or travelling on business?" The following afternoon the guests arrived and Eve encouraged Matilda go ahead wishing her good luck. Eve listened to the door opening and she heard a man's voice say, "Sorry we are late but we had

185

a meeting to attend and it ran." Eve noted the man's warm deep tones. She could hear Matilda saying. "Come through to the living room." Her welcoming voice drifted in from the hall. Eve wondered why only one man spoke and it seemed Matilda was directing the conversation towards him when she asked him "Would you like the room with the garden view?" "That would be great," he replied. Eve could tell he was smiling. She wished Matilda took their details and names before directing them to their rooms. Then she heard one of the other men introduce the trio, "I'm Philip Charter, this is Bruce Sussex and Andrew White, we are attending a conference in Galway, it is a follow on to one we were at a while ago." Matilda seemed to be familiar with Andrew White because when he said "I was going to find a hotel for us but when I heard about here, I thought it would be suitable."

Matilda blurted out, "Delighted you decided on coming here Andrew," then she thought of what she was saying and stopped. After that Eve could hear Matilda rummaging, "Just a moment," she said while turning on the computer. 'That's it,' Eve remembered back to the evening she spotted Matilda in the hotel in Galway. She'd known it was her and now it was making sense. She listened as Matilda clattered about making tea and tipping biscuits on to a plate. Philip and Bruce brought their tea to the room saying, "If it's alright with you it has been a long day and we'd like to shower and relax for the evening." Of course, I understand." Matilda continued talking to Andrew then their voices faded and Eve listened to their footsteps going towards the front bedroom. She even imagined there was a whisper but wasn't sure if her mind was playing tricks. She listened and was shocked at what she heard him say to Matilda. He was flirting with her. She knew when he said, "I wouldn't mind spending the evening with you." Matilda responded, "Like we did in the hotel after the last conference." She came back into the kitchen where Eve was standing. She was drowning Eve with information. Matilda did not know Eve heard everything. Matilda continued to say, "They are on business and attending a conference in Galway." Matilda was all business herself. "I'm going home. Eve had a headache and just needed to leave" What was she going to do now? Would she tell her brother about Matilda's carry on or hold back and see what would unfold?

Conor came to rely on Garrett's help lately, because Matilda was away most of the time. He was an excellent business man and he kept the ship afloat while Conor and Matilda attended counselling sessions to fix their rocky relationship. The disagreements between them became more frequent, and each time Matilda would threaten to sell the apartments. In order to keep her happy, Conor took her away for weekend breaks, booking into expensive hotels and lavish restaurants to eat, but it was to no avail they still fought and couldn't seem to see eye to eye in anything lately. They weren't getting along for a while, but in the past six months Matilda was impossible to live with. Conor wasn't sure what caused her to be so unsettled. Eventually, after another one of their raging rows she moved out.

Conor was devastated when he got up on a frosty October morning to find a note on the table with the engagement ring left on top of it. He read the note saying she had moved on with somebody else and that they were finished. Then he freaked out when he read the last part, 'I am contacting my solicitor and will converse with you through him as regards my apartments. We haven't been getting on for ages and you don't listen to anything I have to say, so what's the point of staying together? We are different people, so it's for best we go our separate ways.' Beads of sweat came through his forehead and he felt his legs almost buckle. He didn't know where to turn how was he going to tell his parents, or sister? Did her brother Garrett know she was leaving him? He tried her phone there was no reply, he text but still no response. He walked up to Garrett's apartment and after knocking twice Garrett opened the door. "Come in Conor. What happened you look like as if you have seen a ghost." He leaned against the wall and began telling him what happened and asking if his sister had divulged any of this to him. Garrett knew nothing and was furious at his sister for walking out on Conor. "She can't just up and go away like this. Leave her to me and I will see what is going on." He told Conor not to mention this to his parents yet. Conor went back up to his office, feeling a tiny flicker of hope. The day at work went by smoothly, which helped him. It was evening time and he spotted Garrett driving up towards the caravan park and waited outside at the hedge for him. Within the next few minutes the flicker of hope Conor had was extinguished when he heard she had moved in with another man. Garrett continued. I tried reasoning with her but she wouldn't listen to me. She said she wasn't getting on with you for a long while despite working shoulder to shoulder every day.

187

Conor was aggravated and got angry, shouting "How could she get on with me when she was seeing someone else?" Garrett shook his head. "Go up to your parent's house and I will look after the park. I think Eve has just arrived." He tried to explain to his parents who weren't taking in the situation's severity. They advised him to try talking to her in the morning. He did, but nothing worked. When he returned home, he went into the house and sat at the table with Eve who had stayed at home last night. He was pale and shattered looking as he told her it was pointless trying to strike up a conversation with Matilda as it was a futile war of words again. "She literally totally blindsided me" he said sadly. His parents were listening, but not knowing what to say.

CHAPTER 26

C onor's worst fears were confirmed when after weeks of trying to talk to Matilda there was no contact from her and no response to his many calls or texts. Then, one morning after three months had passed, he received a solicitor's letter laying out in black and white her plans to sell the apartments. Even though it was a complicated situation, Conor knew the sale would ultimately go through. He was shattered and explored every avenue possible to stop the sale but failed to do so. Eve threw him a lifeline when after a lot of negations with her solicitor, she sold her house and bought the apartments. After many months and umpteen visits with their solicitors, the transaction was completed and the disastrous episode was behind them. Eve owned the apartments and she moved home and became her brother's business partner. As time passed, they were pleased with the success they had running a viable and growing business together. It had been a challenging time for their parents but they pulled through it. Garrett had tried to remain in contact with his sister as he didn't want to forget how good she had been to him when he needed it but slowly over time she had stopped returning his calls and make excuses why she couldn't meet him. Garrett had put all his energies into working with Conor and the family in trying to improve the business.

One cold frosty morning just after Christmas, Eve was having a lie in as she was feeling sluggish after the New Year celebrations the night before. This month would be quiet in the park and guesthouse. She turned over on her other side and was very snug as she closed her eyes and thought how lucky she was to be off work for two weeks. As sleep was approaching, she almost jumped out of her skin when her brother banged on her door, "Eve are you getting up?" All he could hear was a sleepy voice, "I have no interest in being up early on New Year's day I deserve a rest, get away from the door." Managing the business throughout the year had taken its toll and she needed time to relax and unwind. She fell into a deep dreamy sleep but it didn't last because Conor came back again, "Come on, you can't stay in bed all day." "Oh for God's sake," she muttered with a groan as she tossed away the duvet and rolled out of bed and tore open the curtains. He waited for her to appear in the kitchen where he was sipping a cup of tea with his parents who didn't agree with him annoying his sister. "Wait until she hears the news I have for her,' he said smirking. Eric was watching for his daughter to come down from her room and tear into her brother. Eventually she walked into the kitchen in a cantankerous mood and hit him across the chest. 'Don't talk to me." He looked at her smiling "I have exciting news for you." "Well, it better be good after getting me out of bed, what is it?" Eric was reading the newspaper, he lowered it a couple of inches and his glasses peered over the top of it momentarily, gauging the situation as he glared from his wife to his daughter. When he noted the grim look on Eve's face he quietly retreated behind the temporary invisibility that the newspaper afforded him. Her brother told her that Garrett won a holiday to Hawaii. She was filling the kettle and didn't turn around. "How on earth did he win that?" she asked. He entered a competition on line last month and was contacted by email yesterday evening congratulating him on being a winner. "It's probably a scam," she said. "No, it's genuine they emailed three tickets to him early this morning. He's over the moon and even better he has invited us to join him." Eve looked at her brother with an expression that said 'not sure.' Conor reading her mind said in a high-pitched voice "Come on the holiday, it will do you good, we all need a break and it's free!" he exclaimed, his enthusiasm level stuck on slightly overexcited. "It's good timing," their father pointed out from behind the paper. "Go with them. You had a busy year, a change of scenery will be good for you." The following morning, she announced at breakfast she had decided to travel with them. The week passed quickly and as she was dragging her suitcase out to the car, she wondered why she brought almost a quarter of all her clothes and a half dozen pairs of shoes for just seven days. She hoped she wouldn't have to discard half it at the airport because it felt heavy to her as she lifted it down off the bed.

Garrett pulled up outside and opened the boot. She walked over with her luggage and as he lifted it in he remarked, "Gosh you must have brought the kitchen sink," and he laughed. Eve remarked when her brother threw his travel bag into the boot of the car, "You're travelling very light" "I brought enough to get by it is only for seven days, I see you brought enough for a month!" They drove towards the airport, caught the flight that brought them to their destination early the next morning. After signing in, they each went to their room tired, but excited to explore. Eve opened up the door of the balcony directly beside her double bed, looking out she saw there were three interconnecting pools, surrounded by palm trees and filled with the most alluring blue water that looked so wonderfully cool. She gazed out towards the ocean, a warm breeze was blowing and the sun shone a highly coloured orange.

It was breath-taking and she pinched herself to see if she was dreaming. The hotel was on a hill and a little above the beach, giving a perfect view of the cove far beyond. The shoreline curved around in a gentle swoop creating a private bay with soft, white-crested waves that lapped at the white sand. The water shimmered, shifting from bright to light turquoise and all the way into deep dark indigo, as the waves swept away from the shore and moved off in the distance leaving an enchanting panorama of the ocean blended with the sky. She went back into the room and hurled herself across the bed, silenced her phone and passed out on top of her duvet burying her head in the nest of pillows. Jetlag had claimed its first victim. Eve was awakened by a gentle knock on her door, she sat up with her eyes closed and wondered for a brief second where she was. Then she jumped out of bed waving her hands in the air "Yes, yes I'm in Hawaii." She hurried over and opened the door, "Are you coming down for a bite to eat?" Conor asked. "Go ahead I'll be down shortly." After a refreshing shower, she emptied the contents of her case onto the bed. She brought several dresses over to the long mirror trying to decide which one she would wear. She decided on a cream one she bought online last month. It was an elegant short dress with lace cap sleeves, low cut front and back, it made her feel flirtatious. She arrived downstairs half an hour late to Conor giving out that they were waiting for her. Garrett couldn't take his eyes off her then he commented, "You look beautiful tonight Eve." She blushed slightly, thanking him.

She was chuffed that he noticed the effort she put into getting ready for dinner. They ordered food and while waiting for it to be served, they ordered drinks. It gave her the chance to notice how dapper Garrett looked tonight, his brown eyes and curly hair made him look attractive. She left her hand on her chest for a split second so as not to be noticed. Thinking to herself, 'Be still my heart.' Eventually, servers appeared from all corners of the dining room passing out different foods on skewers and platters with veggie bowls on the side. When dinner was finished and after a couple of cocktails Eve stood up stating, "I'm going to my room to chill out, I think the tiredness is after hitting me." When she reached her room and went inside, she slipped into her pyjamas and filled a glass of wine from the small fridge provided. She went over and slid open the balcony door, stepped outside the sky and sea was completely black with nothing but a slim streak of reflected moonlight running across the waves to cut through the night. She sat there until tiredness overpowered her, going over to the bed she slid under the cool, crisp sheets and shut her eyes.

Surrounded in pitch black, and absolute silence, it was pure bliss. The following morning she woke refreshed and excited for the day ahead. After breakfast they were whisked away by the tour guide on a sightseeing trip. They were taken all around the island where they viewed spectacular scenery and ended up the day dining in the 'Cove Restaurant' in the hotel. There was a fine crowd already seated and a small band set up. As they played more and more people arrived as the music was so inviting. Conor moved away from the table and joined some women at the bar that he had already met on the beach earlier. Garrett asked Eve to join him in the residents lounge for one more drink, she did and one drink led to another as they were engrossed in conversation. Garrett moved closer to where she was sitting. She wished her brother would appear soon but he didn't. Garrett whispered, "Eve, it's really great having you with us, I'm enjoying your company." He was glaring at her, spontaneously he lifted his hand to touch hers. "Garrett, I really enjoy your company too but let's leave it at 'just friends,' it's a lot less complicated."

He lifted his hand away saying, "Well, at least, let me walk you to your room." As they walked along, he reminded her they were going surfing tomorrow morning and in the afternoon would indulge in a spa treatment. As they arrived at the room door, he paused and so did she but then she said rather quickly, "Good night sleep well." He walked away towards his room exhilarated, with the thought that maybe she liked him too. The following evening, Garrett surprised them. "We're going hula dancing tonight." Eve cried, "No way." Conor encouraged her, "Come on sis, be a sport hula dancing is a tradition here on the island, surely you are capable of a few hip swirls." She crinkled her nose up at him "Maybe." "You'll look good in a grass skirt," Garrett commented. When he was looking at her, he noted even though they'd only been here a couple of days, she was already glowing with a golden tan and a smattering of adorable freckles over her tiny nose. Secretly, he thought, 'Gosh, she's beautiful.'

They enjoyed the next few days relaxing under the sun-drenched sky. As it was the last full day of the holiday, they went early morning swimming. Eve ran and gave Garrett a cheeky push sending him face first into the sand. She continued to run until she reached the sea and continued running towards the waves. The water was icy against her sun-burned skin as it hit her body. She submerged herself and swam, when she turned back Garrett was right behind her and they swam back to shore together. As they reached the edge, he caught her wet hand and squeezed it, "I enjoyed that." She couldn't help admiring his lean well-toned body, suddenly she realised she was staring at him, she quickly turned and looked straight on towards the sand dunes and grass hills where they were heading.

Later that afternoon, Eve and Garrett walked in the treatment door room together. A pretty Hawaiian woman wearing a loose pink trousers and white t-shirt waved them through to a darker circular room lit only by candles. Garrett was going to a different apartment, but before he parted company with her, he leaned over and whispered in her ear, "Romantic isn't it?" She wished he didn't say that and responded, "All spas are like that as far as I know." Then Garrett went down the hall for his treatment. The therapist said, "I'll step out make yourself comfortable under the covers. Lie face down on the bed with your face slotted into the cushioned cradles."

The treatment lasted for one hour and was pure bliss. Eve felt so good after it and told her brother afterwards the therapist found knots and tight muscles she didn't even know existed. Garrett was gazing at her as she talked until Conor stared at him and broke the gaze. After dinner, she lazed on the sun lounger and relaxed, it was the last night of the holiday she wanted to use every minute admiring the view and soaking up the atmosphere. As she lay back and closed her eyes, she reflected over the past week that was most enjoyable. She appreciated Garrett sharing his holiday with them. She liked him and found out he was fun to be with. She didn't realise Garrett was standing near her until he pulled up the second sun lounger to lie beside her. He was whispering to her, it was easy to see he was flirting. Her heart thumped, she just smiled and was lost for words. She was glad when Conor rushed in, "Come on down to the beach bar and drink to the last night on the island." Eve lifted her head "Let the two of you go ahead I'm having an early night." Garrett stood up and walked away with Conor, he squinted back and flashed a tender smile her way. She felt confused and wasn't quite certain how she felt about him. She lay back and stayed there until the sun slipped away and sank beyond the horizon, and there was nothing to be seen but a slash of orange reflecting off the sea. They had an early start the next morning and arrived home late into the night.

Business was booming for Conor and Eve and their parents were proud of them. Garrett still occupied the apartment and was in a good position financially and helping with the business. Eve was delighted for the twins who were in jobs that they loved and both with boyfriends. They were now living in Hugh's house as was their father's wishes and after a lot of legal complications eventually it was signed over to both of them.

Eve had plans to get on to the property ladder again and was on the lookout for something suitable close to her home place where she would be near the business. She was seeing a special someone but was keeping it under her hat for now. She intended to dedicate this year to the business and building it up to a higher standard. This morning she was up bright and early and looking across at the hills noted a low haze hung over the sea, giving the expectation that another beautiful day was poised to unfold. Later, while Eric was in the garden, he spotted a fancy sports car driving up to the office where his daughter spent her working day. Eve loves when he surprises her at work. That night, when Eric's daughter finished up from the office he mentioned to her that he noticed a car driving up to her but she fobbed him off by saying that it was a representative from the heating company. "I see," Eric said, but didn't believe her.

Eve was going out with her secret man this evening and was looking forward to spending time with him. After a glorious time together and night began to fall, it was time for her to go back home. He wrapped her in his arms and pulled her close, his lips met hers in a long lingering kiss as he held her closer. She went back home feeling jubilant.

CHAPTER 27

The weeks rolled into August; it was early afternoon and all guests were out for the day so Eve set off for her usual walk; the sun shone bright and the day was warm and still. After walking for a while she sat on the bench beneath the oak tree down by the river near to the guest house. She watched butterflies fly past, bees buzzing, and bugs crawling at her feet. She breathed in the smell of summer and enjoyed the fresh air and sunshine that August brought with it. She was lost in the moment's beauty and didn't notice him walk up.

"Hello." The voice pulled her out of her reverie, shielding her eyes against the sun she looked towards him "Afternoon," she laughed, she was thrilled to see him. They both gazed at each other thick with expectation. She could see love radiating from his eyes. She pointed to the bench, "Sit here with me." He sat down and his hand slipped into hers naturally. They stayed there for a long while, talking and observing the wildlife, they talked and talked and she couldn't remember a time when she'd been happier. Something deep within her told her he was going to be a very important person in her life. She was in love with him and hoped this was the start of something big. She was going to let her parents know this evening that her secret man was Jack, the therapist. He was looking at her and wondering why she was lost in thought.

Jack had something to say to her and didn't intend to let the evening pass without speaking his mind. His voice quivered, 'I have something to say to you. She looked at him puzzled and didn't speak. "I'm going away next year." She was shocked. "In fact, I hope to be on my honeymoon." She felt faint and was still looking at him, disbelieving his words. He opened his mouth to speak, his phone rang, "This call is urgent I need to answer it, but don't move till I explain." "Answer it," she said, and got up off the bench and walked away from him. He put up his hand and covered the mouthpiece. "Wait, Eve please." She continued on walking. 'What kind of fool was I thinking he was going to propose soon, while all along he was planning to get married to somebody else?' She was devastated, she thought he had the same feelings for her as she had for him, she truly loved him. He continued talking on his phone and she noticed he was walking slowly after her. She walked with speed then she sped up her steps when he called out to her, she knew he was finished on the phone. He was breathless when he caught up with her. She looked around at him with fire in her eyes. "Please listen to what I was about to say to you before my phone rang" there was utter panic in his voice. She screeched at him with fury, "I don't want to hear it, you are no different to the rest of the rats I wasted my time on!" She threw her hands in the air "Get away from me."

He stood there while she dashed off at speed. He decided not to follow her while she was in an angry mood. He had to instigate his body to move. He wished now that he hadn't gone about asking her to marry him in such a roundabout way, because she took it up the wrong way altogether. He went back home with hopelessness in his heart. Eve walked back home to the guest house. She walked into the kitchen beside herself with rage. Her father was looking out the window red faced. "What's wrong with you?" she asked. "I'm slogging here on my own all day I'm exhausted. Conor is gone to a meeting with the bank manager and Garrett took off this morning without a word to anybody. When I contacted him he said he was having his car tested and had to rush off." Eve was of little support to him. "Well, I'm here now and you may put a stop to your hysteria."

Later she spotted Garrett driving into the park, and her mother arrived home later. Conor came up to the house to let his parents know how the meeting went, they were delighted for him that it went according to plan. Eric noticed Eve's phone ringing several times, he pointed it out to her. "I'm tired and going to ignore it until tomorrow." Conor was surprised "Answer it Sis, maybe it is one of the twins trying to contact you." "No, it's not. I checked." Julie felt her daughter was in a sombre mood and wondered why but didn't dare ask. Not long after that she went up to bed, her father asked the others if they knew what was wrong with her. Julie shrugged her shoulders, "Just having a bad day I suppose." Eve lay there looking up at the old lamp shade, it had cracks in it just like her relationships with men, there seemed to be always something missing, that special spark, that special someone that would make her fall into his arms and feel it was the most natural thing to do. Eve thought she had that with Jack until today when he announced he was going away on honeymoon. She stayed awake all night and thought about going away from this place altogether and starting a new life for herself but she knew realistically she could not let her parents down at their age and what about the apartments she had invested all her money in? No, she would have to stay for the foreseeable future. She turned over on her side and sleep crawled up on her near morning.

Garrett thought about contacting Eve and asking her out even though she gave him the brush off several times. He was crazy about her and hoped eventually that she would accept his invite. He walked down by the river flowing at the end of the garden it held nothing but silence except for the sound of ducks between the lily pads, with their webbed feet rippling in the still water. His eyes blazed and stung as he watched a sinking sun turn from gold, to almost silver. He pondered, 'Was all hope fading for him finding a soul mate?' With hot tears flowing, he bent his head and pulled his fleece jacket tight around his body and listened to the evening breeze whistling through the trees. He was off work for a week but had planned nothing special.

It was a very busy week in the park with Garrett away on holiday. Eve was glad he would be back to work Monday. It would leave her with less pressure. She snuggled up on the couch with her parents either side of her in arm chairs watching the television as her phone chirps for the fourth time. Messages were coming in thick and fast, so she sat up and peered at the screen, reading that all four were from Jack. She took a steeling gulp of her coffee before scrolling to the earliest text, that he wanted to meet up with her.

She text him later and agreed to meet him next week at the White Swan restaurant. The following week she was on her way to meet him and had arranged to stay with her friend Majella afterwards for the night. He was in the restaurant thirty minutes early sitting at the table fidgeting with a serviette. He couldn't ever remember being so nervous before. He jumped when he saw her walk in the door; she came and sat down at the table. He had a momentary panic in his stomach, 'Would his voice sound for him at all. How would he tell her she had made a big mistake that day at the river?' He looked at her with soft eyes. She tried to keep focused and just listen to what he had to say.

She was waiting for him to speak when he didn't she blurted out ,"Well what have you to say to me that was so urgent that needed four texts late on a Friday night?" His voice sounded wobbly. The server stood there, she handed Eve a menu, but Eve handed it back saying, "Just a glass of water please I'm not hungry." He was disappointed when she refused to order food. He was unsure of what to say next, or how to approach the last meeting they had, it was obvious he was being careful how to select his words. His face darkened slightly when he said, "Eve. Please let me start off where we left off when my phone rang and I was abruptly cut off that day down by the river, it was a misunderstanding that never should have happened but you wouldn't let me explain." She looked at him with sheer scepticism written all over her face. Her body shook fiercely, "Go ahead spit it out." "I'm getting married to the most wonderful, amazing, beautiful woman in the universe." She sat gazing at him flabbergasted, speechless." I'm asking will you marry me?"

Her mouth opened with nothing but a gasp. She felt an electric pulse in her chest as if she was after receiving a bombshell and it almost knocked her over. She looked stunned. He caught her by the hands, they stood up and he took her in his arms. It was clear to see she regretted walking away from him that day. He held her, tears were trickling down her face, she thought how wrong she was and felt terrible, all those awful thoughts she had about him. The ill feelings she had, not answering his calls or texts she told herself he was a monster. She kept gazing at him, it took those moments to digest his words. She apologised for not being more understanding when he called out to her that day to wait. "You are forgiven, it is water gone under the bridge. All that matters now is your answer." "Will you marry me?"

She leaned forward and placed a long lingering kiss on the lips. "Of course I will, I couldn't think of anything that I'd want to do more." The evening turned out to be magical and they ordered dinner among the cosy atmosphere of lightly burning candles and soft music. When dessert was served, Jack took a black velvet box bordered in gold from his pocket and placed it on the side dish.

Inside was the most beautiful gold ring with a large stone set among shinning smaller diamonds. "I hope you like it and that it fits," he said with emotion in his voice. He slipped it on her finger, "It's perfect," she said. She lifted her hand in the air admiring her ring as Jack surprised her further with an overnight stay in the Glenlo Abbey Hotel outside the city.

They arrived there early evening, it was cool and breezy, and the wind had blown flower petals over the drive way like confetti waiting to greet them. The sun was fading, the air was pure and invigorating with that intangible strengthening quality which the air of the sea seems to possess in an extraordinary degree. As they walked towards the entrance Eve inhaled great breaths in, wallowing in the moment. After drinks in the bar, they went up to their suite and closed the bedroom door. There was a momentary silence between the two of them as they lingered in an embrace. She whispered "You are my rock, you changed my world the day I met you." She noted his eyes sparkle when she spoke like he was drinking her in. "You are my world now," he said "I'm hypnotized by your presence." They kissed again clinging longingly to each other and the night was theirs to cherish.

The following day, Eve prepared to go home alone to let her family know about Jack. The problem was they did not know she was seeing him; they thought she had forgotten him and he was in her past, now; she was going to shock them by telling them she was going to marry him. She arrived home late evening. Her parents were sitting in the living room, her father reading a crime novel and her mother putting the finishing touches to menus for dinner for the coming Saturday evening. Eve came in and sat down on the couch and sipped her tea. She waited for the opportunity to tell her news; she hoped they wouldn't be annoyed that she had kept them in the dark for so long. Then, a plan materialised inside her brain, she sat up straight and pulled herself out towards the edge of the couch so she was facing both her parents. "The twins are coming to visit tomorrow evening, I was planning on cooking a special dinner for them in fact I'll cook for all of you." Conor walked in the door just at that moment asking "Am I included in that?" knowing that he was. Eric asked curiously ,"Is there an occasion?" "Just dinner, we seldom get together and Thursday evening is quiet." Early the next morning Garrett was trimming the hedges when Conor walked over behind him and waited until he stopped,

Garrett mentioned he was planning on meeting with Matilda hoping to reconcile. He knew Conor probably didn't want to hear that but he explained he didn't want to be estranged from his sister again.

The twins arrived early all excited; they loved their stepmother Eve, and thought of Eric and Julie as their grandparents for sure. Josephine asked, "Will Garrett be over too?" Eve said, "No, it's just family." Julie prompted "Maybe you should ask him he is almost part of the place," Conor who was standing listening intervened explained that Garrett wasn't free, anyway. Eve seemed relieved with the news. By eight o'clock all sat down to a delicious meal. After dessert was consumed and coffee served, Eve spoke nervously, "I have something to tell you all, which was my reason in getting us together here this evening..." She paused trying to gather herself and not sound so shaky. She continued, "I have been going out with Jack for a quite a while now and even though the road has been bumpy, we are in love and he asked me to marry him." The twins screamed together, "What did you say?" I said, "Yes." They jumped up and hugged her all excited. The relief she felt after was splendid. Her parents sat there dumb founded they didn't speak and she wished they would say something. She got up and ran up to her room and back down within seconds with the ring on her finger. Her mother was smiling and said, "If you're happy that is all that matters." Eric stood up and hugged her, "Congratulations what a surprise." Then, Julie took the news in and went over to where her daughter was standing and wrapped her arms around her. Conor said, "You kept that silent," internally he was disappointed because he thought Garrett and Eve would be become an item, he knew well that Garrett was very keen on his sister. Eve's Father didn't divulge that he knew his daughter was seeing somebody, he knew very well that the fancy car calling to Eve's office would never be a company car a rep would be driving.

Having met with Matilda and talking out their issues, Garrett was relieved that they could move past what had happened and re-establish their sibling relationship, he really had missed her. As he drove along, a light bulb moment flashed in his brain. He would go over and ask Eve out on a date, finally he thought to himself, everything was turning out wonderfully for him. He had grown to know and love Eve over the years. Conor was walking across the yard when Garrett drove up the avenue, "I'm just back from Eve's, she cooked an enormous meal for us, but think I over indulged. Come in for a nightcap with me and I'll tell you about the night."

When they went in and had the drinks in their hinds Garrett said, first let me tell you how I got on with my sister. Conor had no interest in hearing her name but listened to Garrett anyway just to please him. Conor tried to let Garrett know what had happened during his night. "I want to let you in on some good news" he said. "Sounds interesting, I'm intrigued, what is it?" Garrett answered inquisitively. Conor knew he couldn't sugar coat the news so he decided to just say it as it was, "Eve shocked us all after the meal by telling us she got engaged to Jack." Garrett listened in disbelief, his insides rattled and his stomach twitched, he was in utter shock he thought out loud 'she can't be.' Conor knew by Garrett's body language that he was devastated. When he had his drink finished, he excused himself and left. He lay awake for most of the night going over in his mind the way he jelled with her and how they worked in harmony each day. He had no inkling that she was seeing anybody, with the benefit of hindsight he wished he hadn't been so sluggish in approaching her but on the other hand she had given him the brush off several times. It was too late for him now, he had let her slip through his fingers. The way she would smile and flirt with him on occasions led him to believe she was into him but obviously not, Jack was the person she desired. How could he work with her now, not when he had feelings for her and she had no interest in him, he put his heart into this place and had felt like part of their family? He decided there was nothing more for him here so he decided he would have to quit his job and go away and find work elsewhere, he had savings and could rent an apartment. He couldn't see any other way, it would be impossible to be so close to Eve knowing that they would never be together.

The next morning at first light he packed some clothes and left. He would have the rest of his belongings collected later. It was almost ten o'clock in the morning when Conor called over to Garrett's apartment, he was taken aback when he got no reply and found a note left on the window sill with the keys of the door. Conor went up to his parents and told them the news, they were very upset and couldn't fathom out what happened. When Conor contacted Garrett, he wasn't budging he told him he had lost the girl he wanted and nothing made any difference to him. He explained he didn't want to work in proximity with Eve so he had to finish working in the park he refused to return. Eric commented they would never get someone as efficient as Garrett and maybe it was best to leave him a few days and when he has thought it through he might realise that he has acted hasty and come back. Conor was agitated, "I think he is gone and won't be back. He had his eye on Eve for a long time and was heartbroken when she got engaged to Jack, he believed that Eve and himself would eventually be together."

Garrett moved into a one bed flat in Galway and finally got a job in a tourist office on the outskirts of the city. He kept to himself initially but Matilda was encouraging him to meet new people and invited him out with her and her friends. She knew it would take some time for him to move on from Eve but she was happy to support him at his own pace.

The month of June started off in turbulence for Conor. Yesterday had been an upside-down day after a guest complained the drinking water gave her a nauseated stomach. He needed to take a sample and bring it to the laboratory for testing later in the day. It was important to get the results back before the scheduled group moved into the park tomorrow evening. His next problem caused him an amount of stress because there was a build-up of ice on the deep freeze. It badly needed to be defrosted but it was impossible to find time to get around to everything and his parents were full time in the guest house. Garrett was sorely missed.

The crunching of wheels on the gravel alerted him to a visitor, he went out to see who it was, as he wasn't expecting anyone at this hour of the morning. He was after filling a mug of tea and the toast had just popped. A girl jumped out of the car, pushed her sunglasses on to the top of her head. As Conor walked up to her, she stretched out her hand, "I'm Sue O'Neill from the Health Board, just carrying out a routine inspection. Am I talking to the owner?" "Conor Wallace, part owner as my parents are still involved in the family business." She asked rather authoritatively, "Who handles the day to day running of the park?" He hesitated afraid of giving her any wrong answers, "Well I suppose that would be me most of the time." They chatted for a few moments before she informed him she would have a look around for herself. She asked him before he went about his business if it was alright to go up to the guesthouse first. He walked a step behind her and sent a quick text to his mother and hoped she read it, there was nothing else he could have done in the circumstances. She got the text and cursed out loud, Eric asked, "What the hell is wrong now?" She told him and with that Conor and the health inspector walked into the front hall. Julie took off and left Eric standing there in the kitchen to meet and greet the girl with Conor.

Julie rushed into the nearest bathroom and flushed the toilet, pulled out clean towels and hung them on the towel rail then she got the brush and ran it through her hair and applied a little lip gloss, she wished her face wasn't flushed, her blood pressure was surely raised she thought. After going down and meeting the inspector she calmed down considerably. Conor introduced her as Sue O' Neill and she seemed to be friendly enough. She went about checking the house first, then outside in the park and lastly the offices. Conor's parents were on tender hooks for the two hours while she scrutinised every corner of the buildings. When the inspection was completed, she went back up to the house and reported what needed their immediate attention.

She said rather sternly, "It is not acceptable to let a build-up of ice go to that extent on a deep freeze. There are water pipes coming from the sink that need to be covered, extra shelves are needed in the office to accommodate the amount of paperwork and books left on the floor. The trees close to the caravans need to be trimmed and there is water lodged in corners that would need to be drained." She was concerned when she spotted warning notes on taps saying water not fit for drinking, she enquired about the problem and Conor explained he was taking a sample to the laboratory this very afternoon to have it tested. Conor's parents were overcome with the amount of problems she detected. Eventually, she shook hands with Eric and Julie before she went back up to the office with Conor to sign the papers on the report.

She sat at the desk opposite him and handed him the documents that required signing and she planned to be back in one month. He walked over to where she was standing and stretched his hand out to hers. "I hope all will be in order the next day." As she turned to go her note pad slipped to the floor, they both bent down together to retrieve it, she could feel the heat from his breath as she stood up quickly and let him pick it up, she took a step backwards but stumbled, quickly he reached out and steadied her. She gave a nervous laugh as they both stood in awkward silence.

Later that evening in the office, Sue's colleagues noticed she was brighter than usual, normally she complained about the inspections she had carried out but this evening she was acting differently. They wondered what had brightened up her day. They didn't have to wait long because she couldn't contain herself, telling them all about Conor, "He's single, good looking and running a very successful business." Martina, one of her work colleagues, asked "How can you be so sure he is single?" "Oh he is, because his mother told me that her daughter was involved in the business as well, she said they were both single up to now but her daughter was getting married next year." The girls laughed at her, slagging her she should be called detective.

A month passed quickly and Sue was due back for the final inspection. She arrived late afternoon. Conor was away he didn't expect her today even though it was the exact month since she was here last. Julie met her and after she double checked everything and was satisfied, she went back into the house and handed Julie the final report. She seemed to linger longer than expected, so Julie felt she should offer her tea. Eric stayed outside wishing they would soon decide to stop talking and she'd go because there were guests booking in within an hour. She stood up to leave and Julie walked her to her car. Eric came walking up towards the house and noted Sue turned her head to look towards Conor's office. Silently she wondered why he was not about the place today, this was her only chance to see him again. As she drove out the gate, there was his car cruising up the hill at a fast pace, she tipped the brakes and reversed back, stopped and rolled down the window.

He pulled up beside her "Hello there, I wasn't sure of the exact day that you were returning." "Not to worry as I met with your parents and I have good news for you, the business is now fully compliant and you definitely meet the health boards requirements, well done." He was relieved and thrilled, much work had happened in the last month to ensure that it would pass the inspection. She kept lingering and making chat about nothing in particular. He chanced cheekily asking, "Maybe we could meet for coffee in town one day next week?" Sue said "I have a meeting next Wednesday evening we could meet in the Eyre Square centre around four o'clock if that suits you?" The following week, they sat having coffee and chocolate doughnuts deep in conversation that

Wednesday. Conor suggested a stroll on the promenade afterwards, it was the start of many meetings as friends.

Excited for her wedding day tomorrow and birthday, Eve was up at the crack of dawn and taking a moment to reflect on her life to date, she thought about Hugh and knew that he would want her to be happy. Looking in the mirror in the bathroom, she looked closely at her reflection and noted lines on her face, and pockets of skin beneath her eyes, her hair was coloured hiding multiple white strands but she knew her face told its own story of happiness and grief and now, of course, a new beginning for her and Jack as they start on their journey together. Later that evening on their way back from the rehearsal which went splendidly, before getting into bed, Eve looked through the window and pondered to herself excitedly enjoying the serenity of the moment, 'When the sun rises it will be a new day and the start of my new life with Jack'

The family got up early the next morning, make-up and hair stylists arrived and the house was full of activity. Breakfast was served by the twins, who then helped her into her wedding dress. They had been with her when she picked it out and she knew how important these memories are to cherish. The church, flowers and music were perfect and the ceremony was simple and short. They enjoyed a reception of champagne before sitting down to witty speeches from the best man who was Jack's brother, home from Australia for the occasion. By three in the morning, the newly married couple left for their wedding suite as they were catching a flight to Las Vegas to begin a three-week honeymoon. They thoroughly enjoyed the day and they could now look forward a well-earned break.

The next morning dawned bright and clear, after an early swim in the hotel pool and a wholesome breakfast Conor set off for a brisk walk to clear his throbbing head after a very late night. He had only one person on his mind and that was Sue; he loved her company; she had such a quirky sense of humour and was always upbeat in her opinions and quick to offer a positive solution and her support. He definitely liked her and wanted to see more of her. She invited him to dinner next Saturday night. His family weren't aware he was seeing anyone, but his mother had her suspicions because he had become more exact in his appearance. He was impatiently waiting for Saturday evening. She was more than a friend to him; he was serious about her and he knew she felt the same about him at least he hoped she did.

That Saturday evening, Conor called to his parent's house to let them know he was going out for the evening to visit a friend and may not be back until late on Sunday. After landing at Sue's home, he stopped outside the blue front door of a two-story apartment, with a wrought-iron balcony on the top floor and a pair of bay trees strung with tiny lights stood either side of the door. He walked in the hall door after Sue opened it, a carpeted hallway was revealed with several doors leading off of it. He followed her into the kitchen and noted it was connected to a spacious sitting area with two vintage leather chairs, a large lamp and bookshelves on either side of a small stove on the back wall. 'Dinner is almost ready," she said. "You have a fabulous place here." "Thanks. It is compact and comfortable," she turned around pointing "The study is in here," as she opened the door off the kitchen, "And the bathroom is next to it, there is also a master bedroom upstairs with an en-suite of course and a small walk-in wardrobe." He was impressed. Sue felt it so natural sitting together having dinner with him. After a most enjoyable dinner date, reluctantly he mentioned maybe it was time he left. Straight away she said, "We'll do this again really soon." "I'd like that," he said, after a short while he left disappointed, he had hoped of plans to stay overnight. She could not sleep that night despite how exhausted she felt. It was excitement that kept her awake. She loved cooking for him and being with him but she was playing her cards close to her chest she had been hurt too many times before and was going to make sure this relationship would not end up on the rocks like the other two. There was something genuine about Conor, she felt a closeness to him she couldn't quite explain, or had ever felt on this level before.

The next morning, Conor heard a car drive up right outside his apartment. He looked through the window and caught sight of a familiar figure walking to the door. His heart did a loud drum roll in his chest. He wondered what she was doing up so early on a Sunday morning, but he genuinely didn't care what time it was as he was happy to see her any time. He pulled open the door and greeted her with a warm smile. "I'm on my way to the Christmas market in Eyre Square in Galway would you like to join me for a few hours?" Conor was delighted with the invite and was ready to leave in no time. Sue wanted to know

207

more about this man that came into her life over a year ago. Sue insisted on bringing her car so Conor sat back and relaxed.

Eric and Julie were up early serving breakfast to the guests, Eric opened the door to take a bag out to the bin at the side of the house, he spotted Conor getting into the passenger's side of the car. He went back inside and tried to recall why the car looked so familiar to him, he mentioned it to his wife who was busy cooking, "Never mind who it is, Conor is off today and it's probably one of the lads collecting him to go to a match or maybe racing who knows." "He must have come home last night," he said to Julie. She said, "Serve the breakfast and stop looking out the window." Eric was wrecking his brain trying to remember when he realised, he called back to Julie who was still cooking breakfast, "I know who owns the car, don't you remember that girl Sue O' Neill from the health board that carried out the inspection that's who it is and he is gone with her." Julie smiled and continued on cooking.

Sue was over the moon and was enjoying been out with Conor for a few hours. He was on tender hooks and didn't want to make any wrong move; he liked this girl and wanted to impress her. As they reached the market, they slowed down and they both were aware they had slipped their hands together she noticed he was clasping hers. They talked and laughed all day, as they were making their way back to the car park after a light dinner he asked if she would like to go out to Salthill for a stroll, but it was getting late and she was eager to get home to Morgan her little Yorkshire Terrier who'd be waiting inside the door for her to return. He asked "Where was the dog when I was over for dinner?" "I left him with the dog carer for the night I was afraid you wouldn't be a fan." "I love dogs but can't have any because there are too many people coming and going to our place."

December wasn't the best month of the year for the gardens but the turquoise blue sky made a perfect background for the evergreen hedges, dark green viburnum and glossy laurel. It was one year on from the day Sue asked Conor to visit the Christmas market with her. Conor was sitting at his desk and looking out the window thinking how happy he was that morning. He flicked through his diary there weren't many bookings this month but there was a mountain of end-of-year meetings to go to and accounts to be tidied up before he paid his tax bill. December had rushed in with a flurry of events, the madness of decorating, juggling schedules, and the frustration of shopping. Even though he shopped on line mostly, his mother liked the shopping experience of walking into a store and buying her presents so he made time to take her there before the holiday period.

He was looking forward to Christmas this year because he was hoping Sue would stay overnight during the holidays; he thought maybe New Year's Eve would be a perfect time, with the start of a new year blooming. Sue decided if Conor asked her to stay over at his place during the holiday period she certainly would. As 31st December approached, Conor plucked up courage and invited Sue over for the celebrations and asked her to stay. She was delighted and accepted without hesitation. She could picture herself here on a balmy summer evening with a glass of wine in her hand and Conor by her side as they watched the moon rise over Galway Bay and stretch out over the mountains of Connemara. She stayed over several other weekends until eventually Conor asked her to move in with him.

One summer morning, she woke up in her new surroundings and was greeted by a scene that warmed her heart. All around the grounds was a vista of flowers, pink and yellow roses, trailing purple wisteria and flaming blood-red geraniums spilling from their brown terracotta pots and pushing their bright heads to the sun. When she lifted her head a little higher, she could see beyond the pines and the morning mist was rising like a blanket of smoke towards the sky.

Jack and Eve strolled hand in hand happily together after continuing with their love of walking. They went back inside where Jack spent half an hour on the phone with an estate agent. Eve laughed as he communicated with her via rather dodgy sign language to describe the conversation that is going on between him and the estate agent. They were in deep negotiations recently about a four bed detached residence with its own garden; it had them interested, since they first viewed it.

As they walked around it that first day with its modern decor and cool white interiors she dreamt how she would put her own stamp on it. The next moment she heard Jack talking numbers even though they had agreed to place an offer slightly below their budget. Jack was carried away with excitement and offered more than they had planned. She heard him say, "We are ready to make an offer," then she heard him, "We are offering the asking price." After a minute, he clicked off his phone and went over to where she was standing and lifted her up and swung her around in delight saying, "I think the house is almost ours." She remained silent. "What's wrong?" he said as he left her standing and went to the fridge. "You offered the asking price. I thought we were going to make a lower offer so we could save some money to change some of the décor in the house" she said rather angrily. "I couldn't. A higher offer came in already." With that his phone rang, while talking to the auctioneer he gave Eve the thumbs up. After he clicked off his phone for the second time, he said with a high-pitched voice, "It's ours, we are moving." He went to the fridge and took out a bottle of white wine, half-filled two glasses, handed one to Eve, they clinked their glasses together, "To our new home." Eve was still worrying about the money, but he reassured her that when he sold his house in Salthill it would bring in far more than they were expecting.

Six months later, Jack was turning the key in their new house. He pushed the door open and whisked Eve up in his arms. "Put me down," she squealed. "No, I'm carrying you over the threshold it's an old tradition." They decided to host a house warming the following month and invite both their families and friends. It was a beautiful November morning, the rain of the previous days had washed the air clean. The guests arrived early evening and the party started off in great spirits. The twin's partners, Joshua and Daniel, were helping them in the kitchen as they arranged the food and drinks for the guests. Julie brought hot trays of finger food, while Jack stocked up on a selection of alcohol. Sue came over in the evening and Jack's brother who was home from Australia dropped in later that night. Music and chatter drifted through the air. As midnight approached Eve and Jack walked out into the moonlit night. In the distance an owl complained to his patient listener, they stood there enjoying the sounds of nature. With his arms tight around her, he leaned down and with his mouth warm against hers she wrapped her arms around his neck, she closed her eyes as the world seemed to spin around her at that moment. They stayed entwined with whispers of the places they would visit and things they would see and do together, they knew that life was to be lived. The hum of their family and guests echoed from inside as they turned to walk back hand in hand.

Christmas rolled in like the rising tide. Eve was excited going home to spend the holiday with her family when the park would be at its most beautiful, the winter sun would shine down through the surrounding trees, sending jewel-coloured reflections dancing on the walls of the houses and the glittering fairy lights on the outside trees would create a magical wonderland among the mountains. The twins arrived to the scent of a melange of fruits and vegetables roasting and boiling, sending a tempting aroma through the house.

Christmas morning comprised cooking, sipping wine and the placing of presents under the tree. The smell of homemade chestnut stuffing, turkey roasting, ham cooking in cider, and vegetables roasting topped off with the scent from the plum pudding boiling was mouth-watering. Julie made sure everybody's palate was satisfied. After dinner came the pulling of crackers, the exchanging of gifts, the 'exclamations and the thank yous.' all against the soundtrack of joyous laughter. Board games were played and television viewed, the drinks trolley was rolled in and remained there until the early hours of the morning. With spirits high the night ended and it was time to get to bed. They all agreed the day was absolutely perfect. Each hugged Julie and Eric and all agreed they would do this again for Christmas next year. Little did they know everything was about to change for them as a family.

Early January, Conor's parents took a step back and moved into one of the apartments. They offered Conor the living quarters in the guest house and the option to build on more rooms. He was thrilled and accepted wholeheartedly; he talked to Sue who was very supportive. His parents would still work but with less responsibility and would feel free to take time off whenever they wanted. They were content to see their two children settled and the twins who were engaged to be married next year dropped in to see them every so often and life was good.

CHAPTER 28

Two years went by and Eric and Julie were settled into the apartment. The renovations had started on the guest house and all was going according to plan for a few weeks until Conor's parents saw something unfolding that they weren't happy with. The house was being gutted. Seemingly, the young couple applied for a grant and decided to do a bigger job than first planned. Sue called in to see Julie one morning early, she was sitting at the table finishing her breakfast and Eric had gone to town. As Sue sat down opposite Julie, she quizzed, "I hope you will be happy with the changes Conor and I are making in the guest house." Julie was focusing. "The place is so cramped, we will have to empty all the rooms and make a place for the modern furniture I have ordered. Everything has to be of a high standard or we won't be eligible for the grant." She listed off the changes while Julie listened. "We're hoping to create a light filled open-plan kitchen with dining and living space. That will mean the builders will be knocking down the wall between the living room and kitchen. We are going to extend the box room into a master bedroom for ourselves. I would also love to have a walk-in wardrobe and vanity space at the end of that room. In the plan also the bathrooms will be revamped and Conor is planning on having a specious wet room with fitted black brass shower. The attic will be converted into a home office with a space at the far end to relax and watch television. The exterior of the house will be insulated. The heating system will be upgraded which will mean installing a highly efficient boiler. We are also installing solar panels to the front and rear of the house. We intend to keep the decor light and bright and the sliding doors which will set off the kitchen and living area will look out on the lush and colourful garden. Eric has promised he will plant and keep it as always." She was so excited telling Julie, Julie could hear it in her voice and see it on her face. But Julie became tearful and Sue reached across the table for her hand. "I know it sounds like an awful lot of change and we don't want to upset you but we want to put our own stamp on it. We want to modernise it." Julie responded, "I understand, it's just hard because of all the memories we have had in the house, it feels like the end of an era." Eric and Julie discussed the changes to the house later that evening. Eric panicked, worried that it wouldn't be ready for the season ahead instead of making money, they would lose out on guests.

A month passed and the builders had moved in. This was Julie's first time to walk down to the building site to view the situation. The roof was off the house and the walls were knocked. Eric voiced his concerns but Conor insisted it would be ready for the season. "I'm working tirelessly day and night to keep the build under control. It will be fully finished in twelve weeks that will give us time to get the painters and decorators on site." His Father asked, "When will the grant come through?" "When the build is fully completed?" Julie was annoyed and said, "Make sure you don't leave it too late like you did with the other building years ago costing me a substantial amount out of the money I got from Matthew."

Conor ignored her when she mentioned her money, he knew he would have to reimburse her soon. Slowly but surely after the second month of the build, Julie and Eric calmed down and agreed with the changes the young people were bringing to the place. Sue assured Julie that her involvement would be vital in running the business because she was the heart and soul of the place. Julie was chuffed she had come through a difficult few months trying to come to terms with the change but was feeling a little comfort now that Sue was planning to include her in the running of the guest house.

The next day, she went into Galway and treated herself to a new outfit then went out to the Salthill to walk and breathe in the salty fresh air off the sea. It was cold and windy, she didn't care it was just what she needed to clear her head of the lethargy and depression that had invaded her for the past eight weeks. In front of her there was a couple with their children and a frisky terrier they called Rolo having fun as they skimmed stones on top of the waves. As she stood and watched, she spotted a plane in between the clouds travelling over the sea. She felt energised looking up at it and had a light bulb moment thinking, 'I could be in that plane flying out to another country enjoying the sunshine and freedom in fact I could take off whenever the fancy took me. Eric wouldn't want to go but she knew she would get him around to her way of thinking.' Her outlook was looking much more positive than yesterday as she walked on with a pep in her step. The following day after breakfast, Eve took her to town and bought her two new suit cases just to have them in the house at least it would be a start to a new way of life for her parents, travelling would be fun. Julie hid the cases from Eric, time enough he would have to fall for her plans.

A few weeks later, she decided to make an appointment with the doctor to have a full check-up. She felt a weakness occasionally and had done nothing about it so now was the time before they went travelling. After twelve weeks the build was finished, inspected and signed off, the grant was paid into the bank account a short time later. Julie and Eric congratulated the young couple on their achievement in creating a beautiful and classy guest house and they both admitted that they were happy to be proven wrong. That night, Julie was delighted and announced to Eric she was booking a weekend away for both of them. Eric was hesitant at first but then agreed to go, he felt Julie deserved it after the worry of the past while. After Eric went up to bed, she browsed through the internet to see where would be a suitable destination, after a lot of thought she decided to stay in Ireland this time thinking that they had plenty of time to go further afield later on. She booked a bed-and-breakfast in Dingle, County Kerry and paid a little extra for a sea-view room. Before she went up to bed, she went into the back room and cut the labels off the cases. Tomorrow she would start packing them, she was so excited to be able to be free enough to get the odd break from now on. She went to bed happy and slept soundly.

Eric was up and out early while Julie slept a little later than normal. An hour later, Eric went back up to the house for breakfast, he was stunned when he found Julie passed out on the kitchen floor she was a grey colour and not responding, he immediately called an ambulance. Then he called Eve but got no reply so he rang Conor and told him in a frantic voice that Julie had passed out. Luckily, the ambulance arrived shortly after, Eric knew it was serious when they wheeled her into the ambulance and the paramedics connected her to a heart monitor, and gave her injections and oxygen. At the same time, they kept reassuring Conor and Eric that they were looking after her and she would reach hospital quickly. Eric was relieved when before the door was clasped shut she lifted her head slightly and nodded at them. Eve rang back, Eric was distraught as he explained what had happened and told her she needed to make her way to the hospital as soon as possible. Eric and Conor drove behind the ambulance, leaving Sue to look after the business. Jack and Eve arrived a little later and met Eric and Conor who were waiting in the emergency department heavy hearted. The doctor on call walked over to Eric and after asking if he was the next of kin told him his wife was admitted to the coronary care unit and asked him to go over to admissions where they would take necessary details. Before the doctor walked away, he said to the family that he would speak to them shortly.

There was no word from the doctor for the next few hours. Eric sat there staring at the ground, the others were silent with only a couple of words passing between them. Eventually, Eve walked up to the CCU and stood outside the door hoping a doctor or nurse would come outside, when they didn't she went to the nurse's station and enquired for her mother, she felt it was too long to be left sitting with no information on her condition. The sister in charge of the unit called the doctor to have a word with the family. Eve followed him back to the waiting room which they had been moved to an hour ago he stood in front them and spoke with a kind soft voice. "Julie is stable at the moment, we discovered a weakness in her heart and her blood pressure is elevated. There are more scans and an angiogram to follow. I would advise you to go home and we will call you if needs be." "How serious is her condition?" Eric asked. "She is very weak at the moment, the next seventy-two hours are critical," the doctor explained. Then the doctor looked at Eric's sad face and offered, "If you would like to step into the unit for a moment follow me."

After they went home and Eric went inside his own door, the shock hit him. 'She seemed fine yesterday planning holidays,' he looked at the two suit cases and swore when she came home and got better he would never refuse to go any place with her again even foreign holidays which he disliked. They would have plenty of outings from now on. He was a matter-of-fact type man who cried very little in his lifetime but now a few tears trickled down his cheeks. He went to bed with a picture of how frail she looked tonight connected up to many machines and he drifted in and out of sleep until morning. Julie's condition worsened with each day, she became weaker and slipped in and out of consciousness, the doctors did all they could for her but because of complications she passed away with her family by her bedside.

In the months that followed, Eric was heartbroken and spent many days sitting in the living room crying and not having the energy or interest to do anything. It was on one of those evenings that Eve walked in and spotted him looking at the suitcases with a bleak expression written all over his face and his voice sounded quiet and tired. She lifted the suit cases and took them away and told him that while he kept looking back at the past, he could never move forward into the future. She understood more than most how he was feeling, remembering it all too well herself. A month from that evening, he focused on working around the grounds. His children were a wholehearted support and Sue was nothing but kind to him. After the first anniversary of Julie's was over, Eric demeanour brightened up, business was booming and Conor took on staff in the guest house. Sue was involved in the bookkeeping and Eric kept busy keeping the grounds immaculate.

As time moved on, so did Eric as best he could. He began socialising again. He renewed his friendship with Paddy and they started attending races, matches and the odd game of cards together. It felt good to be going to the pub and having a few pints with his friends. His life was taking some kind of structure, he was getting back on track. He missed Julie but she wouldn't have wanted him to sit in a corner sullen for the rest of his days. Paddy and Eric began going to the card game twice a week, Eric enjoyed the company and he felt less lonesome.

Then one night, he noticed Eleanor, Paddy's sister walking into the hall with a group who had travelled there on a bus. As they walked in, she looked directly at him and nodded; he lifted his hand and greeted her; she continued on walking towards her table he didn't speak to her anymore that night and Paddy didn't mention her name either. Seeing Eleanor again after all this time made him feel conflicted within himself. He remembered back to when times were very difficult between himself and Julie and how he was willing to move forward with Eleanor such were his feelings for her. She had changed when she won the Lotto money and he had felt hurt by the way she treated him. Equally, he wasn't proud of how he had behaved towards his own family especially Julie, even to this day he felt guilty about it. After attending the counselling sessions with Julie they could move forward together and their relationship definitely improved, he was thankful for that at least. He worried that when he did eventually see Eleanor, it would stir up old feelings he had for her but it didn't. It just reminded him of a difficult time in his past and how through his own stupidity he nearly lost his family. He decided he would be polite and respectful towards Eleanor but that he didn't want to encourage any potential feelings.

The following three weeks passed with no sign of Eleanor at the card game, he wondered if his presence had unsettled her and she was avoiding him. He decided he needed to clear the air with her as he didn't want any awkwardness between them. He arranged to call to Paddy's house, hoping he could talk to Eleanor separately at some stage during the visit. Paddy and himself discussed everything from the weather to latest GAA fixtures, Eleanor contributed every so often and by the end of the visit seemed to be more relaxed in his company. When he was leaving, he made an excuse to chat to Eleanor outside. He explained he hoped his friendship with Paddy hadn't upset her. To his relief, Eleanor felt the same as he did, she was worried that he wanted to rekindle their romance and she was unsure how to tell him as she was now in a solid relationship with Paul for some time. They decided they were thrilled just to be friends.

With the arrival of spring, Eric was delighted to be able to get out into his garden again. He loved this time of year and the burst April brought with it. He picked some primroses and placed them on each table in the guest house to bring freshness to the dining room. Julie never failed to have fresh flowers for her guests and Eric continued it on for her. Later that evening, Sue let Eric know how she appreciated it and she would miss him if he wasn't there to add the final touches to the garden and guest house before guests arrived. He found it hard to comprehend that he was nearing eighty years of age, he still felt young at heart, thinking he was only about sixty.

The months rolled by and Eve insisted on hosting a party for Eric's eightieth birthday in her own home. Eric woke to the sound of chattering and laughter of the families that had arrived last night to the caravan park all getting

217

ready for the day ahead. The guest house was buzzing with guests and Eve was over early to help Sue in the kitchen, the twins would arrive later in the day. Eric got out of bed quickly, the lawns had to be mowed and flowers watered before noon. Then he needed to go to town and have his hair cut and maybe a new outfit would be on the cards. A sigh escaped his throat, he closed his eyes. 'How could he be eighty already, time had flown away so quickly?' He thought of his past and his new present, it seemed as if he was after entering a different world. Then sadness took over for a moment, losing Julie before this milestone birthday was heart-breaking. She was his support, his source of strength, and guiding light she kept him on the straight and narrow path, it was a shock when she died, especially when they could unwind, relax and enjoy their retirement. Today Eve had planned a family gathering in her place he felt lucky to have people in his life that cared enough to plan an event in their home just for him alone.

Eve and the twins were well and truly in the preparation mode when Conor and Sue arrived to the house. She gave them instructions to lay the tables with the platters already prepared. Eve put together crackers, artfully swirled with herb-mixed cream cheese, decorated with tiny chunks of wild salmon. The twins had an array of mixed sandwiches, savoury bites, and canapés complimented with side salads. The drinks chest stood inside the door laden with wine, beer, spirits and soft drinks. Sue ordered a large fresh cream gateaux and decorated it with sparkling candles. The party got started about six o'clock, with friends arriving shortly after. They laughed, talked and reminisced until near midnight when Sue brought out the birthday cake and a chorus of happy birthday could be heard around the locality. Eric became overwhelmed, Eve walked over to where he was standing and folded her arms around him. A bubble of happiness rose inside of him, it was good to have his family here with him tonight. Conor stood behind him and prompted him to say a few words. He straightened up and with his children's support he thanked Eve for hosting this enjoyable night and his family for standing by him and being there for him through thick and thin. After he was finished, Sue cut up the cake and the twins handed out drinks. Eric needed a breather and went outside and down to the front lawn, he lit a cigarette and as always promised himself it was his second last one! Taking a long drag he savoured the immediate soothing effect and then he exhaled tilting his head upward, it was when he took a second puff that he noticed Eve walking down towards him. It was too late to quench the cigarette and get rid of it anyway she would smell the smoke so there was no escaping it. She stood beside him and entwined her arm in his. "Why are you out here alone smoking, I thought you gave them up, you know they won't do your lungs any favours?" He stared in front of him at the old chestnut tree. "Tonight was emotional for me and a smoke relaxes my mind and helps me to chill out.' She didn't argue with him, tonight was his to enjoy. He leaned over and kissed her tenderly on her forehead. "The gathering was beautiful thank you," as he finished the cigarette and they went back inside. It was long past midnight when each person went their own direction. Eric was happy to have Eleanor and Paddy back in his life and celebrating his big birthday with him tonight. It felt good to have friends of his own age to socialise with. Eleanor and himself were respectful of each other's separate lives and yet could enjoy each other's company and have a good laugh which kept Eric young at heart. The day had ended and he had enjoyed every minute. Life wasn't looking as bleak for him as it had after Julie's death. Everything was exactly as it should be, Conor and Sue were planning to marry in the future and it was good to see the next generation coming up behind and all paving their own paths in life, Julie would have been so proud of them too.

As the last light of the August summer night cast its rays across the darkening blue sky, Jack and Eve sat back and relaxed as they gazed out their big window over the vibrant sea. The horizon was vividly pink, gold and deep red. She reached out to where Jack was sitting next to her and took his hand. Outside just over the field, there was a rush of wings in the twilight, as sea gulls swept overhead after being disturbed by a large eagle that had strayed away from the distant mountains which had merged with the darkening vibrant sky. The moon cast prisms of silver light, illuminating shades of lavender, green and gold on the mountain sides and they spread like a patchwork quilt across the peaks.

In whispers of love, she hugged close to Jack and looked up at his lean, handsome face and kind eyes that had come into her life after Hugh died. He held her close and she closed her eyes, enjoying just being in the moment. As the moon faded leaving the sky turning a pale grey, he wrapped her closer in his arms and buried his face into her hair. The controls of the TV fell and were left forgotten on the floor. They walked to their bedroom and didn't sleep a wink that night. As six o'clock in the morning approached and the sun came peeping through the horizon, they could hear the seagulls chattering in the distance and the odd hoot of a ship going out from the docks in Galway making its way to sea. With the sound of that ship they fell into a deep sleep nestled together knowing the world was 'their voyage.'

THE END